The Loneliness of the Long-Suffering Mother

The Loneliness
of the
Long-Suffering Mother

DAVID HOLLAND

Troubador Publishing Ltd
Unit E2 Airfield Business Park,
Harrison Road, Market Harborough,
Leicestershire LE16 7UL
Tel: 0116 279 2299
Email: books@troubador.co.uk
Web: www.troubador.co.uk

ISBN 978-1-80514-348-2

British Library Cataloguing in Publication Data.
A catalogue record for this book is available from the British Library.

Printed and bound in Great Britain by 4edge Limited
Typeset in 11pt Minion by Troubador Publishing Ltd, Leicester, UK

One

It was nine o'clock in the morning and Ros stood looking down into the toilet bowl where her husband Ted had deposited a giant floater. Although she was a veteran of these outrages, this fresh one had made her wince and turn her head away once more, and after multiple flushes the old debate was raging inside her: let it liquefy or poke it to pieces with a stick. She went over to the sink where a tube of toothpaste – rolled all the way up to its capless top – lay snugly in the hairy plughole. Standing on tiptoe, she could see through the clear glass pane at the top of the frosted window. The burnt umber rooves and brick chimney stacks and the TV aerials of hundreds of semi-detached houses stretched away to a small wood in the distance. Ros remembered pushing her son Pete down all the streets and alleyways of the estate to get to that little wood, where there was a play area with swings for toddlers, each toddler being held in place by a chain fastened across the protuberant little stomach. In her memories it was always a warm day and his woollen mittens were off

1

and swinging at the ends of their elasticated bands as she pushed him to and fro. Her little blue bubble was a grim creature these days.

It being mid-April, the trees were still bare of leaves and Ros could just make out a tall pylon poking through the canopy of the wood. This was the Broadmoor Psychiatric Hospital warning siren which was tested at ten o'clock on Monday mornings. Every time the baleful droning began, Ros was reminded of the air raid sirens that she used to hear in Reading at the start of the war, when she was still a little girl. After ten minutes of silence the all-clear would sound, this eerie wailing reminding anyone who could hear it that only a few miles away in Crowthorne were incarcerated hundreds of the clinically insane, itching to get out and eat your eyeballs, or so the more passionate parents told their children.

Ros's breath misted the glass until she could see no more. She went downstairs, poured herself a coffee and took it into the back garden. At the sight of her, sparrows and blackbirds flew into the chilly blue air. Looking around, she saw that daffodils and primroses had seeded themselves among the shrubs. The azalea was covered in carmine buds and the stems of her tulips were bending under the weight of their deep purple flower-heads. From among the glossy green leaves of her camellia, she plucked the blooms that – sodden with dew – had turned the colour of caramel and threw them under the privet. She had positioned all of these plants – and other favourites such as lupins and irises – so that she could see them from the kitchen, the scene of her greatest labours, and where a blood-red ranunculus stood on the windowsill next to a bottle of Fairy Liquid.

Her garden was small and she walked round and round it in her yellow mule slippers, her arms tight across her chest to stop herself shivering, her mug in one hand and a cigarette in the other. She'd been used to having a chocolate digestive with her morning coffee, but she'd recently noticed that she was displacing more tonnage whenever she had a bath, and that when she got in and launched the yellow plastic duck that she'd kept since Pete was a baby boy, it ran aground on her stomach before it reached her chin.

The coffee warmed her up and the first cigarette of the day – although she didn't smoke much due to a suggestion of Ted's – made her light-headed and agreeable. She peeked over her neighbour's wire fence to see if Mrs Morris was there but the old dear wasn't up and about yet. On the opposite side was an old wooden fence with concrete pillars and behind it a screen of tall holly bushes – planted to conceal an electricity substation – which hid the house of her other neighbours completely. Beyond the fence that connected these two boundaries was a long row of semi-detached houses like Ros's own.

She tilted her mug to make the last drops of coffee into a smile and dropped her butt in. After a hiss a complete silence fell over Ros's world, as though all the birds in their bushes and all the worms in their holes had fallen asleep, until somewhere further up the road a car door slammed and Ros guessed that a mum was on her way to the shops or to the school where her child had arrived but then fallen ill.

She washed her coffee cup and went upstairs to make Pete's bed. In his room there had been a collision between

3

childhood and adolescence. On one wall was a picture of the womble Uncle Bulgaria next to a poster of Raquel Welch wearing a white bikini, while on the opposite wall a chart of chemical symbols had been stuck above a shelf of Ladybird books. In a corner there was a pile of fantasy fiction and an Airfix model of the famous World War Two battleship HMS Hood. A Monopoly board and its pieces were spread out on the floor next to the game Kerplunk, obviously an attempt to devise a new game from the wreckage of two old ones. Little hillocks of unwashed clothes lay around the unmade bed. In another corner there was a half-inflated Space Hopper over the face of which Pete had painted a Woolly Mammoth being attacked by Stone Age men with spears under the word DEATH. A strong, acrid smell led Ros to a pile of clothes on the floor, under which was one odorous long sock, blackened as though it had been set on fire.

Among the tangled bedclothes she found a small plastic cap which she screwed onto a tube of acne ointment by the bedside, and also the album *Never Mind The Bollacks* by the Sex Pistols which she knew had been leant to Pete by his friend Dan. Ros prayed there and then that Pete didn't become a part of this strange and anarchic movement that she was always hearing about on the news and that he just carried on liking the Electric Light Group or whatever they were called. Before she left the room she found a piece of paper and wrote on it in large letters, PLEASE TIDY YOUR ROOM, FROM MUM, and pinned it where Pete was most likely to see it, over Raquel Welch's breasts.

As she went down the stairs Ros thought of the perfect antidote to the Sex Pistols and the looming apocalypse.

She got the carpet sweeper from the cupboard under the stairs, took it into the living room and placed her favourite record on the turntable of the hi-fi. She waited in the middle of the room and as soon as 'I Couldn't Live Without Your Love' by Petula Clark started playing she began sweeping along to the music and hopping from one foot to the other to keep time. When Petula came to the final chorus... 'I couldn't live without your love, now I know you're really mine'... Ros sang into the handle of the carpet sweeper, throwing her head back so she could see – now that she was standing directly under the lightshade hanging from the ceiling – that the pearl-grey bulb was furred with dust.

In the silence after the song ended Ros stood looking through the net curtains at the empty street. She was panting and smiling but once she'd tucked her hair behind her ears the smile faded.

I wish I had a cat for company, she thought, but she knew Ted didn't like them.

She took a duster out of her pocket and wiped the wood top of the telly. Crouching down, she could see her reflection in the screen. She was wearing a green paisley headscarf, a pink woollen cardigan and black slacks. Her hair was the colour of dark autumn leaves. Her eyes were light green, large and fringed by black, naturally long lashes while on her cheeks – without make-up this early in the day – clustered the childish freckles that she'd hated as a teenage girl but which her mum and dad had always loved. Ros was proud of her looks but the curvature of the screen enlarged and elongated her nose.

I look like a sea cow, she thought.

She went to the fruit bowl and rearranged the apples so that the next time Pete reached for one he would naturally select the reddest and juiciest. Something caught her eye and she moved closer to the window. A small white van had parked by the kerb outside her house and a young man – maybe in his early twenties with ginger hair and blonde eyebrows – emerged from behind it holding a vacuum cleaner. He put it down, trundled it across the pavement and then ran it across the lawn in the direction of the front door, his mouth slightly open and his wet underlip quivering from the effort.

Poor boy, thought Ros. I don't want a new vacuum cleaner.

When she opened the front door he was wiping his feet on the mat in the manner of someone running while standing still. He was wearing grey polyester trousers, a white shirt and a blue kipper tie tugged loose. He looked at her and grinned with one corner of his mouth as though at that time of the morning his professional smile wasn't fully charged yet, but instead of introducing himself he said, 'Hello missus,' and started to bundle himself into the house, lugging the vacuum cleaner and forcing Ros to retreat.

'Oh, you're coming in then,' she said, a little shocked but naturally amiable.

Immediately to the right of the front door was another door of whorled glass panels. The young man barged through this and straight into the living room where he sat down in the armchair by the front window, with his knees apart and the vacuum cleaner erect between them. As he moved past Ros she smelt alcohol, and not the stale, vaporous reek of beer either but the medicinal, nose-wrinkling flavour of blended scotch and she knew that the man was drunk. She stood in front of him with her hands on her hips.

'So you're a vacuum cleaner salesman, are you?'

He snapped his fingers and pointed at her.

'I knew you were an intelligent woman from the moment I saw you.'

For much longer than was polite, the man's eyes rested on Ros's breasts, which according not just to Ted and all men but to Ros herself were her most tremendous assets.

'Nice,' Ros could tell he was thinking, but to herself she thought, Poor boy, you need a girlfriend.

The sound of a car going by – the threat of a rival vacuum cleaner salesman in the area – broke the spell and the man roused himself.

'Well here it is,' he said, sitting up and placing a finger atop the handle of his gift to women. 'The brand new Model 181. Streamlined, made of toughened plastic, with a beat and sweep design and a self-adjusting cleaning head. Perfect for carpets and hard floors, easy to empty'… here he pointed to a small plastic switch at the base of the dust bag… 'and fully approved by the electricity board. Or in other words you won't blow yourself up with it.'

'I'm sorry but I don't want a vacuum cleaner,' said Ros, smiling at the same time in order to let the evangelist down easily.

He frowned at her as though to say, 'Where's that intelligent woman who was here a few moments ago?'

'You won't believe the price.'

'Go on then.'

'Forty-seven pounds fifty or if you want it on the never-never, six ninety-five a month for twelve months.'

'For that?' said Ros, nodding at the machine. 'You're right, I don't believe it.'

Now the man was smiling only with his mouth, while the childish eyes were saying, 'Don't you know I'm doing you a favour?' A belch convulsed his chest and blew out his cheeks but with a valiant effort he managed to hold it in.

'I'll tell you what. I'll knock two pounds off. Forty-five fifty and I can't say fairer than that.'

'You didn't tell me your name.'

'Brian.'

Ros had met a few Brians – sensible, reliable sorts mostly – but she had the feeling that life for this Brian was going to be hard.

'I'm sorry Brian but I don't need a new vacuum cleaner. I only bought one a year ago and I'm very happy with it. I'm sure you'll have better luck at another house.'

Brian sighed and looked at his machine. Obviously this woman didn't have a heart and now the redeemer was going to have to be returned to the back of his van instead of lighting up her life.

'Oh well,' he said.

He stood opposite Ros, two heads taller than her, and his one-sided smile turned into a leer.

'I tell you what. Show us your knockers and you can have it for free.'

Ros's mouth fell open and she took a step back. A terrible thought crossed her mind: either Brian had escaped from Broadmoor or he was this Yorkshire Ripper that everyone had started hearing about on the news.

'Get out,' she whispered.

'Is that a 'No' then?'

'Get out!' shouted Ros, trembling now.

She realised that she was pointing an imperious arm at the door and thought she must look like Elizabeth Taylor in *Cleopatra*, sending Mark Anthony away with a flea in his ear after a lovers' tiff.

Luckily for Ros all the fight had gone out of this particular Brian and he turned towards the door, dragging his vacuum cleaner and mumbling, 'Keep your hair on.'

Ros was traditionally slow to anger – the carelessness and rudeness of others tending to baffle rather than incense her – but for once she was beside herself. There was a draft excluder in the shape of a sausage dog by the door and she picked it up by the blunt end and hit Brian over the head with it.

'Hey,' he said, looking round. She hit him again. 'Oi, that hurt.'

'Get out!' shrieked Ros.

'I'm going,' said Brian, but she kept hitting him even as he escaped through the front door, doubled over, with one hand behind his head to ward off the blows and the other holding his machine, and even as he ran across the lawn towards his van, Ros adding another 'Get out!' to each whack of the sausage dog.

Brian ran around to the driver's side, chucked his vacuum cleaner in and jumped in after it, but he must have been able to hear the thumps of the sausage dog as Ros belaboured his van even as he sped off with a screech of tyres.

Ros found herself alone in the street. She noticed Mrs Morris peeking through her net curtains to see what all the fuss was about and then her friend Pauline from across the road came out looking anxious. The next thing Ros knew, she was in Pauline's hallway, babbling about what had happened. Pauline's daughter Jane was there, still sucking her thumb at nine years old and wearing nothing but yellow cotton pants at ten-thirty in the morning, and also Norman her husband, a civil servant off work with a hernia, wearing blue pyjamas and smoking a pipe. Pauline was wearing her grandmother's mauve, satin, floor-length dressing gown and was gripping her hair with both hands in horror. Despite her distress, Ros had time to think, They're a funny family.

'I thought he'd escaped from Broadmoor,' squeaked Ros.

'I didn't hear the siren,' said Pauline.

'I thought he was the Yorkshire Ripper.'

'We're a long way from the Ripper's stamping ground,' said Norman, trying to calm the ladies.

'You must tell Ted,' said Pauline.

But as Ros recrossed the road she thought,

'I can't tell Ted. He'll find the man and murder him with one of his own vacuum cleaners.'

She went into the back garden and had a cigarette to calm herself and a chocolate biscuit for comfort. At eleven o'clock the new wonder plane, Concorde, went over on its way to New York. Today Ros imagined that the famous actor Roger Moore was on board and at that very moment was being handed a glass of champagne by a blushing stewardess.

When she'd finished her cigarette and chocolate

biscuit she went into Ted's shed – freshly creosoted by Pete in exchange for extra pocket money – and after a quick rummage found a bamboo stick just the right length for tackling her husband's floater.

Two

That same night the grim creature was lying in bed reading the fat, paperback version of *Lord Of The Rings*. On the cover, the title in large red letters was superimposed over a road winding its way through a mountainscape of needle-sharp pinnacles and terrifying abysses. Pete often stared at that cover for minutes at a time before starting to read, letting his excitement build until the urge to rejoin the Hobbits on their great romantic adventure became irresistible, and once he'd started reading he'd wish he was there with them and being the bravest of them all in the war against the goblins and faceless necromancers, and yet knowing at the same time that this could never be because he lived in a different world and was really just a boy lying in bed.

On this night, however, the hardships of Frodo Baggins and his fellows seemed trivial compared to the horror of his own situation, and after a while Pete stopped reading altogether, so distracted was he by memories of recent weeks and so consumed was he by the question,

'When did it all go wrong?' He had the feeling that it had started the night of the disco at the youth club, when he had stood in front of the bathroom mirror to check his spots and found that – compared to the spiral arms and local clusters that afflicted the other boys at school – a whole constellation of bright red suns had dawned on his face.

He'd blamed the image in the mirror on the stark and unforgiving light in the bathroom, and by telling himself that it wasn't true was able to set off for the youth club with hope in his heart. He called out 'I'm off, then' and darted through the side gate before his mum – seeing that he was only wearing a shirt – could capture him and bundle him into a thick, sensible jumper that his friends would laugh at. He walked quickly with his hands thrust deep into the pockets of his brand new jeans, trying not to catch sight of his face in the wing mirrors and windows of the cars parked along the road.

It was a cold evening and there was a deep blue glow behind the street lights that had just come on all over the estate. In the houses that he passed the standard lamps were on in the living rooms where footsore salesmen and bank clerks had loosened their collars and were watching TV with their wives and children, black-and-white TV except for where a new Japanese model threw fluorescent colours onto the net curtains.

He turned into an alleyway where dusk was falling. A younger boy on a bike appeared out of nowhere and teetered along beside him.

'Where are you going?'

'Up the youth club.'

The boy didn't say anything else, but Pete noticed him looking curiously at his new jeans, which had wide flares and narrow turn-ups. Then the boy sped off and Pete watched his bottom bouncing up and down until he swung out of the alleyway.

On the breeze he could smell batter and vinegar when he was still two streets away from the chip shop on the main road. Someone had rubbed away a porthole in the steamed-up window and through it Pete could see faces he recognised from the neighbourhood, one of them a punk girl with black lipstick who was biting a saveloy in half. As he walked by a schoolfellow came out.

'Oi, Turner, you going up the youth club?' When Pete nodded he said, 'Wait for me,' and fell in beside him.

The boy held out a bag of chips and Pete took one – almost liquid with grease – and popped it into his mouth. They didn't say a word to each other, just kept each other company while they pulped their chips, until the boy said, 'My friend lives here,' and swung down a path.

Left alone, Pete wondered if tonight would be the night when he got to dance with a girl for the very first time. He was at the point in adolescence where the absolute necessity of having a girlfriend – not just to satisfy his own desires but to gain the respect of friends who'd already had girlfriends – and the seeming impossibility of ever getting one were excruciatingly counterbalanced. One moment he'd think, 'How can they resist me in my new jeans,' and the next – considering the state of his face – he'd doubt if he'd ever have the courage to ask a girl to dance in the first place, never mind the miracle of one saying 'Yes.' And so as Pete got closer and closer to the youth club, the balance tipped dreadfully towards the probability that he was going to live the rest of his life as one of the lonely.

Night was about to fall and the street lamps were bright orange and haloed as Pete reached his destination, where the white lights of the porch lit up the faces of about a hundred boys and girls milling around outside. He realised that some of the boys he didn't recognise at first were actually schoolfellows who – liberated from their uniforms – looked older somehow. Pete went to a boys' school and so never associated with girls on a day-to-day basis, but he recognised some of the girls in the crowd from their attendance at the youth club. Beside them, the girls who he'd never seen before seemed more glamorous, and it was one of these beguiling creatures who he hoped to dance with. People had started to go in and every time the door opened he could hear 'Sound And Vision' by David Bowie being played.

Pete spotted his friends Dan and Adrian sitting on a wall next to some fifth formers from his school and went over to them. When they spotted his new jeans they all smirked.

'You should have got straights,' said Dan.

Pete looked down at his brand-new jeans and then looked at everyone else's jeans and realised that he was the only one who wasn't wearing straight Levi's with cuffed bottoms. One of the fifth formers had spiked black hair and was wearing a black leather jacket over a Ramones T-shirt. He sneered at Pete and shook his head, making the safety pins in his nose and ears twinkle. Pete had noticed Dan and Adrian hanging around with these fifth formers a lot recently but had always thought that it wouldn't be long before he was included as well. Now his two old friends jumped down off the wall and stood next to him for old time's sake, Adrian slapping him on the back as though to say, 'Bungled again.'

The three of them had been friends since junior school. They lived on the same estate and had stuck together like musketeers through the bloody transition to secondary education. Adrian was chubby, with a big bottom and blonde hair and a sense of humour that was on the wicked side of cheeky. Dan was the young god of the estate, tall, with wide shoulders and a precociously large Adam's apple for a fourteen-year-old. He'd been wet shaving since he was twelve and could grow a man's moustache in two weeks. Pete was as tall as him but with skinnier shoulders. He had the black, strangely woolly hair and brown eyes of his father but the tender mouth and chin of his mum. He was the most intelligent but also the laziest.

When they went into the hall 'Boogie Nights' by Heatwave was playing. The room was dark, illuminated only by the strobe lights which sent circles of multi-coloured dots spinning over the polished wooden floor and the bodies of the people on the dance floor, girls mostly at this stage of the evening, dancing in self-conscious pairs or inward-facing circles of four or five.

'It's loud!' Pete cried.

He could feel the beat thudding in his stomach and the floor vibrating through the soles of his shoes. From out of the darkness faces jumped when struck by coloured beams. Apart from when the lights struck him Pete felt that his spots were invisible and – feeling braver – he began to examine the faces of the girls on the dance floor and those lining the walls, searching for the one, unaware that he himself was being assessed from the corners of long-lashed eyes and from beneath creamy brows. In the pulsing and strobe-lit darkness the girls grew confused, one moment seeing three handsome young boys standing there and the next, three hounds sitting up with their tongues hanging out and their little front paws bouncing up and down to the music.

'Well, who do you fancy?' said Dan.

Pete had noticed a girl dancing with her back to him. She had long black hair and was wearing a red cotton dress that fell to just below her knees, with a slit in the back from her neck to her waist. He liked the way the fabric of the dress moved silkily over her hips and thighs as she hopped nimbly from one foot to the other in black high heels. When she finally turned towards him, her eyes – beautiful but grave – swept over him, so that almost in the same moment he thought, 'She's noticed me,' and, 'She's forgotten me already.' He loved the slimness of her waist and the two heartbreaking dimples in her cheeks, but what he admired most of all were her breasts, the pertness and amplitude of which reminded him – subconsciously – of his mum's.

'Nice,' said Dan, following Pete's gaze. 'You should ask her to dance, definitely.'

'Not for a fast one,' said Pete, panicking.

'Of course not, wait for a slow one.'

Pete had to wait almost an hour for the next slow dance. In the meantime the nascent punk rockers in the crowd kept badgering the DJ to play something by the Sex Pistols so he played 'The Combine Harvester' by The

Wurzels to annoy them. He kept the dance floor full by playing hits such as 'You Make Me Feel Like Dancing' by Leo Sayer and 'Dancing Queen' by Abba.

Pete watched Dan and Adrian dancing with their long-term, on-off girlfriends Karen and Wendy and wandered around, eventually joining a group of boys who had hidden themselves behind a stack of moulded plastic chairs. They were all rockers with long hair – known locally as the Greenies because they looked as though they washed their hair in snot – and were taking it in turns to drink from a small tin barrel of Watney's Ale. A boy with Black Sabbath written on the back of his denim jacket handed the barrel to Pete, who took a couple of glugs while the Greenies nodded solemnly to tell him that he'd passed the test and was now – lucky boy – as depraved as they were. Pete knew them as a drowsy, harmless bunch who'd be among the first to be discovered throwing up later that evening.

At some point Pete poked his head outside and found a group of people watching a couple kissing in the corner. At the end of the lane that led down to the youth club a group of older boys and girls who Pete didn't recognise were hanging around, talking, theirs faces white under the neon sign of the off license, the visible clouds of breath coming out of their mouths reminding Pete that springtime evenings could be freezing.

When he went back inside 'Jive Talkin' was coming to an end and the DJ said something corny like, 'And here's one for you lovebirds.' 'Love And Affection' by Joan Armatrading came on and Pete saw Dan and Adrian lead their girls onto the dance floor. Karen was so much shorter than Dan that with her head pressed against his chest she looked as though she was listening to his heartbeat, while Wendy – in a well-practiced move – was removing both of Adrian's hands from her buttocks.

The dance floor was emptier now, some girls lingering hopefully while others drifted away to become wallflowers. At the same time as several other terrified boys set off on their own interception courses, Pete headed towards the girl in the red dress, who was walking off the dance floor slowly, her fingers interlaced demurely in front of her, hoping for a tap on the shoulder by someone who looked like David Essex.

As Pete closed in he could tell that the girl had spotted him out of the corner of her eye and – to his horror – she now picked up speed to get away from him. He had to run to catch up with her before she reached the radiator by the wall and instead of touching her shoulder he grabbed it, making her turn.

'Would you like to dance?'

Up close Pete thought that she looked even more beautiful, but the sweetest smile in the world had gone from her lips. Her eyes moved over his face and he knew what she was seeing: a leper without a bell.

'No, thankyou,' she said, and then with a military swivel turned her back on him and perched on the radiator, arranging her dress over her knees.

Smiling stupidly, Pete stood there for a moment among the fallen paper chains and empty drinks cans and then escaped into the darkness. He came across Dan and Adrian looking pleased with themselves.

'Did you ask her, then?' said Dan.

Pete shook his head, avoiding their eyes, and was

aware that after watching him for a while they looked at each other, agreeing silently that there was no hope for him.

All that Pete wanted to do now was go home but he knew that it would look as though he was sulking if he left just then and so he stuck around. It was the time of the evening when the DJ played more and more love songs and Pete had to watch Dan and Karen – who had fallen passionately in love with each other again – through slow dance after slow dance. Finally, while 'Don't Give Up On Us Baby' by David Soul was playing, Pete spotted the girl wearing the red dress in the arms of a boy with – crushingly – a spud-like hooter and ginger hair.

The lights went up and the crowd began to pour out. Pete, aware of his spots, practically ran outside, not stopping until he reached the darkness beyond the porch light. Adrian joined him and they watched as Dan and Karen came out with their arms around each other and then went into a corner and started snogging. When Pete and Adrian got bored of watching they looked down the lane to where car after car was arriving to pick up the boys and girls. The headlights sweeping over the undergrowth illuminated a Greenie puking over his boots, another snogging couple and a row of lads urinating under the stars. Eventually Pete and Adrian heard the loud, wet noise of two suckers being pulled apart and knew that the moistened lovers had called it a night.

Dan joined them and they walked off in the company of the fifth formers that Dan and Adrian were friendly with. A light rain began to fall and Pete knew that his mum would scold him when he got home for not wearing a jacket. As they got to the end of the lane they mingled with the group who'd been loitering there all night.

'What are you doing here, Morton?' said one of the fifth formers.

'Nothing much. What was the disco like?'

'Pretty crap. They didn't play The Stranglers.'

In a pack they headed off down the main road, the older boys laughing boisterously despite the rain. Pete lingered in the rear, looking for an opportunity to slip away unnoticed, but then one of the girls turned round and saw him. She nudged her friend who looked at him and said, 'You've got them bad, mate.'

Now the whole crowd turned round to look, stopping directly under a street light blurred by the downpour, some of the boys wincing as they examined his face. Out of horror and pity no one said anything, and in the silence Pete could hear the raindrops bouncing off his cheeks.

They moved off again, Pete following, and after a few hundred yards Pete went his way and Dan and Adrian went theirs with the pack. It was so quiet in the estate that even when he was a few streets away he could still hear their laughter and the scrape of Doctor Martens. It began to rain harder and by the time Pete got home the flares of his new jeans were flapping around his ankles.

He managed to sound cheerful when he poked his head into the living room to tell his mum and dad that he was back. He went into his bedroom and for the first time in his life didn't turn the light on, but instead shut the door behind him and stood in the darkness.

On the next school day, Pete walked up to the graveyard

at St Michael's church where he, Dan and Adrian always spent their lunch hours. The headstones that had been saved from the rubble of the collapsed steeple were leaning in a row against the wall and his old friends were sitting with their backs against two of these memorials, their legs stretched out and their heads lolling towards each other like two young drunks. As Pete threw himself down beside them he noticed that they both had fags between their fingers.

'When did you two start smoking?' he said.

'Ages ago,' said Adrian, holding up his hand so that Pete could see where the nicotine had stained his fingers orange.

'Want one?' said Dan, taking out a packet of ten Embassy.

'Alright,' said Pete.

He'd smoked cigarettes before and hadn't liked it but now – like a trooper – he lit his fag and managed to inhale without wheezing. His two old friends started to talk about the disco and their girlfriends, Dan reminiscing about how for the very first time he'd nearly inserted a certain finger into a certain orifice.

'And did she like it when you stuck your finger in her ear?' said Adrian.

'Fuck off.'

Pete had the feeling that through such talk they were drawing comparisons between their own love lives and his, but hoped that with a cigarette in his mouth he looked too tough to care.

When he went up there the next day he heard voices and the revving of a dirt bike when he was still a hundred yards away. Instead of marching in, he peeked over the wall and saw Dan and Adrian with the fifth formers, among them the punk with spiked black hair who was always getting in trouble with the deputy head master for wearing his leather jacket instead of a blue blazer. Sitting on the motorbike was an older boy, some school-leaver who Pete didn't recognise. From thirty yards away Pete could smell the hot white smoke that was jetting from the exhaust as the boy throttled up. To entertain everyone he was standing on the pedals and bouncing the bike up and down on its black studded tyres. Dan and Adrian were wincing from the noise but were dead impressed, Pete could tell, Dan pointing out to Adrian the mighty front springs.

When the boy turned the engine off there was a ringing silence. The smoke drifted away and cigarettes were handed out and lit. Some of the boys looked around to see if anything else was going on in the world and just in time Pete ducked out of sight.

When he crept up to the churchyard and peeked over the wall the next day he was relieved to see that Dan and Adrian were there on their own. They were both smoking but Dan didn't offer him one, so Pete had to say, 'Give us a fag, then.'

'Get your own next time,' said Dan, handing him one.

Dan and Adrian talked to each other a bit but didn't include Pete, and then for a long while no one said anything at all. Pete resorted to scraping the lichen off a headstone – revealing a Maud and Josiah – and to break the silence said, 'I wonder what it's like to die.' By way of reply Adrian started throwing Wotsits at him, one at a time, peppering his head, and for the very first time in their ancient friendship with eyes full of fury instead of love. Pete batted the Wotsits away or picked them off his lap and popped them in his mouth, chomping comically, pretending to join in with the joke, but in the time it took for Adrian to empty the packet a friend had became a stranger.

Adrian hadn't spoken to him since that day, although they had nodded to each other across the classroom. Once, Dan had met him in the corridor and cried, 'Watcha, Pete. I'm late for physics. See ya,' but he was a stranger now also.

Pete closed his book, turned out the light, snuggled down into the darkness and thought, 'Well, at least I've got *Lord of the Rings*.'

Three

It was the evening rush hour and Ted was driving down the Reading Road in his custard yellow Ford Cortina, with his elbow out the window, smoking. Now and again a fellow motorist – usually a woman – noticed the wide, handsome face, the black hair peppered with flecks of grey and the long and deadly moustache and thought, 'It's Burt Reynolds!' His hands looked huge in their leather driving gloves and the cigarette tiny between his fingers. He was a large man, broad through the shoulders and solidly built, and with big brown eyes, but Ted was the gentler sort of giant. He looked calm, just another bear driving home through the ashy dusk and looking forward to his pie and chips, and drowsy from all the red tail lights blinking on and off ahead of him, but inside he felt not forty but fifty, middle-aged, doomed, and with a flock of troubles squawking inside his head.

There had been chaos at work. Just as everyone was getting ready to go home, a lorry – returning from Poland – had broken down as it was passing under the brick archway that was the entrance and exit to Dickie's Haulage. As the yard manager, Ted was summoned and found twenty mechanics – desperate to get to the pub or home – shaking their fists at Lenny the driver who was too scared to get out of his cab. It had only taken Ted ten minutes to attach a tow rope and drag the lorry into the yard, but there had almost been a riot and an hour later he could still hear the curses of his staff ringing in his ears.

The yard covered an area the size of a football pitch and was surrounded by Victorian brick walls ten feet high. Beneath the walls were piles of discarded engine parts, ramshackle wooden sheds and hills of old tyres. In the centre of the yard was a massive brick building as long as – but lower than – an aircraft hangar, with a corrugated iron roof supported by blackened steel girders. It could contain three rows of six heavy haulage trucks parked end-to-end, with an inspection pit under each lorry. Ted's office was a little glass-walled cabin held aloft by scaffolding just inside the main door of the hangar. If he stood up from his desk he could look all the way across his domain and check if anyone was shirking instead of working, while if his mechanics looked up they could shout as though he was Caesar, 'We who are about to get oily, salute you!'

Thanks to the oil crisis, Ted had recently been forced to let seven of his men go, reducing his workforce by a third, while because he was only allowed a part-time secretary he had to do a lot of the bum-numbing paperwork himself. Further, due to the sort of boss's brainwave that leaves the workforce in a pickle, Dickie had secured the contract to service all the municipal bin lorries as well. This had been just about manageable when the lorries were coming in one at a time, but when the bin men went on strike Ted's contact at the council had called him and said, 'There's six lorries just sitting here doing nothing, Ted. You might as well have them all.'

So there they were, parked with their noses to the wall and their great empty arses out, stinking up the yard. Ted didn't know which was louder: the grumbles of the men or the shrieks of the river gulls as they dived into the abysses in the backs of the trucks.

Then the other day two rozzers had walked into the yard. They'd sniffed around for a bit and then, after asking for the manager, had ascended to Ted's aerie and introduced themselves as Detective Sergeant Naylor and Detective Constable Fenton. Ted, who was familiar with plod from his borstal days, had saluted, snapped to attention, and said, 'Evenin' all,' even though it was eleven o'clock in the morning. The sergeant, with his hands thrust deep into the pockets of his flasher's raincoat, looked wearily at Ted as though this was the final confirmation that there was no respect for authority anymore. The constable had his notebook out and his pen at the ready while his eyes darted around the room, looking for clues among the paperclips.

Ted sat down behind his desk and waved the policemen into the two chairs for visitors.

'So what can I do for you lot?'

'You are… ?' said the sergeant.

'Ted.'

'Ted, we're looking for some stolen fuel pumps.'

'Fuel pumps for diesel engines to be exact,' said the constable.

'One hundred of 'em. They went missing from a shipment from Germany. Ten thousand quid's worth.'

Ted had been swivelling from side to side in his battered leather executive chair with his hands behind his head, but now he stopped.

'Are you suggesting that my company maybe in possession of these nefariously purloined goods?'

The sergeant smiled horribly, like one old rat knowing another old rat when he sees one. They stared at each other for so long that the constable thought his sergeant had dried up.

'Not at all,' said the constable. 'We were just wondering if you might have heard something, or been offered the parts by someone who might be of interest to us.'

'No one's been through here with dodgy goods.'

'I presume you can account for everything that's here,' said the sergeant. 'The relevant paperwork and what-not.'

Ted had turned round and begun to peruse the shelves behind him while tapping his moustache thoughtfully with a finger. He kept the cops in suspense for so long that the constable began to writhe with impatience.

'Ah,' he said eventually, taking down a file labelled Stock/Invoices. 'Here it is.'

He opened the file, turned it round and held it towards the sergeant who leaned forward.

'Holden and Stanwyck of Wolverhampton,' said the sergeant. 'Well, that all seems to be in order.' He stood up. 'You'll let us know if you hear anything.'

'If I come across the perpetrators I will not only

apprehend them myself but bring them to you in chains.'

'No need for that, Ted. Just give us a call,' said the sergeant, leaving his card on the desk.

Ted stood up and watched them make their way across the yard just as two empty tipper trucks roared in, their perpendicular exhaust pipes gritting the sky with diesel fumes, the vibrations causing the windows in his airborne office to rattle in their frames. His mate Alan came in.

'Are they who I think they are?'

'Not 'alf.'

'What did they want?'

'They're looking for some stolen fuel pumps.'

'Why did they come here?'

'I would've thought that was obvious,' said Caesar. 'They're eliminating the reputable businesses from their enquiries first.'

And on top of all that, Ted had got home that evening and been informed by his wife that Pete had started wearing a motorcycle helmet to school.

'Why?'

'To hide his spots, I expect.'

'They're not that bad, are they?'

Ros had always known that it was the father who was traditionally the last – even after the milkman and next door's cat – to notice the travails of his child, but Ted's obliviousness shocked her.

'They're very bad.' Ros handed him a note. 'And he forged a letter.'

Ted read:

Dear headmaster,

This is to inform you that our doctor, Dr Blisland,
has recommended that Peter Turner, my son, wear
a motorcycle helmet in order to contain the swelling
from a fast-growing and life-threatening brain
tumour. While this will on the one hand make him
an object of scrutiny, it will on the other save his
schoolfellows – especially the more sensitive ones –
the distress of seeing the offending lump on a day-
to-day basis.

Please bear with us at this difficult time.
Yours faithfully,
Rosalind Turner

Ted trudged up the stairs, trying to picture his son's face covered in spots but all he saw was his little 'chubby chops,' the chuckling, fresh-faced, knee-high boy who would never grow old. The only thing that he'd noticed about Pete recently was that he'd stopped laughing at his jokes. He'd been disappointed but not dismayed, remembering how during his own adolescence there'd been the leaden realisation that there was nothing funny about parents. Ted didn't know that his son had stopped laughing altogether.

When he went into Pete's bedroom he found him lying on his back with his hands behind his head, the electric-blue helmet on and the visor down. To get to the bedside he had to hop over a Pan Book of Horror Stories, a black plastic rook and a pair of yellow swimming trunks. Ted leaned down and slid the visor up, revealing sad brown eyes and the bridge of the nose bearing one little spot.

'You're too young to have a motorbike, you know.'

'I don't want a motorbike.'

'Then why are you wearing a helmet?'

'Safety reasons.'

Ted looked around the abode of the hermit and realised they had the same poster of Raquel Welch up in the yard. He rapped on the helmet.

'Where did you get it?'

'I found it.'

'Where?'

'By the side of the road.'

'Are you sure. I mean, there's not going to be some massive biker turning up on the doorstep saying that his helmet's been nicked?'

Pete sighed. 'If you're wondering if I've taken to a life of crime, Dad, the answer is a definitive 'no'.

'Well, don't wear it to school tomorrow or there'll be trouble.'

Ted half turned to go and then said,

'You don't wear it playing football as well?'

'I do. You've got no peripheral vision but when you head the ball it goes fucking miles.'

'Don't swear,' said Ted, leaving the room quickly to hide his grin.

When he got home the next evening, Ted found Pete lying on his bed again, this time without the helmet. The only light came from a lamp on Pete's desk, leaving his face in shadow, but even so Ted gasped at the state of his skin, where a galaxy of red dwarfs was spread over a white universe.

'I see you've ditched the helmet.'

'Much to the detriment of my heading.'

Ted noticed a bruise around Pete's left eye and leaned forward. 'Is that… ?'

Pete turned his head away.

'Whacked in the face by a football.'

Ted straightened up and stood there looking down at the lad. He wanted to believe him but at the same time he could tell the difference between bruising caused by knuckles and bruising caused by a ball. He remembered all the fights that he'd got into during his own youth, when because of his size he'd inflicted more shiners than he'd recieved. Pete's injury was the result of a fist being inserted into his eye socket at lightning speed.

It was alright for me, thought Ted. I was big and could look after myself. Pete's too slim, he's got no upper body strength, he's too sensitive. I should have taught him to stand up for himself, to look people in the eye. But when did I have the time?

Ted took a deep breath, a torrent of fatherly advice on the tip of his tongue, but then his shoulders slumped. He was just too tired, and powerless in the face of his son's misery he simply said, 'That's alright then,' and walked out.

The kitchen was full of steam from boiling potatoes. Ros was standing at the counter, wearing a pink headscarf and a sweating apron covered in pictures of garden birds. Husband and wife looked sorrowfully at each other and Ted said,

'Now he's got a bruise as well.'

'It was a punch.'

'He said… '

A knife snapped at the chopping board as a pork pie was halved.

'It was a punch!'

Ted knew she was right but he was determined to contradict her, for the same reason that he'd stayed in the car – bracing himself – for ten minutes after he'd parked on the driveway. He knew that Ros was the perfect mother, an excellent wife, was good-looking, intelligent and hard-working, but for the past few weeks these qualities had oppressed him. It had something to do with how trivial was the domestic world that she patrolled so sweetly, compared to the vast, industrial world in which he and his mechanics sent Dickie's trucks out on their great journeys across Europe.

'Don't be ridiculous. He's been clobbered by a ball.'

'How can you be sure?'

'Because he told me.'

'You don't think he made that up to hide the unhappy truth?'

Ted watched her, fussing over the dinner, fussing over everything.

'No, I bloody don't.'

Ros stood back from the stove and whirled a tea towel around her head to dispel the steam. She faced Ted with her hands on her hips. Despite the hot and humid air she looked cold and beautiful.

'Dinner will be ready in ten minutes.'

The next evening Pete was sporting a bruise over his other eye. Ted was in the kitchen again, his moustache damp from boiling vegetables.

'He's being bullied,' said Ros.

'How do you know?'

'I wormed it out of him.'

'Who by?'

'A boy called Mick Burnley, and I know where he lives.'

'I'm going round there,' said Ted, turning his fists into rocks.

'Don't. You'll make things worse.'

Ted knew that she was right but he said to himself, 'If it happens just once more I'll go round there and have the father.'

The rest of the evening was spent quietly. They all watched telly together until Pete went to bed about nine. Ros had a bubble bath and then went to bed herself. She opened her Catherine Cookson at the point where the local squire, Sir Barnaby Nightshade, was reigning in his steed beside the lock keeper's daughter and, concerned for the poor girl's virtue, read on avidly for a while but then her mind began to wander. She'd just realised that the cream-coloured dots on the bathroom mirror were flecks of pus from when Pete had stood there and exploded one of his spots. She was scared that if he went on like that he would be permanently scarred by his acne.

Ted came to bed and resumed his Wilbur Smith. He'd got to the point where the hero, a gold prospector travelling through darkest Africa, was making passionate love to his girlfriend in a tent while nearby the local tribe sang a lament for one of their number who'd been trodden on by an elephant. It wasn't a very exciting part of the story but he read doggedly on, hoping to come to a bit where someone else was eaten alive by a wild animal, but eventually he couldn't help himself, and yawning like a lion he let the book flop into his lap. It was only then that he became aware of the great silence beside him, the silence that always descended when Ros was turning something over in her mind. He felt scared whenever Ros was worrying herself to death. In the past when – not divining the depth of her anxiety – he'd said something light-hearted to cheer her up at times like this, she'd looked at him balefully.

In the lemonade glow of the bedside light, the cream that she'd used on her face made her cheeks shine. He could smell the citrus of her bath bubbles and the lavender bag that she kept in her bedside drawer. He'd fallen in love with her because when she was having fun she laughed so hard that her eyes closed – or in other words – went temporarily blind with happiness. It was the contrast between the face he'd been smitten by and the face she wore now that put Ted on high alert.

'Try not to worry,' he said.

'I'm going to the doctor's about it.'

'He's already been to the doctor's.'

'Perhaps there's something else they can do for him.'

In bed Ted wore pyjama bottoms and no top. He'd let go of his book and was rotating his thumbs through the hair on his chest. Ros was reassured by his thick arms and the great soft moustache. Then, as she did every night, she got out of bed and opened the curtains so they could see the night, and then opened the window a little bit so the room didn't get stuffy. Through the same window they often heard a song thrush – which Ted roared at on Sunday mornings if he was having a lie-in – blackbirds in the evening, while all through the summer the smell of honeysuckle came in. Once the deep electric hum of the last London train leaving Earley station had faded away, all was quiet. As Ros padded back from the window in her yellow nightie, Ted lifted up the bedclothes to gather her in.

They lay there side-by-side with their eyes open, the combined heat of their bodies warming the bedclothes. Ros watched the net curtains, filled by a breeze, then subsiding dreamily.

'He's turning into a recluse,' said Ros.

'Yes, what's happened to Dan and Adrian?'

A sharper wind hissed through the holly leaves.

'I had spots,' said Ted.

'So did I.'

'Beauty spots in your case.'

Silently, they agreed that this was a nice thing to say but at the wrong time. Ted shifted his bulk so that he was turned towards Ros.

'He'll be alright, I promise.'

'That's so easy to say.'

'I mean it.'

'I want to help him now.'

Ted detected the shrill note in her voice and realised that she was in agony. They didn't say anymore after that but lay there without sleeping for ages, united in grief for the lad still living.

In the early hours of the morning – wakened by the grinding of her teeth – Ros got up to go the toilet. Once she'd had a piddle she didn't go back to bed but sat there, thinking hard. She remembered Pete as a toddler with his thumb in his mouth, and how once when she'd tried to pull it out it had been as hard as pulling a cork from a bottle. She thought of how he used to wriggle like a worm when his dad was cutting his toenails. She remembered that when he was five or six he'd gone through a phase of wanting them to draw pictures of lorries piled high with vegetables for him, and Ted saying, 'Strange, but he's obviously going to be a costermonger.'

She hadn't had a conversation with him for weeks. Every time he came through the back door after school he would chuck his Adidas sports bag into a corner so Ros could take out his lunchbox, and then run up the stairs, his mum calling after him, 'You didn't eat your apple.' Standing in the kitchen she would hear his door close and then the Sex Pistols: carnage in musical form. He'd told her that he didn't even like the group, preferring The Electric Light Bulbs or whatever they were called. So why does he listen to it? thought Ros, fearing that he'd caught the rage that was going from one young person to the other like a virus.

One day, about an hour after he'd come home, Ros – desperate for some interaction with him – had burst into his room with the excuse that she was looking for dirty clothes. She couldn't see him at first because the curtains were closed and he was lying as still as death on the bed, but when she reached for the light switch he said, 'Don't.' She hopped about the room with the plastic laundry basket tucked under one arm, reaching down for socks, pants and vests, and chattering away, trying to remind him what happiness sounded like.

'Nanny and Grandad are coming for tea this weekend. Won't that be nice.'

Silence.

'Your dad and I were thinking about going to The Rose

for dinner tomorrow night.' The Rose was a Berni Inn that served Pete's favourite meal: gammon and chips with a pineapple ring on top. 'Won't that be splendid?'

Silence.

'Did you play football at school today?'

The silence wasn't simply an absence of noise: it emanated from her once-beautiful son like an odour, driving her from the room.

Now that Pete's personality had disappeared like a sun behind a cloud of misery, Ros felt as though there'd been a death in the family, which in turn meant that her son needed to be saved. Ros couldn't imagine just then how she would be able to bring this about, especially now that within the constraints of their present relationship they no longer talked to each other. That night, surrounded by the silent plumbing of the bathroom, she realised that if she was going to help him she would have to tread carefully around him or – like a god – bring about the miracle of his resurrection in mysterious ways.

Four

It was going to be another dry day so Ros decided to boil some of Pete's underpants, and a pair of Ted's as well, in order to dissolve some stubborn stains that the ordinary wash hadn't removed. She brought some water to the boil in her old enamel saucepan, added the underpants and some soap powder, and gave the mixture a stir with a big wooden spoon.

After a coffee and cigarette she took up her crochet work. Recently she'd made a white maxi dress with gold and blue sleevelets for her friend Carla, and a yellow one for herself to use as a cover-up on the beach. She'd made little lambs and monkeys for the children of neighbours and a colourful vest for Mr Morris next door. She liked the activity because it reminded her of when her mum had taught her to knit during the war. Reading had taken a pounding from the German bombers a few times and Ros remembered emerging from their house into air heavy with brick dust and going down into the shelter to find women knitting by candlelight.

The only frustrating thing about her hobby was that small, crocheted gifts tended to go missing. For a start the cosy that she'd made for Ted's whisky bottle had disappeared, and then the multi-coloured bobble hats that she'd knitted for him, her dad and Pete had been mislaid, innocently according to the recipients but faithlessly according to Ros, which was why she was now crocheting replacements to give as punitive Christmas presents.

She was unemployed around this time because she'd quit her job. For seven years she'd worked for North Sea Fish, a company that imported frozen fish, packaged it and sold it to local supermarkets. The logo on the packets was a cartoon haddock with a big smile on its face, saluting with its fin. This employment gave Ros £35 a week and Ted the opportunity – whenever he was testing the bounds of his captivity – to call her a fish wife.

It was a small business with about twenty men and women working in the packing plant, and five women – including Ros – working in the office, a Portakabin resting on breeze blocks in the yard. Ros had always thought the din was greater in the office, what with the typewriters bouncing on the wooden desk tops at each thump on the keys and the tuneless dinging of the bells. It was freezing in the winter and baking in the summer, when the ants used the gaps between the threadbare carpet tiles as highways. It was heads-down work most of the time but at lunchtime they chatted, listened to Radio 2 – easy listening music – or maybe Ros crocheted some more of a baby whale.

A door opened into the office of the manager, Phil, a fat, unsociable man who could never keep his shirt tucked in and who'd naturally earned the nickname Fillet. He wasn't a tyrant but the girls were scared of his sense of humour. One April Fool's Day he'd come to work dressed as a woman, with a blonde wig and balloons for breasts. In the middle of the afternoon he'd walked into the office, cried. 'Oooh, you are awful!' and burst the balloons with a pin, making Eileen and Cilla jump out of their skins.

One day Ros went into his office with some invoices. Phil was by the filing cabinet next to the door so she put the papers on his desk and started to walk out. Just as she was about to go past him he slapped her bottom so hard that she was propelled from the room. Gail, her friend, looked up from her typewriter. Blushing furiously and scared to look round in case Phil was watching her, Ros walked back to her desk and sat on her stinging behind.

The next morning, while Phil was out of the office, Ros left her notice on his desk. For the next four weeks she contrived not to speak to him and on the few occasions when she did catch his eye – half-expecting to see shame – she met only indifference and a couple of times defiance. On her last day at work she phoned in sick so that she didn't have to go to her leaving do. A week later Ted dropped in to pick up her present, a pair of hand-made ladies gloves. When Gail phoned after a couple of months she got Ted, who took a message, but Ros never called her back.

She never told Ted the real reason why she quit. 'I just feel like a change,' she'd said blithely when he asked her. Ted didn't realise that he was looking at the new Elizabeth Taylor. He wasn't worried because he was earning good money at Dickie's and knew there was plenty of work about in the offices of light industry for experienced secretaries like Ros.

If he did get one clue that she was unhappy around this time he didn't connect it to her job. Partial to walloping Ros's bottom now and then himself, he'd come through the back door one evening, cried, 'Hello Dolly!' and indulged himself fully, but instead of replying with the usual, 'Oh, Ted,' Ros had shouted 'How dare you!' and slammed a saucepan of vegetables down on the draining board. He didn't dare go up to her for the usual kiss while she was standing there with her back to him, batting the steam away from her face with both hands. He crept away wondering what on earth it was that he'd done wrong.

Ros took the freshly boiled underpants and hung them on the line, the click of the wooden clothes pegs against her teeth the only sound for miles around. She was thinking about the day that Ted had taken Pete to the dentist when he was about nine years old. She'd had her hands in the sink when they came back and said, 'Well, how did you get on?'

She'd turned round to find Pete cupping his face with both hands, a look of anguish on his face and his top row of teeth protruding at a sickening angle and now a sickly green colour. Behind him, his dad was moaning, 'My son, my son, what have they done to you?' and clawing at his face with his fingernails.

'What's happened?' shrieked Ros.

'The dentist has been clumsy with his instruments!' cried Ted.

'Mum, they say I'm going to be like this forever!'

Then to Ros's horror the teeth had shot out of Pete's mouth and hit the fridge.

'A miracle!' cried Ted.

By now, of course, Pete was choking with laughter, while her husband's shoulders were bouncing. She'd biffed and boffed them until they'd run from the room and then picked the teeth up. 'Joke gnashers,' it said on the gums.

Now she went up to Pete's room to find those teeth. She knew they were there somewhere because she'd seen them countless times over the years. She found them in a glass jar full of marbles, took them into her bedroom and tried them on in front of the mirror. She jumped, but then got the giggles. She tried to say her name out loud and found that the only way she was able to do so was by pitching her voice high, through her nose. She tied her hair back in an officious-looking bun, dressed herself in an old, shapeless trouser suit that flattened her chest and made her bum look big, and slipped on plain black shoes.

'The perfect representative of the local council!' she screeched in her new voice as she went down the stairs.

She left the house and turned down the first alleyway, which was like all the other alleyways on the estate, with a tarmac path bordered on either side by white gravel dotted with dog turds – solid or liquid according to the digestive health of the depositor – while here and there euonymous or ivy poked through the wooden slats of the fence on either side.

Halfway down the next alleyway Ros almost bumped into an old man who reeled back and flattened himself against the fence at the sight of her gruesome chompers. Once she'd passed by him she spat them out and put them in her handbag.

On the Reading road Ros dipped her head into the first warm wind of the year. An empty milk bottle played a little tinkling tune as it bumped along the kerb. When a sheet of newsprint wrapped itself around her leg she walked backwards for a while to let it fly. She knew why all the gutters were choked with litter. It was because the road sweepers had come out in sympathy with the bin men. Ted reckoned that he'd seen a rat as big as a dog at the yard, and according to Pete there were mice nesting in the ink wells at school. Her dad was always saying, 'This country still hasn't recovered from the war.'

With her destination just ahead she reinserted her teeth. Mick Burnley, she knew, lived in a caravan parked next to the Methodist hall, a long low building with brick walls and a crucifix at the apex of its triangular wooden roof, and which doubled as a scout hut and a ballroom dancing studio.

It was a long, dirty white, rectangular caravan, one side of which abutted a giant privet hedge choked with brambles. The door was on the other side, facing the Hall, and was reached by a path that snaked through long grass, bypassing an old bicycle frame and a perambulator containing a pile of sodden baby clothes and a plastic cutlery tray. A garden gnome laughed at Ros from among the weeds growing up around the rusty tow bar. The curtains were drawn across the window that faced the road. In these dismal surroundings Ros's courage began to fail her and for the first time she hoped that no one was in when she knocked.

There were two steps up to the door, the first of which was an upside-down biscuit tin and the second a plastic table for toddlers. Ros stood on the second step, knocked loudly, and waited. There was a long silence and she thought, 'Thank God,' but then she heard the creak of a chair, a grumble, and footsteps thudding across the floor. The door flew open, outwards, sending Ros flying through the air to land on her newly enlarged bottom.

'What are you doing?' snapped an old lady in the doorway.

'You knocked me over!'

'Don't you know the door of a caravan opens outwards?'

'I do now.'

Ros climbed to her feet, dusted her bottom and picked up her handbag while the old lady looked down at her. She was stout – in her sixties guessed Ros – with thin grey hair and a bookie's pen stuck behind her ear. She was wearing a long black skirt, one pink slipper and one yellow slipper, a green tea towel around her waist and a grey wool cardigan, the bottom corners of which were pendulous from all the bits and bobs stuffed into the pockets. She was tubing a cigarette paper with her forefinger and using the other hand to pluck a packet of tobacco from her cleavage.

Now erect, Ros took a deep breath.

'Are you Mrs Burnley?'

'Who wants to know?'

'My name is Barbara Amplethorpe and I'm from the department of social services.'

'You're a new one.'

'New to the area but not new to the profession.'

There was a silence while the old lady regarded Ros bitterly.

'Well?' said Ros.

'What?'

'Are you Mrs Burnley?'

'If you want Mick's mum, she's dead. If you want Mick's dad, he's in Parkhurst. If you want me, I'm his gran, Violet. If you want Mick, he's at school.'

'I'm here about Mick. I wonder, Violet, could we talk inside?'

At this point Ros stepped forward and for the first time Violet – obviously short-sighted – beheld the terrible teeth.

'My God, what happened to your… '

'A birth deformity,' said Ros, seizing the opportunity to go on the offensive. 'One which I've learned to live with entirely for the sake of others.'

'You poor woman,' mumbled Violet, and shuffling backwards she waved to Ros to come in.

To the left was a three-sided sofa around the dining table, while to the right was the kitchen and beyond that a corridor which led to the bathroom and – Ros guessed – the bedrooms. The portable telly on the table was turned on but with the sound down, while on the seat of the armchair facing it was an overflowing ashtray. The whole place reeked of cigarette smoke but it was tidy, with faint furrows made by the hoover in the thick cream carpet and wet cereal bowls stacked neatly on the draining board.

Ros sat on the sofa and Violet took the armchair. She lit her roll-up, pulled hard on it and blew smoke out of her mouth and then both nostrils, subsequent puffs emerging with every word.

'So what's the dopey fucker done now?'

'I'm afraid there's been an accusation of bullying.'

'Who by?'

'The parents, I suppose, at least according to the headmaster.'

'That headmaster! Do you know how many times he's caned Mick this year? Three already! And he can't miss, you see, with an arse that size.'

Ros's teeth almost shot out but she managed to control herself.

'My concern, Violet, is that bullying at school can lead to misbehaviour in society, and even criminality. I know the headmaster has talked to Mick but bearing in mind their relationship... I wonder if you could talk to him.'

'I've talked to him a hundred times...'

There was a small gap between the drawn curtains and Violet's eyes narrowed as she spotted something outside. Ros looked too and saw a big boy dressed in the blue blazer of Pete's school coming down the path towards the caravan. He was a skinhead, with small eyes, a muscular face and hands the size of mallets.

Violet jumped up, scampered down the corridor and returned with a pillowcase. She opened a cupboard, took out a cabbage and dropped it into the pillowcase, then twirled it around until there was a big white ball on the end of a twisted rope. At first Ros had thought, 'Mick's bunked off school, I didn't think of that,' but then she found herself thinking, 'Ah, he's forgotten his packed lunch and Violet's getting it ready for him. Funny sort of packed lunch, though: a cabbage...'

The moment that Mick ducked his head through the door, Violet swing the cabbage and clobbered him with it.

'FUCK!' GRAN! WHAT ARE YOU DOING?'

'How many times have I told you to stop bullying people?'

'I HAVEN'T BEEN BULLYING NO ONE!'

'This lady says you have!'

More blows rained down on Mick who tried to escape by running away, but Violet leapt after him, the commotion made by the both of them rampaging down the corridor causing the caravan to rock from side to side. Ros – rooted to the spot at first – followed, crying feebly, 'Stop! Both of you. Please!' and found them in the furthest bedroom, Mick cowering on the bed and Violet swinging the weaponised cabbage around her head. Ros tried to grab it but tumbled onto the bed herself. She vomited her teeth but with her face pressed against the bedclothes managed to push them back in without anyone noticing.

Somehow they found themselves back in the living room. Ros snatched the cabbage from Violet and ordered Mick to sit down, which he did.

'I don't know. I really don't,' she said. 'You're as bad as each other.' She put her hands on her hips and looked at them. 'Violet, I have to say that berating your grandson in this manner will only make matters worse. And Mick, the reason I'm here is to appeal to you to stop bullying this boy at your school. I'm afraid to say that if you don't, you may be taken out of school and placed in another institution.'

Mick was sulking by now, his nose almost touching the formica tabletop. Suddenly Ros felt sorry for the great oaf and sitting down opposite him reached out and took his hand. The human touch caused a fat teardrop to roll down Mick's cheek while Violet – wondering where all the tenderness had gone – just stood there with a lump in her throat.

'Can you do that for me?' said Ros, softly.

'I'll try, Mrs…'

'Mrs Amplethorpe,' said Violet.

'I'll try, Mrs Appleforp.'

'There's a good boy,' said Ros. She stood up. 'Well, it's time I went, but if I hear any more bad reports I'll be back, you know that don't you, Mick?'

'He knows,' said Violet.

'Now I suggest you both have a nice cup of tea. And Violet…'

'Yes?'

'Boil that cabbage before you do any more harm with it.'

When Ros got home there was a row of clean white underpants waiting for her on the line. As each pair landed in the laundry basket she said out loud, 'Thanks Mum!' in imitation of an advert for washing powder that she kept seeing on the telly, in which a perfect little boy and girl were electrified by their mother's prowess at stain removal.

'It was exhausting being Barbara Amplethorpe,' she said to herself as she sat down in the garden with a biscuit. The warmth of the day melted the chocolate so she had the luxury of sucking it off her fingertips one-by-one.

Five

The following day, Ros set out on another mission, this time to see the man who'd been evoked by Pete in his heartfelt epistle: Dr Blisland. He was a tall man with calm brown eyes and a white, Abrahamic beard, who always wore a dark suit with a red handkerchief poking out of the breast pocket. Ros had always been reassured by the way he sat there tamping tobacco into the bowl of his pipe while he listened to her, and how after lighting up he'd disappear inside a cloud of smoke for a while, like a druid behind his cauldron. Over the years he'd cured two bunions of hers, advised her to have a hysterectomy when she started to suffer from heavy bleeding, treated Pete's hayfever and then his acne, and on the night that Ted had left the pub through a closed window, charged round to their house to set his broken nose. To do this he'd first applied dressings to the traumatised area, and then positioned a small wooden splint either side of the nose, the whole arrangement looking like a miniature coffin on top of an oval bun of bandages, and the sight of which provoked much ribaldry from wife and son.

'Mum, do you think Father will ever look the same again?'

'Who nose?'

'Mum, would you describe Father as an inquisitive sort of person?'

'If he wasn't nosy before he's certainly nosy now.'

'Very bloody funny,' Ted would honk through his swollen appendage.

Dr Blisland and two other doctors occupied a large detached house on the Reading Road, where the living room had been turned into a waiting room and two of the bedrooms into consulting rooms. In the wide, wooden hallway was the reception desk where Ros gave her name.

'I'm afraid Dr Blisland's away,' said the receptionist. 'Dr Bangalore will see you today.'

'Oh,' said Ros, flummoxed for a moment, but then remembering the importance of her mission she said, 'Okay,' and went into the waiting room.

She found two people sitting on opposite sides of the room. The first was a man in his thirties wearing a cheap polyester suit, sweating horribly and holding a handkerchief over his nose like a rep with the Black Death. The second was an old lady sitting with a large black handbag balanced on her knees by way of a defensive bulwark, and her head turned dramatically to one side as though she'd been hurled against the wall by a hurricane of germs. This was Mrs Leopard, who Ros knew. She was about seventy years old and was wearing a dark blue trouser suit and dandy red shoes. Her eyebrows had been artificially raised so that she wore a surprised look and her handsome face was perfectly made-up, giving her a haughty air – the man opposite was clearly frightened of her – but Ros knew her as an immensely kind woman with a playful sense of humour.

'Hello, dear,' she whispered as Ros sat down next to her.

'How are you, Mrs Leopard?'

'Dizzy spells, dear. I expect it's high blood pressure.' She leaned closer to Ros. 'Have they told you Blisland's ill?'

'They said a doctor Bangalore. Do you know him?'

'Never heard of him but he's obviously an Indian which is fine by me. Oh they're a fine race! You probably know that I was out there with my husband during the war. 1944. The battle of Kohima. What a bloodbath! But thanks to those Ghurkas… What men!'

Mrs Leopard had been in charge of the nursery that Pete attended when he was four years old. He'd been such a quiet, shy little boy and Ros had been so worried about him – he gets it from me, she reflected – that every lunchtime she used to cycle down to the little cottage school and hide behind a tree, from where she'd observe him standing in a corner on his own, shredding his fingernails with his teeth, watching all the other little girls and boys playing merrily around him. Sometimes he spotted her and would run towards her, but she'd shoo him away, hissing, 'Why don't you play with the others?' One day Mrs Leopard caught her and scolded her. 'I know you're worried, Ros, but you're over-protecting him.' Then she'd said, 'Just make sure that he can't see you when you come. Peek through the bushes.' Which is what Ros had done until the wonderful day when she saw Pete wheeling around the playground with his arms flat out at the head of a squadron of playmates.

'And how's your Peter?' said Mrs Leopard.

'He's fourteen now.'

'Such a shy little boy, wasn't he. And then he became happy, don't you remember? I bet he's a handsome young man now.'

'Oh, he is,' said Ros.

A voice over the tannoy said,

'Mr Monroe to room two.'

The man with the Black Death went out and Mrs Leopard peeled her face off the wall.

'And why are you here today, if you don't mind me asking?'

'I'm here about Pete.'

'Oh?'

'To get something for his hayfever. Ready for the summer.'

Ros picked up a copy of Woman's Realm and they looked at it together until Mrs Leopard was called. Before she left she took one of Ros's hands so that their faces were close together.

'I'll always remember you cycling down the lane in the sunshine, darling, so beautiful and so full of care.' At the door she looked round and pulled a face. 'If you hear me scream it's because Dr Bangalore's got cold hands.'

After ten minutes Mrs Leopard passed the waiting room on her way out and Ros was called in. Dr Bangalore was small and portly, about fifty-five years old, with dark brown skin and brown eyes and bald apart from a semi-circle of white hair around each ear. When Ros came in he trotted towards her, waved her into the patient's chair and then trotted back behind his desk. When he sat in Dr Blisland's great oak chair his feet barely touched the ground. He was a smoker of cigarettes, a dainty one, hardly inhaling and blowing out formless clouds of smoke, like Joan Crawford in an old movie, Ros thought.

'What can I do for you, Mrs Turner?'

'I'm actually here about my son Pete.'

'Is your son a patient here?'

'Dr Blisland prescribes something for his acne.'

'And what does he prescribe?'

'Triclosan.'

Dr Bangalore pulled an unhappy face.

'Is it helping his condition?'

'Not at all.'

'You should have brought him here so I can see for myself.'

'That's part of the problem. I can't get him out of the house.'

The doctor stubbed out his cigarette, linked his hands across his tummy and dipped his head in thought. 'Such a shame,' he muttered. 'Such a shame because acne is a chronic condition that can persist into middle age, while the psychological effects can last even longer.' Looking up and seeing the scared look on Ros's face he held up his hands. 'But those cases are extremely rare, Mrs Turner, I assure you.' Then he jumped down off his chair and began to pace up and down in front of Ros. 'Now, we know that Pete's current treatment isn't working, so logic tells us to try something else. Do you agree?'

'I suppose so.'

Dr Bangalore stopped by his desk to take a cigarette out of the packet, but instead of lighting it he walked up and down while holding it in the air.

'Now Mrs Turner, if you'll permit me I'm going to take you on a journey to a country far away from here, to the land of my ancestors, in fact. You see, once upon a time in India a guru was travelling through the countryside when he came to a village where everyone – even the teenage boys and girls – had wonderful skin. He couldn't understand why this was until the day he noticed that the dried elephant dung that the villagers used as fuel in their homes had, when ignited, a particular smell. The next day he followed some elephants into the jungle and found that they were eating an extremely rare plant with little blue flowers called Wort Of India. He concluded that it was the presence of this plant in the smoke from the elephant dung that caused such beneficial effects on the villagers.'

Dr Bangalore lit his cigarette and sat down again. His story reminded Ros of a fantastical tale from the Jungle Books and she wondered if he was like one of those medieval quack doctors who passed off useless elixirs as miracles. On the other hand she was a little spellbound by this amiable and passionate little man, and sat there smiling drowsily, wondering what to say. The doctor registered her bemusement.

'Ah, you didn't expect to hear a story like that today, did you?'

'So what you're saying, doctor, is that we should go to India.'

'No, Reading.'

'And where can I get elephant dung in Reading?'

Dr Bangalore chuckled and shook his head.

'It's not elephant dung that you want, Mrs Turner. It's the little blue flower.'

'So you can get it in this country.'

'It is cultivated and used in many parts of the world but not often by mainstream medicine. For instance, someone like Dr Blisland, with his more orthodox background, would never think of prescribing it.' Dr Bangalore suddenly looked serious. 'Which is in no sense a criticism. I have known him for many years and he is a fine fellow and a fine doctor.'

'Well, if you think it'll help, I'll get some.'

'Good.'

Dr Bangalore wrote some notes and an address on a leaf of his prescription pad and tore it off.

'The people who run this chemist's are friends of mine. They put an extract of Wort of India into an ointment which can be applied to the skin.'

The next thing Ros knew, she was standing by a stone trough full of blue geraniums just outside the door, tucking the prescription into her handbag and thinking that providence had been kind to her, thanks to her encounter with the new doctor. But as she walked away doubts began to creep in. Was the treatment legal? Was it expensive? Did Dr Bangalore recommend it to all acne sufferers or was he using Pete for experimental purposes? She walked in a daze, like a child who'd just climbed down from a storyteller's lap, her body in the everyday world and her mind holding an elephant by the tail as it crashed through the jungle.

She needed some groceries so instead of taking the alleyway to the estate she went past the Redan and down to the supermarket, where she took a trolley from just inside the door and headed down the first aisle. Ros loved her family and knew that they loved her back – after their own fashion – but she also knew that, very simply, men lived to eat, and that except for when thoughts of loved ones intruded, they thought about nothing but food all day long. So she never did less than a mighty shop when it came to providing for the men in her life. She got potatoes for chipping, fishfingers, orange squash, chocolate cake and sugar puffs – all of Pete's necessities in other words – and then salad stuff, pies, toilet roll, tinned fruit and a bag of apples for them all, a dozen light ales and a bottle of scotch for Ted and a bottle of Cinzano for herself, and finally – knowing the importance of cheese to growing boys and English yeomen – a brick of cheddar.

When she got to the till there were two punk rockers – a boy and a girl – paying for cigarettes and booze. The girl was fat and was wearing holed black tights, a white PVC miniskirt and a black string vest over a red bra. Ros knew the boy from when she used to go into the packing plant at North Sea Fish on Friday afternoons and hand out the wages. He was about six-foot-three with spiky blonde hair, a pale handsome face and shining blue eyes. His black combat trousers were slashed to pieces but his Ramones T-shirt was intact. His real name was Mark but because his girlfriend's name was Sugar everyone called him Lump.

They'd never met outside of work before and it took them both a few moments to get used to the novelty of seeing each other in civvies, Lump without his white overalls and green rubber boots on, Ros divested of her sensible secretarial clobber.

'Hello, Ros. What are you doing these days?'

'Still looking for another job.'

Lump, Sugar noticed, seemed riveted by the dimples in Ros's knees and – taking umbrage – hit him over the head with the wine bottle she was holding.

'You slag!' cried Lump.

'Wanker!' screamed Sugar.

They grabbed each other by the throat and began a shoving match, dislodging a rack of chewing gum by the till and causing a great pyramid of tins of baked beans to cascade all over the floor.

'Oi, you two, pack it in!' shouted the manager as he came over.

Sugar and Lump let go of each other and, smirking, formed an orderly queue at the till. Ros went and stood behind them, stepping around the manager and an assistant who were picking up all the cans from the floor. The girl on the till looked uneasily at Lump and Sugar as she checked the prices on their items, and for a while the only sound was the leathery hum of the conveyor belt.

'So why aren't you at work today?' said Ros to Lump.

'I had to sign on, didn't I. Then we went to The Redan but they wouldn't serve us snakebites so we're going to make our own. Then we're going to the woods to pick some mushrooms.'

'But they've got mushrooms here,' said Ros, indicating the vegetable section.

Sugar and Lump looked at each other and grinned.

'No, we're after *magic* mushrooms,' said Lump.

'Ah,' said Ros, as though now she understood, while thinking to herself, 'Aren't they a bit old to be reading Enid Blyton?'

The rest of the day proceeded normally. At about half past four a small thunderhead came through the back door. Ros wanted to put her arms around him but knew that he would flinch from the touch of love. The thunderhead proclaimed – as usual – that it was starving and went straight to the cupboard that contained the crisps.

'Hey, you're not having any of those,' said Ros. 'Dinner will be ready soon.'

After pausing for a moment Pete cried in a plummy accent, 'But surely, mater, aristocratic families enjoy an aperitif before dining.' and took out a jumbo-sized packet of cheese and onion. Ros took the packet, bashed Pete over the head with it then exchanged it for a miniature packet of Frazzles.

The thunderhead was followed an hour later by a grizzly bear, and Ros was treated to a perfunctory kiss, some desultory conversation and – on asking him if he'd enjoyed his dinner – a grunt.

At about nine o'clock, just after Pete had gone to bed, the doorbell rang. Ros went to answer it and found two large, grim-looking men on the doorstep, their faces the colour of mustard under the porch light. They were both wearing raincoats and had their shoulders hunched up against the drizzle. The leading man held up his warrant card.

'Detective sergeant Fenton and detective constable Naylor. Is Mr Edward Turner in?'

Ros frowned and thought, 'Edward Turner? Who's he?' but then she cried, 'Oh, you mean Ted. Yes he's here.' Then her face fell. 'Why? What's happened?'

'If we can just have a word with him.'

She left the policemen there and went into the living room. Ted was standing up, his moustache looking even blacker now that the skin of his face was so pale, and realising that the sound of the men's voices had brought him to his feet, Ros felt scared for the first time.

'There's two policeman here to see you.'

'What do they want?'

'How would I know?'

Ted hesitated, like a bear who'd just got wind of an even bigger bear, but then he said, 'I'll go and see,' and left, shutting the door behind him.

He took the policemen into the kitchen where they began to talk, their deep, steady voices vibrating the whorled glass in the living room door but not allowing Ros – who was standing with her ear pressed against it – to make out the words. It was Pete, standing on the landing in darkness and wondering who the men were, who could hear snatches of what they were saying.

'Your name keeps coming up, Ted.'

'Coming up where?'

'Among the people we've talked to.'

'They say, "A big man, with a moustache."'

'And another man, with a bald head and glasses like Eric Morecambe.'

Ted snorted, 'You should be looking for Ernie Wise, not me.'

'This isn't a time for levity, Mr Turner.'

There was a long silence. Pete guessed from the amount of tobacco smoke drifting up the stairs that at least two of the men in the kitchen were smoking.

'Well, that's the situation, Ted,' one of them said eventually. 'The next time we have any sort of conversation it'll be down at the station.'

'I just can't help you, lads,' said Ted, and even though Pete couldn't see his father, he knew he was shrugging with one big shoulder. Even so, a chill rose from Pete's toes and went all the way up his legs, as though he was standing on a precipice. He tip-toed back to his bedroom and wailed inwardly like a child,

'They're going to take my daddy away.'

Ros heard the men coming out of the kitchen and hopped away from the door so that they wouldn't see her shadow behind the glass. When Ted came in he found her standing in the middle of the room, looking frightened.

'What did they want?'

Ted looked at the telly, which was on but with the sound turned down.

'Oh, they're looking for some stolen goods.'

'Why did they come here?'

'They think I might have heard something.' Ted sat down with a big sigh. 'Turn the sound up.'

'Well, have you?'

'Me? God no.'

Ros didn't believe for a moment that Ted had stolen anything, but she did suspect – due to his evasiveness – that he knew something and had lied to the police and her to protect a pal of his in the industry. In bed that night the great boiler of a man that she'd slept beside for seventeen years, who usually burned steadily all night long, kept flaring up and dying down as though disturbed by winds from the outside world.

Six

Like many adolescent recluses, Pete spent lunchtimes in the library, where he felt safe from Mick Burnley and public scrutiny of his face. For a while he'd gained a sort of notoriety as the boy who wore a motorcycle helmet to school, but the torture had never stopped altogether. In particular, a poster of a famous volcano kept appearing on the school noticeboard on which the words 'Mt Etna' had been replaced by 'Turner's face' and the word lava by the word 'pus.'

Among the other monkish pupils often to be found in the library was Edmunds with his club foot, long-legged Walker who had spasms, and poor Tyler in his wheelchair, with his hands always at right angles to his wrists, his head leaning to one side at a brutal angle and his tubed tongue sticking out. Pete ignored these other hermits and read Lord of The Rings. He wished he was a great hero like Aragorn but felt like an orc in school uniform.

'So how far have you got?' said a voice one day.

Pete looked up and saw Timothy Herbert, another boy

who spent a lot of time in the library because he didn't have anyone to talk to. Timothy was short for his age, had little legs, a large head and a stocky body. He wore glasses with thick lenses, a hearing aid in each ear and had a severe side parting in his greasy black hair. With his hands thrust into the pockets of his blazer, he stood there smiling benignly down at Pete like an old professor.

Pete wondered how this complete non-entity had dared to accost him but he didn't ignore him. He held the book up so Timothy could see that he was about a third of the way in. Timothy bit his lower lip and wrinkled his nose so that he looked like a rabbit.

'So I guess you're coming to the end of the first volume. The Fellowship has found sanctuary in the realm of Lorien.'

'How did you know?'

'Oh, I've read it five times. I've read The Silmarillion four times.'

Pete was impressed but didn't say so. He was more worried that people would notice him talking to Timothy Herbert. He looked around and sure enough, Tyler in his wheelchair was regarding them with a wet eye.

Pete pretended to read on and after a while Timothy wandered away.

Two days later Pete looked up from Lord Of The Rings and saw that Timothy had sat down opposite him. In his left hand he was holding a book called History's Greatest Unsolved Mathematical Problems and with his right hand he was doing calculations on a piece of paper. His face was glowing and he was humming like an early computer. Pete didn't really want to talk but he couldn't help himself.

'Do you understand that book?'

Timothy looked up.

'I understand the concepts but I'm not trying to find the solutions. I imagine that whoever eventually solves any of these problems will have a similar experience to Gandalf at the entrance to the Mines of Moria, where the password to enter eluded him but then turned out to be devastatingly simple.'

Pete was flattered because Timothy was obviously treating him as someone who was his equal in intellect.

Timothy went on, 'Do you like maths?'

'No.'

Timothy looked at Pete's book.

'Looks like you've finished volume one of Lord of The Rings. Hurry up a bit though. Then we can talk about it.'

Pete didn't like the sound of this because it presumed that they had some kind of future together. When he looked round in the hope that no one was watching them, he met the eyes of Edmund's who'd clearly identified him and Timothy as another David and Jonathan.

The next time that Pete went into the library, Timothy was already there. He was about to ignore him when he noticed that he was holding a copy of ELO's new album, *Out of The Blue*.

'You've got it!'

'Yesterday.'

'What's it like?'

'All the tracks are brilliant.'

Pete was about to ask if he could have a look when Timothy bowed and presented it to him. Pete thought that Jeff Lyne was some kind of god who'd arrived in the spaceship depicted on the front cover of the album, and realising that Timothy thought the same, admitted to himself that even friendless swots could have good taste. He handed the album back and then became aware of a commotion behind him. He looked and saw Edmunds with his club foot pushing Tyler in his wheelchair straight towards them. Edmund's eyes were bulging out of their sockets while Tyler was clapping with his wrists and dancing from the neck up.

'Let's have a look, Herbert,' said Edmunds.

Timothy winked at Pete, handed the album over and then sat there looking pious and lordly, as though he'd just bestowed the gift of eternal life on two of the dying. Pete smiled, and noticing the smile, Timothy smiled back, and for a while the two regarded each other fraternally.

The next time that Pete went to the library, Timothy wasn't there. He sat down in his usual corner and opened Lord of The Rings but after a while became aware of an unusually deep silence in the room. He looked around and saw that every boy was holding an open book over his face like a mask, and then he saw why: Mick Burnley was there, standing in the middle of the room and looking vexed, the crinkles in his forehead reminding Pete of a giant chip. Mick walked up to a boy called Dobbs, who was always in the library not only because he had acne like Pete, but ginger hair as well and so – as everyone said – was the unluckiest boy in the world.

'Oi, mate.'

Dobbs peeped over the top of his book but was too frightened to speak.

'Oi, are you listening?'

'Please leave me alone.'

'I just want to ask you something.'

'What?' squeaked Dobbs.

'Is this the library?'

Dobbs looked around at the thousands of books on all the shelves and thought that Mick must be having a laugh. This presented Dobbs with a dilemma: how to show his appreciation of the joke while his toes were curling with horror. But really there was only one thing for it, so he began to laugh. It was a long, shrill, hair-raising laugh that echoed down all the long corridors of the school and even made the headmaster – sitting at his desk a third of a mile away – look up suddenly. But it was the boys sitting around Dobbs who were the most terrified, because they'd witnessed Mick driving a boy insane before their very eyes.

Dobbs stopped laughing when he realised that Mick's expression hadn't changed, meaning that he wasn't joking after all and that he really was as thick as shit.

'Well?' said Mick.

'Yes, it is the library.'

'I fort so.'

Mick lumbered off and for the next five minutes could be heard stomping up and down between the racks and cursing. Pete counted eight 'Fucks' and ten 'Bollocks'. Then Mick reappeared looking down at a book and walking straight towards the empty chair next to Pete. At this point, Pete covered his face with Lord of The Rings and prayed. He felt someone brush against him and the chair creak as someone sat in it, but once he'd plucked up the courage to look he found that it was only Timothy sitting there. He'd never been so pleased to see anyone in his whole life.

Timothy whispered, 'Mick Burnley's here.'

'I know.'

Mick was standing in front of the desk of Mrs Collier, the librarian. She reached up for his book and said, 'We don't often see you in here, Mick.'

'It wasn't my idea, Miss. It was Foreskin's… I mean Mr Foreskin's… shit… I mean Mr Foreman's. He told me to come and get a book about the army because that's the best place for me.'

Mrs Collier looked at the book.

'But this is a book about Nazi atrocities during World War Two.'

'Well, I fort, if I already know how to commit atrocities before I join up, I won't have to do any basic training. They'll send me straight out with the nuclear flamethrowers.'

'But Mick, armies fight to bring about peace.'

'Peace!' Mick threw out his arms in shock. 'Oh, that can't be right, Miss. That can't be right at all.'

'Wait here.' Mrs Collier walked off and came back with a book called Careers In The Army. 'I think this is more what Mr Foreman had in mind.'

She stamped the book and handed it to Mick, who wandered off, flicking through the pages. When he got to where Pete and Timothy were sitting he stopped and mumbled sadly, 'There aren't as many pictures in this one.'

He looked up just in time to catch Pete peering round the edge of his book and recognised him by the ugly rainbow of purple, yellow and black around Pete's left eye. Even though he was standing only a few feet away, Mick waved and cried amiably, 'Hello, mate.'

Now Pete was in a dilemma similar to Dobb's. Was this

new, amiable Mick a genuine incarnation or just the same old Mick who not so long ago had socked him one in the maelstrom of the playground. 'Just be polite,' thought Pete, at the same time remembering the proceedure for dealing with a ferocious dog: stay still, don't run. From behind his book he said, 'Oh, hello.'

Mick pointed at Pete's eye.

'I did that, didn't I?'

'You did.'

'Sorry about that,' said Mick, looking bashful.

Pete couldn't believe his ears and realised – from the way he was fiddling with his hearing aids – that Timothy couldn't either.

'Still, it's getting better.'

'Oh, yea, I'll be as right as rain soon.'

Mick looked at his book, his lips protruding thoughtfully, and then said, 'Do you want to hear a joke?'

'Ok.'

'What's that revolting growth on your neck?'

'I don't know.'

'Your head.'

There were snorts and sniggers from the boys round about and then Mick walked off looking mightily pleased with himself, naturally for one who'd just made a new friend and brought the house down as well. Timothy said, 'He got you there, Pete.'

Pete blushed, not because of Mick, but because it was the first time that Timothy had called him by his Christian name.

Now and then Ros would pick up Pete from school in her

white Mini Clubman Estate. It had missing wheel trims and shuddered when it went round corners but she loved it like the second child that she'd never had, and even did a weekly oil and water check, much to Ted's amusement. She didn't pick Pete up every day because she knew that he wouldn't want to be seen as a mummy's boy, but she knew he was pleased when she did turn up, though obviously he didn't show it.

One day when she was waiting for him, as hundreds of pupils flowed past her and out of the school gates, she searched the faces of the boys for spots and every time she found a young fellow with even a few, let alone a hundred, she thought, 'Thank God.'

She saw Dan and Adrian and wondered where Pete was, and then spotted him walking towards her with his head down, trying to hide his face but listening to the boy walking beside him, a strange, serious-looking boy with big glasses and a severe side parting. As Pete climbed into the car, the boy stood and watched, biting his lower lip and wrinkling his nose so that he looked like a bunny rabbit. It worried Ros that Pete was keeping such strange company.

'Is that boy a friend of yours?'

'Who, him? No, not really.'

When they got home Pete opened the garage door so that Ros could drive in. He went through the back door which led straight into the kitchen and began making himself a bowl of Sugar Puffs. When Ros came in she found Pete sitting at the kitchen counter using a table spoon to eat Sugar Puffs out of a large yellow tupperware bowl that she normally used when preparing cake mix.

She reached into his school bag and took out his lunchbox. She was pleased to see that he'd eaten everything – the cheese and pickle sandwich, the crisps and the big piece of chocolate cake – but it worried her that he was following it up with such a large bowl of sugary cereal. She leaned against the draining board with her arms folded and watched him – tickled for the thousandth time by the opiated eyes and bulging cheeks of the adolescent boy eating cereal – and in the end decided not to say anything. She knew that all the extra sugar wasn't helping his skin condition but at the same time she didn't have the heart to deny him any of his treats.

They ate their dinner off their laps while sitting in front of the telly, just the two of them, this being the third night in a row that Ted was going to be late home from work. Two days before, he'd phoned Ros at about four o'clock and told her to keep his dinner in the oven. 'It's mayhem here,' he'd said. 'I'll be back about nine.' In the background she could hear great booms and the echoing shouts of the men in the shed, and Ted's goodbye was drowned out by the scream of a power tool cutting metal.

The day before, he didn't phone until eight o'clock in the evening, saying, 'I'm on my way now.' He was in the pub, or so she guessed from the dull hubbub of voices behind him, the barman's 'Who's next?' and the fairground clunks and clangs of a pinball machine.

'You could have called earlier!' Ros had shouted.

'Sorry, love. I had to stay behind to supervise the boys doing overtime.'

'I hope you haven't had a lot to drink if you're driving.'

'Only two pints of shandy.'

Ros knew that Ted had said these words with a wink at the men around him, having really sunk about four pints of ale.

'Very likely.' she said.

'Honest.'

'I don't believe a word of it.'

'Hey, lads,' he said, turning to the crowd. 'I've only had two shandies, haven't I?'

'No!' they roared.

Comments were made for Ros's benefit.

'More like ten pints!'

'You're better off without him, Ros.'

'I've never seen such depravity!'

Then the line had gone dead and Ros wished that they had a dog, so when Ted got home she could point at it and say, 'Your dinnner's in there.'

By the time Pete went to bed, Ted still hadn't called and this time Ros began to imagine that he'd had a fatal car crash on the way home or got arrested by the policemen who had come to the house. When the phone did ring at about half past nine she snatched it up and cried, 'Ted?'

'It's me.'

'Where have you been?' Ros wailed.

'Don't panic. I just got held up again.'

Behind Ted this time there was nothing but silence and his voice sounded far away. Then she distinctly heard the wrap of knuckles on glass – so he was in a phone box – and Ted go 'Sshh!'

'Where are you?'

'At work.'

She told him to hurry home and put the phone down.

A floorboard creaked on the landing and she looked up to see Pete's bare feet and the bottoms of his pale blue pyjamas in the darkness. In the voice of a little boy who'd just woken from a nightmare, he said, 'Was that Dad? What's going on?'

'He's been held up at work again. Don't worry.'

Now Ros was sure that something was up – Ted's lie about his whereabouts had confirmed it – but through the fog of marriage she couldn't divine what, although she was sure it wasn't another woman.

When Ted got into bed Ros kept her back to him and pretended to be asleep and he had to lean right over her to kiss her cheek. His lips were warm but his moustache was damp and cold as though he'd been outside all evening.

Seven

Ros heard that they were recruiting at Huntley And Palmer's biscuit factory in Reading. After her interview she walked across Elm Park to her parents' house which was an old terraced, two up-two down that had been modernised by the corporation in the mid sixties, so that on the ground floor there was now the parlour, a small dining room, a kitchen and a WC (replacing the outsde loo), and upstairs two bedrooms and a bathroom. The alterations meant that her parents had been able to stay where they were instead of moving into a tower block 'built from the rubble of the war', as her dad said.

She had her own key so she went straight in and found them sitting side by side on the sofa facing the telly. Betty, her mum, said 'Hello, Ros,' but neither her or her dad, Charlie took their eyes off the screen. Bountiful Bob the game show host, with his copper-coloured skin and fluorescent teeth, had just told a loving couple that they'd won a caravan. The wife had gone daft with excitement while her husband was clearly hoping that the top-heavy blonde leaning out of the caravan's front window was part of the prize. As the credits rolled, Bouniful Bob pushed them through the door of the caravan and a second later they reappeared next to the blonde and began waving nuttily at the delirious audience.

Ros stood there with her hands on her hips, looking from her parents to the telly and back again.

'What are you watching this rubbish for?'

'Oh God, Hitler's here,' said Charlie.

He tried to sound cross but really he liked nothing better than to be scolded by his heavenly daughter. He was a short, round-faced, portly man with a purplish nose, and was sixty-six years old and retired. He'd been a merchant seaman during the war and had crossed the Atlantic six times in the Convoys. 'Torpedoed twice but never sunk!' was his peacetime cry. He used to come home on leave, lift plump little Ros onto his lap and tell her about the great cargoes that they carried all the way from America, such as hundreds of lorries and jeeps, or mountains of tins of fruit, or of beef or beans.

'One night,' he told her, 'I was up on deck keeping watch in the freezing cold with a great big icicle hanging off the end of my nose, and below me there were a million socks and I wasn't allowed to put a single pair of them on.'

'Poor Daddy!' Ros had cried, clinging passionately to him.

'But I said to myself that when I get home my dear little Ros will give me a cuddle and that'll warm me up.'

After the war Charlie had been a sexton at the local church and then a postman until the day he retired.

Ros's mum was only a couple of puddings short of

being as plump as her husband but it was from her that Ros had inherited her chestnut colouring and good looks. Vestiges of an English rose remained in her bashful brown eyes, rounded cheeks and delicate chin. She sat there smiling up at Ros with her arms folded across her big bust, her legs crossed at the ankles and a pink fluffy slipper dangling from her toes.

Charlie got up, puffed over to the telly and turned it off. Then he looked solemnly at Ros.

'It is time!'

Ros saw the look in his eye and turned pale.

'No, Dad.'

'Come on, love. You know it's what you want.'

'I'm forty.'

Her dad moved towards her with his hands out.

'Mum, help,' said Ros, but her mum just sat there watching and smiling.

Ros had gone weak at the knees so she couldn't run. Slowly, her dad backed her against the wall and enveloped her in his arms. Like great spiders his hands crawled down her back and then – pouncing on her ribs – began to tickle her. Ros squirmed and sank to the floor, emitting high-pitched squeaks like a mouse under a hawk, but she couldn't escape the spiders until – finding the strength from somewhere – she wriggled free and crawled behind the telly. Her dad followed her, and unable to reach her with his hands now, began to torment her with his toes.

'Did you forget that you are one of the ticklish? That you always have been and always will be one of the ticklish? And that it is the fate of the ticklish to be tickled?'

After a while he stepped back. 'Arise, oh little one! Your ordeal is over.'

Whimpering, Ros crawled out from behind the telly and got to her feet, her hair all over the place. Half blind from the tears that had made runnels in her make-up, she grabbed a cushion – still warm and concave from the imprint of Charlie's bottom – and bludgeoned him with it. Cowering, he dashed for the door and fled through it.

'It's time for a cup of tea.'

They took their mugs into the little walled back garden. A square of mowed lawn was bordered on two sides by vegetable patches and on the other two by flower beds. The warm, early summer sun was trapped here so that already Charlie's runner beans had twined halfway up their bamboo frame, and the lavender was busy with bees from dawn until dusk. In the corner stood an old metal dustbin, its top covered over with a soft green cloud of carrot leaves. When mature, these locally famous vegetables were as wide as tea cups at the top and descended three feet into the compost.

They did a circuit, Charlie pointing out things to Ros and making sure she couldn't see inside the shed, where a crocheted, multi-coloured bobble hat had been turned into an onion bag. They unfolded some picnic chairs and sat in a row, looking up the garden.

Charlie said, 'Once, Ros, when you were a baby, we left you in your carrycot out here and when we came back a bee was sitting on your nose. You were looking at it with your eyes crossed like babies do. We didn't know what to do, did we, Betts?'

'We thought if we tried to chase it away it might get angry and sting you.'

'What happened in the end?' said Ros, who'd heard the story before.

'Oh, it buzzed off eventually,' said Charlie.

Ros thought of poor Pete, who looked as though he'd been stung by a whole hive of bees.

'We haven't seen Pete for a while,' said Betty.

'I expect he'd rather go out with his friends than see his nanny and grandad,' said Charlie.

Ros explained that Pete's acne had turned him into a recluse, that his original doctor had prescribed a cream that wasn't working and that the new doctor had advised trying a strange potion called Wort Of India.

'Is he eating properly?' said Betty.

'Of course,' said Ros.

'I mean he's not eating loads of chocolate?'

'Well, a bit now and then… '

'You musn't let him have any,' said Betty.

Ros was trying to remember the name of the movie in which her favourite actor, Stewart Granger, had gone to a costume ball and put on an ugly mask to hide his handsome face.

Once they'd finished their tea they went back inside and Ros got ready to leave. The three of them made a crowd in the tiny hallway. Ros hugged her mum but when her dad came towards her for the same she shied away in case he tickled her again, and he had to rummage among the coats hanging on the wall in order to find her face and kiss it.

'I'll bring Pete next time,' she said, stepping into the sunshine.

They watched her walk away and thought how pretty she looked in her yellow twill skirt and white blouse, with her little leather handbag bouncing against her hip.

Ros had an appoinment at Jenny's to have her hair done and as she opened the door to the salon she was smiling at the prospect of being fussed over. The warm and soapy air was full of the tang of hairspray. There were women in recliners with their heads tilted back into sinks, having their hair shampooed, and others helmeted by the great dryers, sitting stiffly with magazines open on their laps. Over the drone of the dryers the hairdressers chatted to the ladies, thatching their hair with rollers or watching their apprentices make decsive snips with one eye closed.

Jenny was Ros's best friend from school, had been the chief bridesmaid at her wedding and was now the owner of her own salon. She was tall, with blue eyes and long blonde hair that was curled and feathered in the style of the TV star Farah Fawcett Majors. She saw Ros come in and they looked at each other the way they used to when they were eight years old and their mouths were full of sweets. They sat side by side in reception and caught up.

Dawn, the girl behind the desk, called over, 'How's that handsome husband of yours, Ros?'

All the girls knew Ted.

'I didn't marry him because he's handsome. I married him because he's good at DIY.'

'I bet he's had to fix the bed a few times,' said Tracy – the salon's vulgar heart – as she passed by.

Jenny washed Ros's hair, sat her in a chair and bought her a coffee. Linda, who always cut Ros's hair, came over and taking sides with Jenny, persuaded her to have two inches off the bottom and the hair nearest to her face feathered.

Ros normally wore her hair down past the shoulders with a centre parting. It was straight all the way down to where the ends curled naturally. She tucked it behind her right ear when she felt pretty and behind both ears when she was full of beans. Ted thought that she was most stunning when she had her hair up, revealing the long, smooth neck that brought a lump to his throat, and was wearing a cocktail dress like a Bond girl in a casino, and she obliged him now and then but generally she felt self-conscious when too many heads were turned towards her. On the night many years ago when they'd celebrated their engagement by going to a posh restaurant, they'd sat near a group of guffawing men who'd spent the evening nudging each other and looking at Ros. This had made Ted even more proud of his fiancee but after a while Ros went completely silent and stopped eating.

'Can we go?' she'd said before their puddings came.

'Why?'

'Please.'

Ted was desolate because he thought that Ros had changed her mind about their future together, until they got outside, where her loving smile returned and she clung to him once more.

At some point Jenny showed her a photograph of her own son, Duncan, who was fifteen years old. He had dark hair and his eyes were blue like his mum's but what really caught Ros's eye was the smoothness of his skin.

'Very good-looking,' Ros forced herself to admit to Jenny as she handed the photo back, while thinking that there was not a boy in the world who possessed the sweetness of her Peter, even with his skin the way it was.

She tuned in to what Linda was saying to Paula, the girl who was working next to her.

'Does your Andy do it?'

'Fart? Of course. All the time.'

'I mean first thing in the morning.'

'Probably.'

'My Jim definitely does. As soon as he wakes up he does this great big fart under the bedclothes.'

'Men have more wind.'

'I know, but they don't have to share it around, do they?'

'True.'

'Anyway, the other morning I'd had enough. He farted and I said, 'Did you have to do that right now?' Of course he goes into a great big sulk. The next morning I woke up and I'm lying there thinking, 'Any moment now.' But for once he doesn't and I think to myself, 'He's reformed.' But then he gets up, goes into the bathroom, sits on the toilet and then does the fart. The neighbours must have heard it through the wall.'

Ros remembered a similar, conciliatory gesture that Ted had made, at a time when he knew that she was cross with him about something. She'd walked into the bedroom one night to find that he'd lifted the bedclothes up – obviously because he'd let one go – and was wafting the stink towards his side of the room. Seeing the sheepish look on his face she'd almost felt sorry for him, but instead of letting him off the hook had glorified in her ascendency for a couple more days at least. These days she took Ted's tremendous early morning guffs so much for granted that she wondered how Linda's marriage survived if she made so much fuss.

When Linda had finished cutting her hair, Jenny came over. She stood behind Ros's chair and stroked her hair where it was feathered, checking the new styling for structure and bounce.

'Do you like it?'

Ros, feeling drowsy from all the pampering, smiled her thanks and then, knowing that she didn't have to pay for the cut, tipped Linda all the same. Once she'd left the salon and walked a few yards, she checked her reflection one more time in a shop window and tucked her hair behind her right ear.

Now it was time to make her way to the chemist's that Dr Bangalore had recommended. After walking for half an hour she found it in one of the back streets near the station. It was a corner shop built of the same deep red brick as all the terraced streets round about. The shelves in the window displayed pills and powders, soap, cosmetics and plastic toys.

As Ros opened the door a bell chimed and a fat Indian lady pushed her way through a bead curtain behind the counter at the back of the shop. She had a face as round as a baby's and wore – for such humdrum surroundings – a thrilling amount of make-up. She was wearing blue silk trousers, a purple tunic and a dozen or so gold bangles on each wrist.

Ros held out the prescription and said, 'I've come for this.'

The woman looked at it and then disappeared behind the curtain. Ros heard her say to someone, 'Look, from Bangalore-ji.'

'Ah,' said a man's voice. 'I'll come.'

The woman returned, followed by a small Indian man wearing glasses with thick black frames and a white lab coat. They stood next to each other and smiled amiably at Ros, the woman chuckling silently and her head wandering faintly from side to side in the most endearing way, Ros thought.

'I see this is not for you,' said the chemist.

'It's for my son.'

'Has Dr Bangalore explained all about Wort Of India?'

'He told me the story.' Ros wanted reasurance from these kind people. 'Is it really true?'

'A strange story, isn't it? But quite true. I assure you that the effects on your son will be entirely beneficial.'

'Well, I'll try it,' said Ros.

While he was gone Ros wandered around the shop. She picked up razor blades for Ted, a box of plasters and two make-up brushes. She brought them to the counter and the woman put them in a brown paper bag. It was so narrow behind the counter that when the woman opened the till the coin tray shot out and boffed her in the stomach. She chortled, bumped it back in with her tummy and handed Ros her change.

The chemist took his time coming back and Ros tried to think of something to say to the woman, who was the first Indian person she'd ever talked to, very few people from India having settled in Earley on the outskirts of Reading. Suddenly she remembered a novel that she'd read once, a romance set during the British Raj, and wondered if it would be okay to ask the woman if she'd ever seen a maharani wearing silk slippers or a tiger dragging a goat from a village, but then the chemist came bustling back in. He had a white tube of ointment the same size and shape as the type Pete already used and had written on the label: Extract of Wort of India. To be applied once daily to the affected area.

'Just before bedtime,' he said.

Ros paid for the ointment and the chemist and his wife asked her to give their regards to their old friend Dr Bangalore. The door jingled again as she left.

That night Pete was reading in bed as usual. He'd just got to the part in Lord of The Rings when Aragorn, Legolas and Gimli are intercepted by the Riders of Rohan and was not in a mood to be disturbed, but then his mum came in looking furtive. He tried to carry on reading but had actually gone blind with fury and couldn't see the words. She stood by his bed looking down at him.

'Oh, your face is bad,' she said, sadly. She held out the tube of new ointment. 'Look, I've brought something else to try.'

Pete took it and felt a twinge of interest. He'd known for weeks that the old cream wasn't working and had only carried on using it out of desperation. But then he saw the word 'Wort' on the label and instead of asking what it meant, decided that it was a misspelling of 'wart'.

'So this contains warts?'

'Not warts. Wort. A wort is a plant or the extract of a plant.'

'Or is it going to give me warts? So now I'll have warts *and* pustules. Or are you trying to replace the pustules with the warts?'

This brought Ros to the boil but she managed to stop herself shouting at him.

'You're being silly,' she said. 'Just try it. I promise it won't do any harm and it might work.'

'No.'

'Please.'

'IT WON'T MAKE ANY FUCKING DIFFERENCE!'

Ted charged into the room, making the floorboards quiver.

'What's going on?'

Ros was about to tell him about the new ointment but then her shoulders sagged and she said, 'Nothing, don't worry.'

'That's alright then.' He looked at Pete. 'Don't you ever swear at your mum like that again. Understand?'

Ros pushed him gently towards the door. When she looked back, the expression on her son's face said that there was no such thing as happiness.

Eight

It was a hot, cloudless day at the yard and some of the lads were kicking a football around during their lunch break. The ball flew through the air easily enough but it didn't roll very well because it was really a crocheted, multi-coloured bobble hat that had been stuffed with newspaper. Ted, who was on his way back to his office, stood and watched for a while, remembering when he used to be one of the mechanics kicking a ball around during breaks, and before that one of the HGV drivers ploughing up and down the A1 every week to Doncaster, Newcastle or Berwick-upon-Tweed.

All the municipal bin lorries had been serviced and driven off and for once the yard looked half empty. Ted looked around at the vast, filthy industrial space that he ran for Dickie and thought that he'd done alright for himself over the last twenty years or so. The big, slow teenager who they'd taken on to sweep the yard and pile up the tyres had become in that time if not a captain of industry then at least a corporal of industry.

In his reverie Ted could see his face miniaturised a thousand times in the oily cobblestones of the yard. Suddenly the ball hit him on the head and he came to.

'Come on, Ted. We need a goalkeeper.'

Ted stuffed his clipboard under his armpit, lifted his chin and walked past the watching men to the steps that led up to his office. Here he turned, declaimed, 'It's lonely at the top but I must return to my responsibilities,' and then ascended through a shower of jeers and greasy rags.

He sat behind his desk with a big sigh and opened his sandwich box, which contained a cheese and pickle sandwich and a chicken and red onion chutney sandwich – both on white bread halved into triangles – a pork pie and a packet of cheese and onion crisps. He washed down these victuals with slurps of coffee from a mug, heaving further heavy sighs every three or four mouthfuls as he gazed out the window.

He thought of Pete and asked himself, 'What's happened to the lad?' He remembered Christmases when – in a little skit – he and Pete would sing 'Bring Me Sunshine'. Once they'd finished the song they would turn their backs on their little audience and – throwing their arms and legs around in the manner of Eric and Ernie – would dance out of the room but only after getting wedged together in the doorway because they couldn't both fit through at once. He remembered a sketch that he and Pete used to perform after dinner, when Ros had finished doing the washing-up and was bringing them a cup of tea.

'My son!' Ted would cry, throwing his arms around. 'I'm feeling rather emotional tonight. Some music!'

'Something Russian, Father?' Pete would cry, hurling himself to the floor.

'Tchaikovsky?'

'No, Rachmaninoff.'

'Who's run off?'

'No one, Father. Rachmaninoff is a composer.'

And Ros would be standing there saying, 'I blame Spike Milligan for this.'

Now his fun-loving son had disappeared behind a mask of boils and a silent stranger had taken his place. Ros had brought the subject up again only the other night, after they'd had an argument in the living room about their three piece suite, a mustard-coloured vinyl affair with orange fabric cushions that they'd had since 1968. Ros, wanting it changed, had told Ted that she'd seen a nice one in Hudson's in Reading and then told him the price.

'How much? For a sofa! Does it do the hoovering as well?'

'No I do the hoovering. I'M THE ONE WHO DOES THE HOOVERING!'

After hanging his head in shame, Ted had found Ros in the kitchen and given her a hug of apology. In a muffled voice she said, 'And I'm worried about Pete. He's become *ancient*.'

'I'm worried too,' Ted had said, picturing his son's boils, but really he was more worried about another giant boil, the one on his soul in the form of a hundred stolen fuel pumps that he couldn't seem to get rid of for love or money. He made himself another coffee, adding Coffee Mate for creaminess – to cheer himself up – and then sat down again, this time heaving the most tragic sigh of all.

He'd been sent to borstal all those years ago for stealing bicycles – usually from outside the offices of the civil service in Reading – and selling them to a bargeman on the Kennet and Avon canal who would chug all the way up to Bristol for their disposal. That Ted had kept on the straight and narrow ever since his incarceration was not to do with the coldness and brutality of the place, but entirely due to the look of dejection on the face of his foster mum, Doreen, the day he'd gone inside. He'd been able to look after himself in borstal because of his size but it was a great soft lump of a boy who'd cried on her shoulder the day he got out, her saying, 'You'll never go back there, will you love?' and him saying, 'Never, Mum. Never.'

Not that there hadn't been opportunities to dabble in the black market. Now and then his best friend Vince – he with the bald head and Eric Morecambe glasses – would say something like, 'Someone's told me about some caravans, Ted. Fancy a flutter?' Or he'd get a call at the yard from some contact in the Midlands who would whisper, 'There's a lorry load of exhaust pipes passing through your manor, Ted. Do you want it to break down outside the yard?' But to all these friendly gestures he'd replied in the negative, thinking of Doreen, and Ros and most of all of Dickie, who'd taken him under his wing and really was a captain of industry, who'd kept Dickie's Haulage going in a bankrupt country through all the grim post-war years and when all the economic miracles were happening elsewhere.

Then earlier in the year Ted and Vince – on their weekly night off from their families – had gone to see Confessions of a Window Cleaner at the Odeon. They'd tippled all the way through the viewing so that when they burst out onto the slick, neon-lit high street they were shouting like teenagers: 'Why didn't we become window cleaners? The full-breasted, accommodating young women we would have befriended! The things we might have glimpsed!'

Coming along the pavement towards them was on old friend of theirs, Barnaby, also pissed and not wanting the night to end. After a joyous reunion they'd gone on to a little drinking club and it was here, at some point in the evening, that Barnaby had said, 'I don't suppose you can do with some fuel pumps, Ted?'

'I can always do with more fuel pumps. It depends where they come from.'

'These ones fell off the back of a ship.'

'So they're at the bottom of the ocean?'

'No, they fell onto the dockside and straight into my loving arms.'

Vince's ears had pricked up at this moment and while he was getting more information out of Barnaby, Ted was thinking, 'Now I can take Ros to see Evita in the West End. New bumpers for the Cortina. A racing bike for Pete.'

'They're worth about ten thousand quid over the counter,' Barnaby had continued. 'You could probably get five if you know the right people.'

'How much do you want for them?' said Vince.

'Two.'

While Barnaby was up at the bar getting more scotches, Ted and Vince put their heads together. For a start they could get the money and secondly they could use one of the vans from Ted's place to pick the stuff up. Thirdly they could easily store the gear at Vince's place and fourthly they both had enough contacts to be able to shift it all at the right price.

Ted was so drunk that when he went to light up another Regal, Vince pointed at the one he already had between his fingers, while try as he might he could no longer picture the faces of Ros and Doreen, his guiding lights, or find within himself the old determination to keep on the straight and narrow. He was thoroughly enjoying the whispering and all the furtiveness – and here was Barnaby putting another scotch down in front of him – and for the first time in twenty-five years felt as free as the boy tearing through the back streets of Reading on a stolen bicycle, looking over his shoulder to see if there were any civil servants running after him, racing down the tow path towards the lonely barge on the canal.

Ted was still technically drunk the following lunchtime when he drove over to Barnaby's to pick up the pumps and hand over the cash. But he was sober enough to think, 'I must be fucking mad,' and actually felt quite sick – both physically and morally – as he saw a decent portion of his and Ros's savings disappearing into the pocket of Barnaby's trench coat.

Still, things had gone smoothly the following night when they'd stowed the haul. Vince sold caravans off a big lot down by the river in Reading and was doing really well for himself as more and more people bought mobile homes for their Continental holidays or the annual summer invasion of Devon and Cornwall. They'd piled the fuel pumps in an old model that Vince had torn the fittings out of and then Vince had secured the door with a heavy lock and chain. 'No one will think of looking in there,' Vince had said, shaking hands with Ted, who'd then left, not realising that this was only the first of many nights when he'd keep Ros in suspense with his absence.

When the rozzers had come into the yard looking for clues Ted hadn't been too worried but he called Vince nevertheless.

'Are you sure this Barnaby's alright?' Vince had said.

'Stalwart,' said Ted. Then he'd thought for a bit. 'Maybe someone saw us all together in that club.'

Vince went quiet and then said, 'Try not to worry, big man, but keep me informed.'

Then of course Holmes and Watson had invaded his house and forced him into a performance worthy – in its blitheness and butchness – of the great Burt Reynolds himself. He'd gone round to Vince's and this time they'd stood in front of the caravan and scratched their heads. Now it looked exactly like the sort of place where Laurel and Hardy would have hidden stolen goods – and very heavy stolen goods judging from the way the tyres had gone flat – while the chunky lock and chain simply said 'ATTENTION POLICE!

'We'll have to move them,' said Vince, and after a couple of slugs of scotch they set about it.

At first they thought they'd divide the fuel pumps between several caravans, in the belief that if the police found some pumps in one caravan, they wouldn't bother to search the adjacent caravans, but when Ted suddenly stopped after half an hour and said, 'I'm not sure the old bill are that fucking stupid,' they'd changed their minds. They'd then transferred all the pumps into one caravan, an irksome process only made endurable by more slugs of scotch and several fag breaks.

'This time,' said Vince, swaying, 'we won't put a padlock on. We'll leave the door open. That'll fool them.'

Ted, trying to focus with one eye shut, also had a brainwave.

'And put a SOLD sign on it.'

When Vince hurled the empty scotch bottle away, the sound of it smashing on the ground penetrated the silence for miles and scattered all the foxes, water fowl, rats and cats that had gathered around to watch the huffing and puffing humans. This was the night that Ted had got home and kissed Ros with a moustache still damp from river mist.

Since then they'd managed to sell a few of the pumps but now Ted was worried that he wouldn't even make his money back. He looked at his watch, saw that lunch break was over and went over to the window. The men had stopped playing football and were now lounging around, some smoking and laughing, other napping in the sunshine. Ted switched on the tannoy.

'Attention all malingerers! Return to your duties immediately!'

Up in his office Ted heard a few faint fuck offs but gradually the reprobates staggered back to work. Then his heart sank when he saw the amount of paperwork on his desk. Still, there was always Vince if he wanted cheering up and he was seeing him that very night, officially this time, Ros having said that morning, 'So you're seeing your old partner in crime again,' not knowing the truth of her words.

They had five pints of Double Diamond each followed by a few whiskies. Sitting side by side they could see each other in the engraved glass behind the bar.

'This is a good one, Ted. You know outside someone's house when you see three white lines making a rectangle and next to it the word DISABLED in big letters. So you're reversing into this space because you can't find anywhere else to park and a bloke dashes out in his wheelchair and says, 'Oi! You can't park there, it says disabled.' And you say, 'Sorry, mate, I thought it said 'Dyslexic.'

This tickled Ted – just as he was about to take a slurp of beer – and his foamy head exploded all over the barmaid's Stranglers T-shirt.

Vince had three daughters aged thirteen, fifteen and seventeen.

'Of course I'm financially ruined and I can't leave a sock on the floor or break wind much, but on the other hand I never have to make my own tea and it's definitely true girls are more fun.'

Ted thought of his silent son and how the silence around him was getting deeper day by day.

Nine

It was the second summer of drought in a row and in the classrooms the boys were baked alive, or if they opened the windows fine sand from Africa blew in and covered their faces and blazers. It was so hot in the early mornings that when Pete passed through the school gates at ten to nine he was sweating already. At home, his underpants dried in minutes on the line.

Four weeks after Ros had picked up the Wort Of India ointment and three weeks before the end of term, Pete's skin was – miraculously as far as he was concerned – looking better, dried out, everyone supposed, by the hot weather. As a result he was slightly less morose and whenever someone looked at him his face no longer felt like a traffic light turning red.

One lunchtime he was sitting in the library as usual with Timothy, Tyler and Edwards. His hayfever was back and when he sneezed explosively in the direction of Tyler, the motes of dandruff blown off his shoulders formed a nebula in the sunlight streaming through the window.

Timothy was doing some chemistry homework, Edmunds was reading The Haunting Of Toby Jugg and Pete was reading Lord Of The Rings, and now and then reaching over to turn the page of the book in Tyler's lap, a volume of illustrations of Middle Earth.

Pete said to no one in particular, 'Do you know anything about hedgehogs?'

Timothy looked up and said, 'Do you mean Erinaceus europaeus?'

'I suppose so, if that's a hedgehog.'

Timothy crossed one little leg over the over and assumed his thoughtful bunny face.

'The European or common hedgehog is nocturnal and omnivorous… '

'Omnivorous?' said Pete.

'Eats anything: beetles, caterpillars, earthworms, although its favourite arthropod is the millipede… er, what else?' He thought for a moment. 'Solitary, life expectancy of about four years… '

Tyler groaned and dribbled while his eyes romped around their sockets.

'Yes,' said Timothy, translating. 'Why the sudden interest in hedgehogs?'

'Oh, I don't know,' said Pete with a shrug.

They all went back to their books but Pete was thinking hard about hedgehogs. He agreed with Timothy that they were nocturnal, but he also knew that when the weather was hot they came out during the daytime in search of water. This was not something that he'd observed, but something that he'd learned from an article in the local paper.

The real subject of the article was a girl who lived ten

doors down from him – and who he couldn't remember ever seeing – who had started a hedgehog rescue society in order to combat the problems of hedgehogs dying in the heatwave. Her name was Fiona Wren, she was thirteen years old and went to the nearby Embrook secondary school for girls.

The article said that Fiona had always been passionate about animals but that she'd become particularly interested in hedgehogs when she came across one staggering around in circles. She explained, 'I told my mum and we got in the car and went to the vet's. I thought Harry – that's what we called the hedgehog – was going to die but the vet gave him some water and he survived. I was really relieved.' Fiona called upon the whole neighbourhood to leave saucers of water all over the place, and if they found a hedgehog in distress to take immediate action.

Next to the article was a picture of Fiona. She was standing next to her mum and holding out a hedgehog, the very one whose bacon she'd saved, Pete presumed. She had long black hair, a pretty face and a mole the size of a pip on her left cheek. These attributes in combination with her determined expression – she was obviously the sort of girl who bossed her friends about – made her, in Pete's eyes, beautiful.

A short while after the article had appeared in the paper, Ros was in Pete's room, making his bed and tidying up. She picked up clothes from the floor and screwed the cap from his tube of acne ointment back on. She pictured his face and smiled at how much less inflamed it was these days. As she was plumping his pillows she heard a rustling sound and found wedged between them a packet of custard creams, which Pete had obviously been feasting on at midnight. Ros had got the job – three day a week in the wages office – at the biscuit factory and now was always bringing home free biscuits with which she augmented the lunch boxes of both lord and master and son and heir.

While having a final look around, she screamed. The picture on the wall of Raquel Welch had been replaced by a poster of a hedgehog, of monstrous size she at first believed, until she realised that it was simply a regular hedgehog magnified many times. Then she noticed a pile of school library books on his desk, with titles such as A Hedgehog's Year, Hedgehogs of The World, and Fauna Of The British Isles. A chill went up Ros's spine because to give up Raquel Welch for the sake of a hedgehog was – in her eyes – way beyond eccentric, even for an adolescent recluse who'd taken to wearing a motorcycle helmet to school.

Ros went downstairs and cheered herself up by jiving along with the carpet sweeper to Petula Clark's Downtown, but over the next few evenings she observed – usually from the kitchen window while doing the washing-up – further evidence of the young prince's descent into madness, specifically him wandering around the garden in the evenings after dinner, sometimes for up to two hours or until dusk was falling. He always took the same route – following the edge of the lawn with the beds on his right – and every few paces would stop and peer at the vegetation, favouring, to her bewilderment, standard shrubs such as the laurel and the berberis over her beautiful yellow roses and pink and white lupins.

She told Ted about his unusual behaviour one evening.

Pete had finished his dinner and left the room but Ted was only half way through his bananas and custard.

'Good,' he said with his eyes on the telly. 'At least he's getting some fresh air instead of spending all his time in his room.'

Ros, who'd been hoping for a more penetrating analysis, turned to go but then thought she might as well wait for his empty bowl. He spooned the bowl clean – he loved his bananas and custard – and only then noticed the expression on her face.

When she came back with his tea he took her hand, still warm from the washing-up water. Despite all the worry about the police and the fuel pumps, which had led him to drink more scotch and be grumpy pretty much all of the time, and the disappearance of the amatory aspect of their marriage – Ros did wake up one morning and felt something hard pressing against her but it was only Ted's Wilbur Smith – he hadn't forgotten that it was the simple things, those small consolatory gestures, that stopped a husband and wife from killing each other.

'Say that again,' he said, softly.

'I was saying that he keeps wandering around the garden, looking at the bushes.'

'Has he lost something?'

'If he has he can't find it.'

'Has he got interested in gardening all of a sudden?'

'He's got a funny way of showing it.'

Ted took a slurp of tea and then wiped his moustache dry with the back of his hand.

'Well one of us will have to ask him what's going on.'

Ros could tell from the way that Ted was leaning to

one side because she was blocking his view of the telly, that this responsibility had fallen upon her. She went outside, got the hose out and began to water the beds. When Pete came out and started to walk around she cried, 'Hello!' as though she hadn't seen him for three years. In the summer evening light she thought that his skin looked even better now, as though there was the ghost of a handsome man behind the disfigurement. 'Are you looking for something?

'Er... no, not really.'

'You look as though you are.'

He started to say something but then shook his head and walked off. The next time he came near her, Ros said,

'Come on, Pete, tell me what's wrong.'

'There's nothing wrong. It's just that... I don't suppose you've seen any hedgehogs?'

Ros was about to laugh but then realised that this was a solemn moment. She wondered to herself, 'Who is this strange and earnest young man?' She noticed Ted watching from the window and would have winked at him, but didn't want to give Pete a clue that he'd been ambushed, however lovingly.

'So that's what you've been looking for. But Pete, hedgehogs only come out at night.'

'Actually, Mum, they come out in the daytime when it's very hot, looking for water.'

'Ah.'

'And the girl... I mean the hedgehog rescue society... has asked people to look out for hedgehogs that might be dying of thirst.'

'Ah, I see.'

The next thing that Ted saw from the window was his wife and son walking around the garden together, now and again stopping to examine some area of shrubbery. He went outside and ambled across the lawn.

'Ullo, ullo, ullo. What's going on here then?' he said, with his hands behind his back and bending at the knees like an old-fashioned policeman.

'The mystery has been solved,' said Ros. 'Pete's been looking for hedgehogs.'

'Why, don't we feed him enough?'

Pete looked at his dad gravely but with compassion. It was obvious that to save him from ignorance he was going to have to give him a stern talking-to.

'It's not funny, Dad. Hundreds of hedgehogs are dying because of the heat and not enough is being done. We're supposed to look for ones in distress and give then some water.'

'Ah,' said Ted, remembering the hedgehog he'd run over only two months before. He even had an aural memory: a squelch.

Looking at Pete in the gentle light of evening, Ted saw that his skin was getting better. 'When did that happen?' he wondered. And the lad was now taller than his mum, he realised, and was bound to be as tall as his dad in a couple of years.

'What's brought all this about?' he said.

Pete hesitated but Ros jumped in.

'You mean you haven't heard of the local hedgehog rescue society, Dad?'

Ted shook his head guiltily.

'It was started by… ' Ros looked at Pete. 'What was her name again?'

'Fiona,' he croaked.

'Fiona, that was it. She only lives ten doors down apparently. Have you actually spoken to her, Pete?'

'No,' he groaned.

'Ah, thought Ted to himself. 'So behind it all is love, and not necessarily for hedgehogs.'

They all went round the garden looking for signs of hedgehogs but couldn't find any that evening. Subsequent evenings were spent in a similar manner, with one or all of the Turners searching the garden for hedgehogs panting with thirst. Following the advice of the rescue society they left saucers of water in a dozen places around the garden and prayed. The saucers were checked by Ted or Ros before they went to work, there being no cathedral bells in the vicinity to bring Pete to the required level of consciousness for early morning inspections. There was much excitement when it was reported that a saucer was empty, followed by gloom when someone wondered, 'But was it a hedgehog that drank the water, or a cat, or a fox?'

It was Timothy who came up with a possible solution to this question when he came round to the Turner's house for the very first time. Ted, who was in the garage draining the sump under Ros's Mini when he heard the doorbell, thought that Ros or Pete would answer the door but when it rang again he realised that he was the one who would have to make the ultimate sacrifice. So he hurled his spanner aside, spat the steel nut out of his mouth, slid out from under the car and lumbered down the hallway, roaring over the combined din of Ros's hoovering and Pete's music, 'Do I have to do everything around here?'

When he opened the door a strange boy stood before him. He had a sharp side parting, big glasses and was wearing a T-shirt with a picture of a blue space rocket on the front. He'd tucked his elbows into his sides and made his hands into a steeple like a neat little choir boy processing into a chapel, but on the other hand was nibbling at his lower lip with the air of a rabbit.

'Is Pete in?' said the boy.

'Yes he is,' said Ted, stepping aside.

In the hallway they faced each other, Timothy looking up at Ted and squinting, despite the powerful glasses.

'I'm Timothy,' he said, holding out his hand. 'I presume you're Mr Turner, the father of Pete.'

'I am indeed the bearer of that burden.'

Ros came in and recognised the visitor straight away.

'Oh, you're Pete's new friend... er.'

'Timothy,' said Ted.

'Hello, Mrs Turner.'

Ted stepped to one side and bellowed up the stairs. 'Pete!'

They heard the music stop, footsteps across the ceiling and Pete's door opening.

'What?'

'Someone to see you!'

Pete came half way down the stairs and saw Timothy.

'Oh, you're here. Come up.'

Timothy waved farewell to Ros and Ted and then jogged up the stairs, holding on to his glasses in case they bounced off his face. Ros and Ted pulled faces at each other that said, 'Strange. Interesting. But nice that he's got a new friend,' and then went back to their chores.

They didn't see the boys again until about an hour later. They were sitting in picnic chairs by the back door, drinking coffee and warming their knees in the sunshine, when they came out.

'Where are you off to?' said Ros.

Pete's face stiffened, as though he'd been asked to give all of his pocket money to charity.

'Out.'

'Out where?' said Ros.

'Just up to the shops, Mrs Turner,' said Timothy the helpful herbivore. 'And then back to my place.'

'Where do you live, Tim?' said Ted.

'Winnersh.'

'Have you got any brothers or sisters?' said Ros.

At this point Pete, mortified by his parents' inquisitiveness and envious of his friends fortitude under interrogation, put his arm in his mouth to stop himself screaming.

'A sister. Jane. She's at Oxford.'

'And what do your mum and dad do?' said Ted.

'My dad's a scientist and my mum's a physics teacher.'

Pete tugged at Timothy and said, 'Come on, let's go.'

'And are you interested in hedgehogs?' said Ros.

'I wasn't especially but I am now that Pete is. Tyler and Edmunds are as well.'

'Who are they?' said Ted.

'Our friends at school. We all like ELO and Lord of the Rings.'

'Ah yes, Lord of the Rings,' said Ted. 'Does it mention hedgehogs?'

Timothy had to think about this. He held his paws in front of his chest like a rabbit sitting up.

'That's a very good question, Mr Turner...'

Ros just managed to suppress a snort of laughter at this tribute to Ted's intellect, but he noticed the look on her face and, reaching out with his foot, trod on her toes.

'... and to be honest I can't remember. I don't think so but seeing as wizards and elves have a great affinity with animals, you would expect it to.'

'Ok, let's go,' said Pete.

But Ros – who Pete now realised loved Timothy more than she loved her own son – hadn't finished.

'Actually, you might be able to help us with something. As you know we've been trying to attract hedgehogs into the garden with saucers of water, but once the water's gone, how would we know it was a hedgehog who drank it?'

'As opposed to Vulpes vulpes or Felis catus? Another good question, Mrs Turner,' said Timothy, this tribute to Ros's brain power giving Ted the excuse to – gleefully – squash her other toes.

Timothy walked a little way into the garden and began to walk up and down with his hands behind his back, the downward angle of his face forcing him occasionally to return his glasses to the bridge of his nose. After a while Ted whispered,

'What's he doing?'

'Thinking,' said Ros.

Eventually Timothy stopped pacing up and down and presented himself before his students.

'After giving the matter some consideration I believe there is a way, which is this. Continue to place your saucers of water strategically around the garden but from now on sprinkle flour around then to an even depth and in the shape of a hexagon, or another multi-sided plane. In the morning – after taking into account variables such as precipitation and wind – the tracks of any animal that has drunk from the saucer will be clearly imprinted in the powder. Further, on examination of the edges of your polygon, you should be able to determine the direction of both ingress and egress of… well… your hedgehog.'

'Ingenious,' said Ted.

'So what we need is flour,' said Ros.

The young scientist thought for a moment.

'And patience.'

For the next few nights the Turner family took the advice of Timothy and set their traps of plain white flour, of which they had an ample supply because Ros wasn't much of a baker. Once again it was Ros or Ted who checked the traps every morning, and yet again they were disappointed, observing the paw prints of cats, the trails of slugs, the dimples from dew drops and the hieroglyphics of birds, but no sign of hedgehog activity.

In record time Ros crocheted a life-sized hedgehog with a brown body and – so she thought – perfectly rendered grey prickles. Knowing that Pete wouldn't accept such a childish gift she left it in a prominent position in the living room, where it stayed for two days before disappearing on the third. The next place she saw it was under Pete's bed, peeking out as though it lived there.

But still no one had seen any real hedgehogs and after

they'd all read the next edition of the local paper, which contained all the data on hedgehog sightings that Fiona had collected, it was clear that out of all the houses in the neighbourhood only the Turner's remained unvisited by Erinaceus europaeus. Ros could see in Pete's face the dreadful certainty that even though she only lived ten doors down, he would never meet Fiona Wren in this life.

Ten

For a few days Ros's ears were like huge antennae, swivelling this way and that in search of local intelligence regarding hedgehogs. The first glimmer of hope came when she was sitting in Pauline's garden one morning, both girls smoking happily out of sight and out of mind of their beloved husbands. Pauline, who was about to go on her annual holiday to the South of France, was making Ros's hair stand on end by telling her about the dreaded squat toilets at French camping sites, and which according to Norman were a form of revenge for the French defeat at the Battle Of Waterloo. Norman, who had, Pauline explained witheringly, incurred his hernia while trying to shift his desk three inches to the left, was now well enough to undertake the epic drive.

Then Jane, fully dressed for once, wandered into the garden to show them a picture of a hedgehog that she'd drawn. After they'd admired the picture Ros said,

'What made you draw a hedgehog, dear?'

'She's going to send it to the local hedgehog rescue

society,' said Pauline. 'In lieu of not finding a real one in the garden.'

'We've been looking for hedgehogs as well,' said Ros.

'They've got two,' said Jane.

Ros's ears sprang erect like a Retriever's

'Who has?'

'This Fiona and her mum apparently,' said Pauline. 'Though why the creatures keep wandering into their garden and not ours is a mystery.'

Shortly afterwards Ros was in her own garden when she got talking to Mrs Morris over the fence. In the blistering heat of an English summer afternoon the white-haired old dear was still wearing a knitted cardigan and thermal slippers. She already knew about Pete's interest in hedgehogs and said,

'At least he doesn't like this dreadful punk music.'

'I don't suppose you know anything about this young girl who lives down the road?'

The inveterate curtain-twitcher thought for a moment and then said, 'The mother drives her to school every morning, I know that. And I often see her in the supermarket on Thursday mornings so I guess that's her regular day. It's funny living on a big estate. I know the names of more footballers than I do people living around here and I don't even like football.'

On the next Thursday, one of her days off, Ros waited for Pete to leave for school, reversed her Mini out of the garage, parked it on the driveway and then climbed into the back seat with Ted's binoculars. She'd never actually used them before and for a while wondered why everything looked further away, until she turned the binoculars around and everything – including the house ten doors down – loomed closer.

Nothing happened for an hour and random thoughts began to intrude on her watchfulness. She remembered a programme she'd seen while sitting with a young Pete – maybe Record Breakers – in which a group of people had tried to break the world record for how many humans could fit in a Mini. 'Twenty? Thirty?' she wondered, and then spent some time imagining the configuration of bodies necessary for such an achievement. She thought of the night her and Ted – early on in their courtship – had tried to make love in the back of a car, an early rustbucket of his parked down the street from her mum and dad's. She remembered his grunts of annoyance and the car rocking from side-to-side as they tried to pull his trousers down, the squeak of her hands sliding over the steamed-up windows and Ted's great roar at the climax of their bitter failure, 'If we were married we'd be able to do this in a bed!' and her going 'Sshhh!' because lights had come on in nearby houses, and her delight at this clumsy first draft of a proposal, this first indication that marriage was on his mind.

The woman who she presumed was Mrs Wren came out of her house at about eleven o'clock, just as Concorde was going over, and like everyone else in Southern England who had the time, she stopped for a moment to watch it arrowing towards the States. She looked up and down the road – a look which under magnification gave the impression that she was looking Ros in the eye – and then turned and headed, Ros guessed, for the supermarket. She seemed to be about Ros's size and was wearing a sleeveless, lilac blouse, white holiday shorts and sandals. 'You poor thing, you've got plump ankles,' thought Ros, who then chided herself for being so uncharitable, and in this roundabout way congratulated herself for having ankles that weren't plump at all.

She dashed inside for her handbag and came out to find that Mrs Wren was some way off but – being an ambler – still hadn't reached the first alleyway. Ros trotted after her until she was at an unobtrusive distance away, and then slowed down to match the other woman's tempo. It quickly became clear to Ros that Mrs Wren was following the usual route to the supermarket from their road, a chain of six staggered alleyways that bisected street after street until it reached the last, dismally long street – on one side of which the odd numbers reached to 351 – which led to the main road and the supermarket.

It was hot in the streets and cool in the dappled alleyways and to begin with everything on the estate looked familiar to Ros: the silent gardens, the bright, burnished cars parked on their driveways, the narrow brown paths across the grassy knolls made by short-cutting children, and the particular concrete pipeline marker outside 54 Marks Road, always lime with algae and damp from the urine of dogs. And as she passed number 181, there was the familiar short-haired, ferrety little dog clinging with its claws to the letter basket and yelping at her, through a flap loosened in its hinges by a million historical yelps at shadows in the outside world.

On the other hand there were new things. Some boys had drawn a picture of an ejaculating penis on a lampost in St Georges Street. Halfway along the next road someone had planted a small palm tree in their front garden to match the tropical sunshine. And on Jubilee Avenue a tortoiseshell cat that she'd never seen before stepped into her path. When she touched its head it closed its emerald eyes and arched its spine so that the journey of Ros's fingertips to the tip of its enchanted tail might last forever.

When she got to the main road she was twenty yards behind her prey. A big lorry stopped to let Mrs Wren use the zebra crossing in front of the supermarket, started to move again and then, seeing Ros hurrying along, stopped again with a hiss of brakes. Ros noticed that the driver was using the method unique to lorry drivers for eating crisps, that of using all the fingers of one hand to take some crisps out of the packet and then eating the fingers along with the crisps. She could feel his baleful eyes following her and pulled hard on the strap of her handbag as though it was the cord of an emergency parachute.

In the supermarket she took a basket and picked up some sliced white bread for Ted's lunches. It was cool in the shop, and quiet, apart from the butcher being jolly to a customer and the two till girls talking about a new nightclub in Reading. She saw Fiona's mum ahead of her, looking closely at a string bag full of lemons, and deduced that she was short-sighted and planning to make a lemon sponge.

Ros had decided to give the boys tinned apricots with evaporated milk for pudding so she found those and then headed for the toilet roll, all the time wondering how she might safely accost Fiona's mum, and frustrated that every time she turned a corner the woman was just disappearing around the next corner. Once, through a gap between the pickles and the mustards on a top shelf, she saw Mrs Wren passing down the adjacent aisle and thought, 'I'll never catch up with her!' Then, as luck would have it, she took a left turn and Fiona's mum was standing right there, reading the instructions on a tub of custard powder. She was a handsome woman, thought Ros, with an oval face and big blue eyes but her lips were compressed into a thin, humourless line, giving her an uncongenial air. Ros crashed straight into her trolley.

'Oh, sorry.' said Ros.

Mrs Wren didn't say anything and carried on reading the instructions, but pulled on her half-full trolley so that it drifted to one side. Ros drove past and then came to a stop about fifteen feet away. An old woman in a pink shop coat was kneeling on a flattened cardboard box and filling an empty shelf with tins of tongue, ham and pork luncheon meat.

'Can I have one of those?' said Ros.

The assistant sat back on her haunches and – without much enthusiasm – handed Ros a tin of ham. Ros took it and when she felt Mrs Wren pass behind her cried to the assistant, 'This ham looks delicious. Is it a new variety be any chance?' hoping that Mrs Wren would stop to see what the new innovation was, but the woman passed by.

'It's just Spam,' said the assistant. 'We've been eating it since the war.'

'Oh,' said Ros, and dropping the tin in her trolley, hurried after Mrs Wren again.

She followed her for a few more minutes and then got angry with herself for prevaricating. 'This is ridiculous,' she said to herself, and the next time she got near to Mrs

Wren she crashed into her deliberately.

'Oh, sorry! I've done it again. What must you think of me?'

The clash of the trolleys brought the shop to a standstill and as the butcher ceased hacking a loin into chops and the till girls stopped their conference a silence descended over the supermarket. All eyes were pointed in Ros's direction and she could sense someone in the next aisle peering at her over a freezer full of ready meals.

Mrs Wren looked warily at this – obviously lonely and unstable – woman who kept bounding up to her with her hands flying in all directions and her hair in a rage, but then she smiled sweetly and said, 'It's quite alright,' and walked away, and at the same time the butcher took up his chopper and the till girls reconvened.

'I'm sorry but I'm sure I recognise you.'

'Well that's obviously because I live around here,' she said, coolly, without stopping.

'I'm sure it's not just that.' Ros snapped her fingers. 'I know, you're an actress. I've seen you on the telly. In Upstairs, Downstairs!'

Still floating regally along, Mrs Wren shook her head sadly.

'I'm not an actress but you might have seen my picture in the paper.'

'That's it!' shrieked Ros. 'In the paper. You're the mother of the famous hedgehog hunter Fiona Wren, The Mary Anning of Earley!'

This outburst tugged Mrs Wren to a standstill. She smiled at the comparison of her daughter with such an esteemed historical personage.

'Well, we're very proud of her.'

'She should get a medal, an award from the Queen.'

'Oh, I don't know about that,' said Mrs Wren.

She looked embarrassed now and, flexing her wrists, pushed off again.

'Actually,' said Ros to her back, 'it's because of your Fiona that my son has got interested in hedgehogs as well.'

'Really,' said Fiona's mum wearily.

'Yes, he's very passionate about the subject indeed.'

This was the first time in her whole life that Ros had used the word 'indeed' and it brought her to her senses. 'She must think I'm mad,' she said to herself, and then thought, 'She's not the only one,' when she got to the tills and saw the shop girls and the manager regarding her warily.

Bravely, however, she got in the queue behind Mrs Wren, who pretended not to notice her all the time that she was bagging up her shopping.

'I'm Ros, by the way.'

'Susan,' said the woman, her throat plumping as she delved in her purse.

Then, without looking at Ros, she swung her shopping out of the bagging area and headed for the door.

By the time that Ros was outside, Susan had crossed the road and was heading back into the estate. She wondered how she would ever be able to catch her up, but then – remembering the trick that she'd discovered when she was a little girl on her way back from the shops – she began to swing her two bags of shopping backwards and forwards, each forward swing having a propulsive effect and increasing her speed.

Eventually she saw Susan halfway down an alleyway and rushed silently after her. Susan, who'd been daydreaming among the midday shadows, jumped out of her skin when she heard a voice behind her.

'Yes,' said Ros. 'He's become very passionate about the subject indeed. He even got a book from the library about hedgehogs. Or should I say Ericaceous expialidocious... I mean... '

Susan, who'd begun to increase her speed, turned and looked down at Ros from the height of a hawk.

'I really don't think Latin names are necessary.'

'Of course you're right,' said Ros.

A moment later they reached the end of the alleyway and Susan – with Ros chugging along behind her – turned right and headed for home. She looked shocked and dismayed when she realised that Ros was following her.

'You don't live down here.'

'I do. Only ten doors down.'

'Oh.'

'Isn't that funny?'

With Susan and her two bags of shopping taking up the whole pavement, Ros had to step into the road so that they could walk be side by side.

'I must say your daughter's very beautiful.'

'Thank you.'

They walked in silence for a while.

'Has she always been passionate about animals?'

'Always.'

After another silence Ros said, 'Any animals in particular?'

At this point Susan – realising that more resistance was

futile – let out a big sigh and said, 'We've got two goldfish, a rabbit, a tortoise, a cat, a dog and now two hedgehogs.'

'Hedgehogs!' Ros caught herself sounding shrill and forced her voice to go lower. 'You've actually got hedgehogs living with you?'

Susan smiled coldly at the turn of phrase.

'If you're asking me whether we've domesticated two hedgehogs, the answer is no.'

'Oh.'

'They're two more that Fiona found. We took them to the vet's and he said take them home, look after them and then let them go.'

Ros could see that they were almost at Susan's house.

'What do you feed them on?'

'Porridge with brown sugar.'

'When do you think you'll let them go?'

'Tomorrow afternoon, I expect. When Fiona comes home from school.'

Susan stopped outside her house, put her bags of shopping down and began to search in her handbag for keys.

'Well, goodbye,' she said, and walked down her driveway.

'Bye!' cried Ros passionately, but as she walked away she thought, 'Prematurely jowly and prone to plumpness,' and this time didn't feel guilty.

And so it came to pass that Barbara Amplethorpe set forth for a second time, with teeth that scared the crows off the lawns, although this time she didn't have to travel very far from her lair, only ten doors down, where the occupant had returned from a shopping trip only two hours before.

As for the occupant, she had heard of the saying 'Caught between a rock and a hard place' but nothing in her life had prepared her for being pincered by a madwoman in the morning and – in the afternoon of the same day – a woman with horrendous teeth, who declaimed when she opened the door, 'Mrs Wren? My name is Barbara Amplethorpe from the animal welfare department. I am here to investigate reports of an illegal menagerie.'

Susan's jaw had dropped at the sight of the teeth and she could only splutter, 'Welfare?… Menagerie?… '

'Please spare me the futile protests, Mrs Wren. I do have local authority power to invade… I mean enter your home if I suspect that animals are in danger.'

A beautiful, perfectly groomed Golden Retriever trotted down the hallway and stood placidly beside Susan. It nosed the air to catch the scent of the stranger but was clearly thinking, 'Well, there's a first: a human with teeth filthier than my own.'

Susan bristled and said, 'Does this dog look distressed?'

Barbara stepped forward – causing Susan to step back – and lifted up one of the dog's ears. The dog rolled its eyes and began to pant.

'Dust.'

'Pardon?'

'A textbook case of dusty dog's ears. A certain sign of neglect.'

'I've never heard of such… '

'Oh come now, Mrs Wren. I only want to check that your pets are in good health. If they are, I will be out of your way in two shakes of a lamb's tail.'

Susan went to protest again, but feeling helpless in

the face of occult forces, she instead stepped aside to let Barbara Amplethorpe in.

Susan's home had the same layout as Ros's. They went down the hallway, into the kitchen – where the crusader paused to inspect the goldfish in their bowl – out of the back door and straight onto the patio. In the corner made by the garage wall and the fence were two hutches, one containing a rabbit with a fidgety nose and the other, two hedgehogs, nestled side by side among some straw and a blanket. Ros leaned down and peered in. The hedgehogs had shrewish faces and little black eyes and their thousands of spikes were tipped with silver. In the hutch was a saucer full of water and outside it was a white, plastic invalid's bowl, grey with the dried smears from some liquid.

Barbara stood up.

'Well, I am pleased to say that everything seems to be satisfactory… but hold on.' Barbara pounced on the bowl. 'Mrs Wren! Have you been feeding your hedgehogs grout?'

'Don't be ridiculous. Porridge oats.'

'I stand corrected, my dear. I stand corrected.'

Susan dug her hands into her hips.

'So is that it?'

'Unless you have anymore animals.'

'Well, we've got a cat but it's probably up a tree.'

'I hope you didn't put it there, Mrs Wren!'

'Of course I didn't. And actually, I don't remember seeing your credentials.'

'My credentials, Mrs Wren, are my passion for animals and the moral vigour with which I condemn the perpetrators of neglect. Now goodbye!'

And with that Barbara Amplethorpe stepped past

Susan, walked down the hallway, opened the door and vanished like a vampire at the touch of the sun.

Eleven

Ted had finished his Wilbur Smith and was now reading The Guns Of Navarone because he'd seen the film on the telly, but even though he'd been looking at the book for twenty nights in a row, he was still – Ros saw when she lifted the book off of his chest – only on page seven. She'd waited until the rise and fall of his breathing was deep and slow, signifying slumber, before attempting this action, further encouragement being the onset of his snores: nasal, pitched high but muffled like the hoot of an owl in woods, a drunken owl judging by the smell of the breeze that bore the hoots towards her. It was a familiar smell around Ted these days and remembering the vacum cleaner salesman as well, Ros concluded that whisky was the tipple of doleful men.

While Ted was sound asleep Ros was wide awake. She'd heard a character say in Starsky And Hutch that the best time to burgle someone's house was at four o'clock in the morning, when the occupants were at the deepest level of sleep and human activity in the surrounding world was at a minimum, but she was in a state of such high anxiety that she couldn't wait that long. She got out of bed, dressed hurriedly in the darkness, sneaked downstairs and went out through the back door. Just before she opened the gate she looked down at herself. She was wearing white trousers, a pink T-shirt and a bright green cardigan to keep out the cold, a combination that made her luminous in the dark. In despair at herself, she banged her head against the wall a few times, triggering a memory: the Milk Tray advert in which a man dressed all in black breaks into a beautiful woman's apartment and instead of stealing all of her jewellry, leaves her a box of chocolates. Ros went back upstairs, dressed herself in black, covered her hair with a black scarf and then tip-toed out again, this time blending into the night.

She looked up the road towards the Wrens' house and reckoned that she had two options. She could either sneak across the nine front lawns that seperated hers from the Wrens', which would involve squeezing past parked cars and fighting her way through thorny hedges, or walk along the pavement with an innocent air and hope that no one spotted her. For the sake of speed she chose the second option and walked quickly down the road, her senses on high alert for the sound of a police car charging to the rescue of the Wrens. Ros had never even stolen sweets from a shop as a youngster, let alone invaded someone's property, and she felt shameless, but also strangely liberated as though she was bobbing along on the surface of life for once, and besides she was impelled by her ferocious love for her son.

In less than a minute she turned into the Wrens'

driveway, noiselessly opened the gate and stood in the passage that led to the back door. It was pitch black around her but up ahead she could see the back lawn – grey in the moonlight – and at the end of the garden the white trunk and silhouette of a silver birch tree under a sky full of stars. The only sounds were her own breaths coming quicker than normal and the rustling of the leaves in the tree.

Touching the walls either side of her, she began to creep along the passage and was almost at the back door when her foot touched something. There was a clink and then the sound of a milk bottle rolling across concrete – loud enough to wake the whole neighbourhood Ros felt – and then a second clink as the bottle came to rest against the wall. Ros heard a yelp and scuffling sounds coming from the other side of the door and realised that she'd forgotten about the Golden Retriever.

She froze, but when a few seconds turned into a whole minute of silence she knew that – thank God – the animal wasn't a woofer, although she could tell that it was still there listening and waiting, probably with its head cocked to one side and its velvety ears up.

She travelled the next few feet in slow motion and only started breathing again when she was kneeling in front of the hedgehogs' hutch. One of them was asleep but she knew that the other one was alert because its little black eyes were catching the moonlight. She opened the door, reached in for the creature but then – looking at her hands – thought to herself,

'How am I going to pick up Mr Prickles without gloves?'

One again Ros cursed herself for not having the

common sense necessary for secret missions. She looked around and saw by the wall a tumble dryer, an old fridge freezer and a bicycle. She opened the tumble dryer and found an old towel, used for drying the dog's paws after walks, or so she guessed from the state it was in. She opened it out, enfolded the hedgehog with it and lifted it up. The creature squealed and then rolled up into a tense little ball.

Ros stood up and came face to face with Susan Wren. She was wearing a bright yellow raincoat over a white towelling dressing gown, and a tartan bobble hat, altogether an eccentric ensemble, thought Ros, while beside her sat the dog on its lead, looking baffled as to why it was being taken for a walk at midnight. It sniffed the hedgehog hidden in Ros's hands and then yawned.

Ros froze, and felt her whole scalp crawling as her hair tried to escape from under her scarf so that it could stand on end. Susan's eyes were black with fury, while bubbles of saliva burst between her lips and a strange moaning sound emerged from her throat as she tried to find the words to berate the thief, who in an attempt to save herself began to jabber.

'Susan! Hello! Yes, it's me again. Silly me. You must be wondering what I'm doing here at this time of night. Well, it's all because of my son, you know how passionate he is about hedgehogs, he's been going on and on about them and I thought, you know, I'll pop round to Susan's and see if she'll let us borrow theirs, but when I got here I thought you might be in bed, so I thought, well, I'm sure Susan won't mind if we just borrow him, and look, I put him in this towel to keep him nice and warm... '

Now Ros noticed that Susan wasn't looking into her eyes, but at a point on her forehead, and with a distant, abstracted look on her face as though her mind was elsewhere.

'She's gone mad,' thought Ros.

Abruptly, Susan turned away and walked into the garden with the dog. Ros heard footsteps on the stairs and guessed from the speed of the descent that it was Fiona. She looked around, saw that the fridge freezer wasn't flush against the wall and squeezed behind it in the nick of time.

Fiona, wearing pink pyjamas, came through the back door and saw her mum in the garden. Ros could tell from the anguished look on her face that it wasn't the first time that she'd come out at midnight to find her mum taking the dog for a walk on another planet.

'Oh no,' groaned Fiona.

From her hiding place Ros couldn't see into the garden but she heard Fiona hiss,

'Mum, wake up! You're sleepwalking again.'

'Ah,' thought Ros. 'So she's not mad.' By this time she was shivering with cold and fear and on the verge of wetting herself, but at the same time a small, nosey part of her was enjoying the spectacle and she only wished she had time to nip through to the living room and inspect Susan's furnishings and ornaments as well.

The next thing she saw was a little procession, Fiona leading her oblivious mother by the hand and Susan leading the dog, which looked over its shoulder at Ros's hiding place before they went inside. Fiona was in too much of a state to notice the animal's behaviour or that the door to the hedgehog's hut was open.

Ros didn't come out for five while minutes. When she did close the gate behind her she was so relieved that she didn't care if she was spotted, and during the walk home actually stopped under a street lamp to make sure that she hadn't squeezed the hedgehog to death in panic. When she unwrapped the animal she saw that it was pulsating gently and therefore alive.

Ros crept into bed so as not to wake the sleeping giant and lay there for ages thinking about how she wasn't cut out for a life of crime, and wondering how she'd been caught red-handed but got away with it. 'Funny family, the Wrens,' she thought. 'A precocious daughter, a mother who sleepwalks, and no sign of the husband.' As she drifted off to sleep she imagined herself walking through the park and coming across Fiona sitting on a bench, crying her eyes out, and putting her arms around the girl to comfort her.

When Pete got home the next day he looked refreshingly unspotty and relieved that the school year had ended. When he came through the back door and found his mum washing lettuce leaves in the sink, he even said 'Hello' first. He consumed a bowl of Sugar Puffs, went up to his room and stayed there until dinner time, listening to his albums by ELO, Darts and 10cc. In his reverie he looked forward to six weeks of lotus eating and no homework, and imagined a naked Fiona reclining on her own bed amongst a sea of toy animals.

Dinner for the boys was salad with beetroot, mashed potato, boiled egg, cheese and a pork pie, which they ate off their laps in the living room while they watched the telly. The house slave – on a diet – just had salad, although afterwards she did have tinned pears with ice-cream along with the men, who forgot to mention how splendid was the fare. However, in a rare moment of thoughtfulness, Ted came into the kitchen and offered to do the washing-up himself, thereby affording the drudge the unlooked-for joy of bringing a load of washing in out of the early evening sunshine ten minutes sooner than expected.

As Ros pulled the towels off the line, she could see Ted standing in the living room window smoking a cigarette and looking sated and calm, his gunfighter's moustache having tamed the West, and at the same time Pete standing at his bedroom window, and who, in the manner of all anguished pubescent virgins looking out across an estate of orderly houses and abundant gardens on a balmy summer's evening, appeared to only see dismalness and disorder.

Ros dropped a towel into the laundry basket and a second later Ted roared, 'Pee… ter!'

She looked up and saw Ted standing in the same place but now with his eyes bulging out of their sockets, transfixed by something. She dashed indoors and encountered Pete running down the stairs. They went into the living room where Ted waved them over and pointed through the window. There, on the narrow concrete path between the window and the lawn, was a hedgehog walking slowly along on its little grey feet. It had beady eyes, sooty hairs on its snout and a tiny nose as round and shiny as a blackcurrant, quivering as it sniffed the air.

The path led towards Mrs Morris's fence so Ted, Ros and Pete ran through the house and out of the back door.

There – unified for once – they stood watching the creature advance towards them until Ros cried, 'Water!' She ran into the kitchen and returned with a saucer of water which she set down in the hedgehog's path. Obediently, it ambled up to the saucer, rested its throat on the rim and began to drink.

'So one of the little fellows has found its way here after all,' said Ted.

Pete just stood there, mesmerised by the sight of the hedgehog and stunned by the change in his fortunes. Ros put her arm around his shoulders and for once he didn't cringe.

The hedgehog, seemingly unafraid of the humans, drank lustily for about three minutes.

'It was really thirsty,' said Pete.

'Where's it all going?' said Ted, expecting the creature to swell up to twice its size after drinking so much.

When the hedgehog had finished drinking it looked up, sniffed the air and then, matter-of-factly, turned round and went back the way it came, a little faster now that it was fully hydrated and so no longer at death's door. Ted and Pete actually waved and Ros cried passionately, 'Oh, bye Mr Hedgehog!'

Then Ted and Ros looked at Pete and Ros said, 'Now you must tell Fiona Wren.'

'I don't know her phone nunber.'

'It's in the phone book.'

Solemnly, they processed into the hallway and Pete took the phone book off the shelf. He began to look through the Rs. Ted and Ros smiled and Ted said, 'It's Wren with a W.'

'I know,' snapped Pete. He began to flap through the Ws. 'Here are the Wrens.' He put the book down next to the phone and underlined the number with a fingernail. He lifted the receiver, started dialling but then stopped and looked at his parents.

'Can't you wait in there?'

Ted was about to protest but Ros kneed and elbowed him until he fell back through the living room door, which they closed and then hid either side of, trying not to giggle. They heard Pete dial the rest of the number, a silence and then a voice at the other end saying, 'Hello?'

Ros whispered to Ted,

'Susan Wren, the mother. A real cow.'

'Hello. Is Fiona there?'

'Who's calling?'

'My name's Pete Turner.'

There was a silence and then Susan said, 'What are you calling about?'

'A hedgehog,' said Pete. 'I'd like to report a hedgehog.'

'Well, you can give me the details if you like.'

Now the heavy silence was on Pete's end off the line. Ros imagined that his face was as long as a horse's. Then a more girlish voice could be heard at Susan's end.

'Who is it, Mum?'

'It's a boy.'

'If it's about a hedgehog then… '

There was the sound of a struggle and then Fiona's voice came through loud and clear.

'Hello?'

'Hello?'

'Are you calling about a hedgehog?'

'Yes.'

'Let me take notes.' There was the click of a pen and the rustling of paper. 'Where do you live please?'

'Forty-seven Coopers Road.'

'That's only ten doors down from me.'

'I know.'

'When did you see the hedgehog?'

'Er, twenty past six.'

'Was it distressed?'

'It wasn't going very fast.'

'Did you give it some water?'

'Loads.'

'And after you gave it some water, did it look better?'

Pete had to think for a moment.

'It looked brand new.'

'Brand new,' repeated Fiona as she wrote the words down. There was a silence and then she continued, 'Actually, it might have been my hedgehog.'

'Really?'

'I was looking after two hedgehogs but this morning my mum left the hutch door open and one escaped.'

'I'm sorry.'

'No need to apologise. It wasn't your fault. Anyway, thanks for calling and thanks for saving another hedgehog.'

'That's alright.'

'Bye, Pete.'

'Bye.'

Ros and Ted heard the receiver being replaced and then nothing else, as though Pete was still standing there, but when they opened the door and looked into the hallway he'd gone.

Twelve

One afternoon Ted was lounging around behind his desk when he had a phone call from detective constable Fenton.

'We'd like you to come in for an interview, Mr Turner.'

'Time to get into character,' thought Ted, and pushing himself away from the desk he glided backwards across the carpet tiles until he bumped against a filing cabinet.

'I'm happy in my present employment, thankyou very much, officer.'

'You know what it's about.'

'And what if I don't come in?'

'We charge into the yard with all guns blazing.'

'Perhaps I'll come along, then.'

Ted phoned his co-conspirator to give him an update on the plodding progress of the police.

'They're still fishing,' said Vince. 'Otherwise they'd have been round with a search warrant.'

'It's alright for you. You're not in the firing line.'

'Just remember, you don't know what I look like, you've never met me and you don't know where I am.'

Ted frowned. 'Sorry, who is this?'

'That's my boy.'

Then Ted made the really difficult phone call, not from behind his desk this time but while prowling around it, now and again lifting up the cord so it didn't knock over his pot of pens.

'Love, all hell's broken loose.'

'What's happened?'

'My car won't start.'

'Oh, dear.'

'And I need you to pick me up from the police station.'

'Why?'

'They want to interview me about those stolen fuel pumps. It's just a formality.'

'I thought you didn't know anything about that,' cried Ros.

'I say 'interview' but what they're really going to do is hypnotise me, to help me remember.'

'To help you remember if you stole something?'

'To help me remember if I've heard anything.'

A long, worried silence came down the line. Ted pictured Ros standing in the hallway, her face dark in the shadow of the cheese plant by the phone, with the reciever at her ear and her fingernails between her teeth. The silence told him that she didn't believe a word of it all, but that she was forcing herself to trust him, for the sake of love. Now – Ted knew – was the time to come clean but instead he heard himself making his tale even taller.

'And I thought the hypnosis might help me remember other things, like where I left that box of chocolates.'

'What box of chocolates?'

'You know, the ones I bought you three years ago and lost on the way home.'

Ted thought that Ros must be standing in Siberia, so cold was the sound of her voice.

'What time shall I pick you up?'

'Oh, about eight.'

'Ok.'

Ros made Pete's dinner and then sat with him while he watched Star Trek. She'd always thought that Captain Kirk was devastatingly handsome but during this episode she hardly noticed that at all. Instead she thought that even though the captain and his crew were besieged by the Klingons, none of their phasers worked and Dr Spock had gone mad, their troubles were trivial compared to the travails of her and Ted.

At half past seven she said to Pete, 'I'm going to pick up your dad. His car's broken down.'

She got ready and then when back into the living room and stood over him with her hands on her hips. Esconced in the chair with the best view of the telly, Pete had achieved – with the rubber limbs of the fourteen-year-old – a near-perfect horizontal.

'Are you going to be alright here on your own?'

'Of course,' said Pete with a sensible face, while picturing the two illicit bowls of Sugar Puffs that he would consume while she was gone.

At the end of an overcast and humid day the heavens opened as Ros was reversing out of the driveway. In her rearview mirror she saw Pauline closing the curtains in her living room and knew she was thinking, 'Where's Ros going at this time?'

She didn't like driving in bad weather and was careful to check the minor functions of her old tin car. The headlights were working because she could see needles of rain in the beams. She set the front blowers to hairdryer volume to keep the windscreen clear and then got the wipers at their highest speed with a bit of luck. However, the rubbery thuds at the extremity of each swipe sounded terminal to her and she told herself to get Ted to look at the things, if, that is, she ever spoke to him again. The rear wiper seemed to have come on of its own accord, and when she stopped at the end of the street and checked her nearside mirror she saw the ruby reflections of her brake lights in a parked car slick with rain.

It only took her twenty minutes to drive to the police station at Earley, a small satellite of the county station in Reading. Among the vehicles in the car park was a panda car with a pale blue body and white front doors, and a black mariah with an electric blue nipple on the roof. The station was in an Edwardian brick villa with gable roofs on every side. The old sash windows had been replaced by frosted glass in metal frames and the wooden front door by a glass door, heavy and stiff on its hinges as Ros found when she pushed her way in.

The reception area was starkly lit by a long, pendent ceiling light, and the grey linoleum floor wet from the passage of previous visitors. Around three sides of the room were wooden benches and on one wall was a noticeboard covered in posters and information leaflets attached with gold drawing pins. Ros searched among the Wanted posters for the evil visage of the criminal mastermind, Ted Turner, but then remembered that he wasn't wanted because he'd already been collared. Opposite was a wooden reception desk topped with glass that reached the ceiling, with at one end an access flap, for the moment leaning up against the wall. Behind the desk stood an officer in uniform and in the room behind him were two pale, overweight men wearing white shirts with the sleeves rolled up, sitting at desks piled high with papers, one of them with his feet up and his hands clasped behind his head, and the other – with a cigarette angling out of his mouth – typing doggedly to his dictation.

The desk sergeant looked up and – being the beaming face of the local constabulary – greeted Ros merrily.

'Hello, my dear. What can I do for you?'

'I'm here to collect my husband, Ted Turner.'

The sergeant looked over his shoulder at one of the other men, who jerked his head to one side, indicating the further recesses of the station.

'He's still helping us with our inquiries, madam. If you'd like to take a seat I'm sure he'll be out shortly.'

Ros sat on one of the benches and dabbed raindrops off her face, and heard others dripping off the hem of her raincoat onto the floor. Outside in the downpour the cars passed by with a hiss that rose to a crescendo and then faded to a whisper, while inside the plainclothes men murmured to each other and chain smoked. Out of the corner of her eye she watched the sergeant move between a wall full of giant file folders and a wooden cabinet containing about a hundred small drawers, each of which contained hundreds of white cards – one of which he would take out and peruse – and bearing the names of criminals, Ros guessed. She was aware that one of the detectives was gazing at her and no doubt wondering what the pleasure of an attractive woman like her would be while her husband was in prison. At the back of the station the shouts of a man were silenced by the slamming of a metal door. Ros began to calculate. If Ted had been dropped off at the station at about six thirty, and it was now past eight o'clock, that meant he'd been in the interview room for an hour and a half, a suspiciously long time. On the other hand if he'd been late leaving work and had only arrived at the station at – say – a quarter to eight, and he emerged in the next few minutes, it had to be because they'd realised that it was all a big mistake and he was free.

'What will they do? Charge him?' she wondered. 'Oh, it won't come to that. It's all a big mix-up.'

In this way – despite being in despair at her husband – she was still trying to get him off the hook.

She rallied herself and sat up straight. Her handbag was on her lap and she took out her cigarettes and – not caring if she looked like a gangster's tart – lit one up. The room was warm and her smoke hung in the middle air.

At half past eight an old man came in. He was wearing a dark blue macintosh, a flat cap and wellington boots. His powerful glasses – pimpled with raindrops – made his eyes look like egg whites in a fish tank, while his cheeks had collapsed in on his toothless mouth. He stood dripping in front of the desk. 'I've come to report a stolen bicycle.'

'Fuck off!' said one of the detectives.

'Now, Percy,' said the sergeant, leaning over the desk. 'Didn't you report your bicycle stolen last week, and the week before that as well?'

Percy didn't have an answer to that. Instead he reversed to the middle of the room and began to jump up and down while jerking his forked fingers in the direction of the policemen and blowing raspberries. Then, as quickly as he'd come, he flew out of the door and into the stormy night.

'I do apologise for that behaviour,' said the sergeant to Ros. He looked over his shoulder. 'And also for the unfortunate language of my colleagues – or as we call them around here – Abbot and Costello.'

The detectives looked up and in perfect harmony cried, 'Oooh! Who's got his knickers in a twist now?'

The clock on the wall ticked round to nine o'clock and still no sign of Ted. Ros went out to the phone box and called Pete to make sure that he was ok. The line was engaged and she guessed that he was talking to Timothy, when in truth – dazed with boredom and desire – he'd dialled the speaking clock. When she got hold of him ten minutes later he sounded sleepy. She told him they were held up but that he shouldn't worry, and that he should go to bed and not set fire to the house.

When she went back inside the sergeant came out from behind his desk and handed her a mug of tea, still with a whirlpool in it. She hugged it to her chest for comfort. He stood by Ros and leaned over her.

'So, have you got any kids?'

'A son: Pete.'

'How old is he?'

'Fourteen.'

'I expect he's into football, is he?'

'Actually, he likes hedgehogs.'

As the sergeant walked away, Ros could tell he was thinking, 'Poor woman. A dodgy husband and a son with strange proclivities.'

When it got to half past nine Ros asked after Ted again and this time the sergeant disappeared through a door. When he came back he said, 'Hopefully another half an hour.'

A young man ran in out of the rain and stood before the desk, blinking the raindrops out of his eyes, searching his pockets and making a puddle on the floor.

'And what can I do for you?' said the laughing policeman.

'I've got a producer somewhere.'

The man took a wet piece of paper out of his pocket and peeled it open. In the conversation that followed, Ros learned that a 'producer' was a form given to him by a policeman, compelling him to attend a police station with documents that proved his identity and ownership of his vehicle.

'All for a broken brake light.' grumbled the young man.

'Shouldn't drive around in a faulty vehicle,' said the sergeant, smoothly. 'That'll be five pounds, please.'

'Christ!'

The young man looked round at Ros for sympathy but she was staring down at her orange tea. He took his chequebook out and leaned on the desk, sucking snot up his nose with great sniffs and dotting the cheque with raindrops, and then left in a drizzly temper.

Five minutes later the door banged open and a policeman burst in with a head under each arm, each head belonging to the writhing and bent-double body of a punk rocker. His helmet flew off and landed at Ros's feet. When he released the heads and the rockers stood upright, they were revealed to be Lump and his girlfriend, Sugar, both of whom stood there panting and looking very cross indeed.

'Filth!' roared Lump at the copper, who shoved him onto a bench.

'Tosser!' screamed Sugar, as the copper hurled her towards the bench on the opposite side of the room.

'Quiet!' bellowed the sergeant, coming out from behind his desk. Ros handed him the fallen helmet, which he handed to his colleague, saying, 'Shame on you, constable. You're out of uniform.'

'Very funny, sarge,' gasped the constable who had his hands on his knees, trying to catch his breath.

The sergeant winked at Ros and said, 'There's never a dull moment here, love.' With his hands on his hips he swivelled slowly from side to side, assessing the carnage.

'So what have these two been up to?'

'Fighting, drunk and disorderly, and theft.'

'Location?'

'The off-licence.'

'Fighting who?'

'Each other.'

The sergeant tipped his head back and roared with laughter. 'Well, then they must be in love!' Then he gestured to the constable. 'One at a time, please.'

While he walked back to his desk, the constable dragged Lump to his feet and hauled him over. Ros noticed that despite his horrible temper, Lump's eyes looked drugged and drowsy, like Pete's when he was eating cereal. Lump noticed her and immediately cheered up.

'Ros! What are you doing here?'

'I'm collecting my husband.'

'Bang to rights as well is he?'

Ros didn't know what this meant and just smiled. The constable clipped Lump around the earhole to return his attention to the waiting sergeant.

'Name?'

'Napoleon.'

There was a snort of laughter and everyone looked over at Sugar who – judging from her dead-tickled expression – had fallen in love with Lump all over again. Ros noticed how fat the girl's thighs were, spread over the bench and wobbling like black blancmanges.

'Real name?'

'Mark Rafter.'

'Address?'

'Buckingham Palace.'

This little joust between the law and Lump went on for quite a while but in the end the law won. It didn't take as long for Lump to hand over his meagre possessions: an empty wallet, one Rizzla, and a quarter-full packet of Golden Virginia.

It was Sugar's turn next.

'Name?'

'Cleopatra.'

Finally the sergeant said to the constable, 'Ok, take them through. And put them in the same cell. Hopefully they'll strangle each other.'

Ros went out to the phone box and called Pete again. He sounded worried.

'Where are you?'

'At the station.'

'What station?'

Ros stood cursing herself in the bitter lemon light and all that Pete could hear was the rain drumming against the panes.

'Er... the petrol station. Where Dad broke down.'

'When will you be back?'

'Not long. Just go back to bed.' There was a silence while Ros thought of a way to succour the doomed youth. 'And remember, no school again tomorrow.'

'Ok,' he said.

When Ros went back inside she found Ted standing in front of the desk. He greeted her with a pallid smile and then continued listening to the sergeant who was reading something to him. Ros heard the words '... receiving stolen goods... ' '... a court date will be set... ' and several dates, all of them in the past. Standing next to the sergeant was another man, wearing a blue and white striped shirt and regarding Ted with snarling eyes.

Ros immediately identified him as a zealous junior detective and thought to herself forlornly, 'I'm getting to know the creatures of this world.'

Ted slumped into the passenger seat with a great sigh.

'You look exhausted,' said Ros.

He went to light a cigarette but then spat it out because he'd been chain-smoking all the way through the interrogation. They drove in silence until he leaned forward and rubbed the windscreen with his sleeve.

'Oh, it's raining.'

'It's been raining for hours.' After a while she said, 'So?'

Ted looked down at the documents they'd given him.

'So I've been charged with receiving stolen goods.'

'Does that mean you'll go to prison?'

Ted remembered Naylor saying, 'You're looking at ten years in Parkhurst, Ted,' but he knew it was a bluff and reckoned the real score would be a year, hopefully suspended. 'Unless,' thought Ted, 'I can get myself a classy lawyer but how will I afford one of those?'

'Don't be daft.'

'What does 'receiving stolen goods' mean?'

'It means that some of the parts we've got at the yard were stolen.'

'Did you know they were stolen?'

'Not at the time, no.'

'Well they can't blame you then, can they?'

'Oh they bloody well can.'

Two of the stolen fuel pumps had been traced back to Ted so he knew that he really was – as Lump had said – bang to rights. On the other hand, during the interview he'd learned quite a lot about the background of the case, certainly a lot more than Fenton and Naylor had learned from him. He knew the name of the freighter that the pumps had arrived in: The Emperor of Hamburg, and even the name of the smuggler who'd organised the sale: Klaus someone-or-other. He knew when the Freighter had arrived in the Port Of London and that other engine parts – crankshafts, exhaust pipes and even big ends – had been stolen off it and distributed around the country. He'd already known that they had a vague description of Vince, but was pretty sure they didn't know about that other link in the chain: Barnaby.

There'd been some tense moments during the long back-and-forth between him and the detectives but Ted knew they were getting desperate when Fenton, suddenly amiable, his voice rising to a girlish pitch, had opened his hands and said.

'Listen, Ted. If you help us, maybe we can help you.'

Ted had thought, 'Ah, so you haven't got much on me at all,' and remembering John Wayne in The Searchers, had pulled heroically on his cigarette and blown a solid ray of smoke directly into the face of detective constable Fenton. The man had lunged over the table at him but was restrained by Naylor. After that Ted had sat back in his chair and regarded his two interlocuters with a bold smirk, saying nothing and worrying more about Ros now, how he was going to face her, and what he would tell Pete if the lad ever found out what was going on.

Ros parked on the driveway and turned off the engine.

'Will you have to go to court?'

'Probably, but not for weeks, maybe months. They'll gather more information.'

They sat in silence, weary and anguished, their breath steaming up the windows. When the cold started to creep around her ankles Ros came to.

'You great oaf.'

'Don't worry. It'll all blow over.'

Then they got out of the car and went up to bed. They even read for a bit, as though nothing had happened, and fell asleep planning to carry on as normal, for Pete's sake.

Thirteen

While Ted's fortunes were plummeting, Pete's were rocketing in the form of an invitation to the annual meeting of the Earley Hedgehog Rescue Society. The invitation was hand-delivered – meaning that Pete had missed seeing the girl of his dreams at his front door – and on it was written '… you are cordially invited… ', an expression indicative of the ice queen herself, Susan Wren, Ros thought as she looked at the card quivering in Pete's hands. The meeting was to be chaired by the president of the Society, Fiona Wren, and held at Fiona's house, sixty-three Coopers Road. There were three items on the agenda: (1) Learn about hedgehogs, (2) Tell us why you love hedgehogs, (3) A plan for the future of hedgehogs. Invitees were requested to contribute fifty pence to the provision of tea and biscuits.

When Ted got home from work that night, Ros informed him of the momentous development.

'Thank God for hedgehogs,' said Ted.

'Good old Fiona,' said Ros.

While they were having dinner that evening, they tried to draw Pete out on his expectations of the meeting.

'I don't suppose there's much more they can teach an expert like you about hedgehogs,' said Ted.

'There might be some species I am unaware of,' said Pete, blithely.

'You'll have to tell us what Fiona's mum's like,' said Ros, her face a picture of innocence.

'What are you going to say when they ask you why you love hedgehogs?' said Ted, halfway through his bread and butter pudding, while thinking, 'We know why you love hedgehogs alright.'

'Well?' said Ros when Pete didn't answer.

Pete, who didn't really want to talk to his parents just then, became agitated and cried,

'I don't know, because they are strange and wonderful visitors from the natural world and a perfect example of how an animal – following Darwin's theory of evolution by natural selection – adapts itself to a predatory environment!'

He went out, slamming the door behind him, leaving Ros and Ted thinking, 'What fervour!'

They were also struck by how Pete seemed to be adopting the more intellectual vocabulary of his new friend, the pocket boffin. In truth, Pete had read those words in a book and memorised them in the hope that one day he could use them to impress Fiona. Almost his first throught on receiving the invitation had been, 'I hope no one else turns up so it's just me and her.'

On the morning of the meeting it was raining again. For the short walk to Fiona's house, Ros wanted Pete to wear a thick overcoat, wellington boots and a deep sea fisherman's oilskin hat that Ted had got from somewhere. With a baleful look Pete reminded Ros that he was fourteen, not four, while with a look of love Ros informed Pete that – in her eyes – he would always be four. In the end, after a chase through the house, a compromise was reached and Pete wore the overcoat but stout shoes instead of wellingtons and a scarf instead of the oilskin hat. He thought he must look like Paddington Bear as he stumped down the road, and underneath all the protective layers felt hot and grizzly and hoped that Fiona provided chocolate biscuits.

He arrived at her house at the same time as a young blonde girl about Fiona's age and a grey-haired old man wearing an old-fashioned suit, a brown bow tie and a trilby which he tipped to them both. The door opened and there was Fiona, looking pert and even more beautiful than her picture in the paper.

'Jane!' she said to the girl. She looked at the old gentleman. 'Professor Pomeroy, thanks for coming.' Then she turned to Pete. 'And you must be… ?'

'Pete.'

'Come in.'

She took their coats and added them to the pile on the bottom step of the stairs, then showed them into the living room. Pete was dismayed to find that there were about ten people already there, none of whom he knew but who all seemed to know each other, judging from the hubbub. No one took any notice of him but there was an especially warm welcome for Professor Pomeroy who – it turned out – was emeritus professor of biology at Reading University and a bit of a local celebrity. Most of the people were adults – neighbours of the Wrens by the sound of it – and there were two children: a beautiful little girl about three years old, standing between her mother's knees, and an eight-year-old boy with big ears, sitting next to his mum. Pete noticed that the boy couldn't take his eyes off Fiona, who was bustling around the room handing out cups of tea from a tray that her mum had brought in, and thought to himself, 'I've got a rival,' and also 'With those ears, no chance.' The Golden Retriever glided in, nosing some and walloping the knees of others with its tail.

Soon everyone was stuffed into a sofa and chairs at one end of the room while at the other end stood an easel. Fiona – energised by the crowd, her expression full of purpose – left the room and came back in with a large board which she placed on the easel. On the board was a hand-painted picture of a hedgehog sitting on top of a green hill in full sunshine. Below the hill was a pleasant valley of cultivated fields, villages, farm buildings, copses and ponds. There were birds in the air and butterflies among the flowers, while every other living creature there – whether it was a pig or a fox or a child in a garden – was looking up at the hedgehog with hoof, paw or hand raised in salute.

There were gasps of approval and the little girl ran up to the picture, cried, 'Mummy, a hedgehog!' and ran back again.

'Isn't that good, Cuthbert?' said the woman sitting next to the boy with big ears.

Pete noticed that Cuthbert was holding a chocolate biscuit and realised that at some point the biscuit tin had gone round and missed him. He reckoned that he'd only ever seen one boy with bigger ears than Cuthbert's: a kid from school – Les Butterfield – whose giant flaps, it was said, could detect the sound of frying chips from forty miles away. Remembering how bad his own acne had been, and anticipating all the torments that Cuthbert would face in the future because of his own dread deformity, Pete began to regard his rival in love more with sympathy than hostility.

A man with long hair and wearing a purple velvet jacket, sitting on the sofa with his arm around his young wife, said, 'Did you do that, Fiona?'

'It took ages.'

Fiona was beaming and frowning at the same time, happy with the praise but keen to remind everyone that her artistic triumph bore a serious message. She pointed at the picture, looked at her audience and said, 'This is the sort of world we want for our hedgehogs. Does everyone agree?'

'Yes!' they all cried, except for Cuthbert who said, 'No!'

Pete felt even more sorry for Cuthbert now, realising that by adding gaumlessness to the big ears, God had given it to the poor lad with both barrels.

Fiona – looking deadly serious – started the meeting in earnest. She confirmed that eveyone in the room had seen at least one hedgehog in their garden, and then listed some common facts about hedgehogs, such as their diet, how far they roamed in search of food and where they were most likely to make a home. Now and again Professor Pomeroy nodded sagely and Fiona would catch his eye in the manner of a student drawing confidence from a mentor.

'Are there any questions?' she said finally.

People shook their heads but Pete just sat there, beguiled by the fact that – in a phrase of Timothy's regarding another beautiful girl – all of Fiona's cones, planes and parabolas were in perfect quantam alignment.

'Now I think we should all say why we love hedgehogs.'

'Because they eat slugs,' said the wife of the man with long hair.

'Which eat our plants,' said two old ladies who looked as though they were great friends.

Professor Pomeroy nodded wisely and said, 'One of nature's benevolent hoovers.'

A tall, thin man wearing a blue V-neck jumper and a white shirt said, 'They're clever, the way they carry their fortifications on their back.'

'They got pwickles,' said the little girl.

'That's right, prickles with silver tips,' said a woman.

'They're good at looking after their babies,' said the young blonde girl.

'Why don't you show everyone your picture?' said Cuthbert's mum. She gave him a large sheet of paper and pushed him gently towards Fiona. 'Just a little drawing he did.'

Solemnly, the little squire walked towards his young queen, holding the picture up like a blazon. Fiona took him by the shoulders and turned him round so that everyone could see. To Pete the picture looked like a football with nails sticking out of it but everyone else thought it was a photographic likeness of a hedgehog, judging from the cries of delight and the ensuing round of applause. Shy but proud, Cuthbert stood there smiling with his chocolatey lips.

He sat down again and Pete realised that it was his

own turn to explain why he loved hedgehogs, but all the things that he'd planned to say had been said by others. In desperation he blurted out,

'I presume that all this time we've been discussing Erinaceus europaeus and not... say... Erinaceus roumanicus or Erinaceus amurensis?'

There was a stunned silence and Pete felt that all eyes were on him. 'They think I'm a show-off,' he said to himself, but then Professor Pomeroy – in a warm and gentle voice that Pete would remember all his life – touched him on the shoulder and said, 'An important distinction, young man, well done.'

'Yes, perhaps I should have mentioned that before,' said Fiona. 'Erinaceus europaeus is the correct Latin name for the common European hedgehog.' She looked at Pete curiously, as though she'd noticed him for the first time. 'Thankyou.'

She then came to the final item on the agenda: a future for hedgehogs. This depended, she said, on everyone encouraging hedgehogs to come into their garden by putting down saucers of water and food for them, and building hedgehog houses in dry, sheltered corners. She knew that everyone there already did these things but appealed to them to persuade their neighbours to do the same, and to be – in effect – evangelists for the hedgehog cause.

'Well, I think that's the end of the meeting. Are there any questions?'

Professor Pomeroy stood up, put his hat on and said,

'With all this food that we're going to leave for our favourite animals, I predict an evolutionary spurt among the creatures, resulting in giant hedgehogs roaming about the estate.'

Everyone laughed and got up to leave. There was a pile-up in the hallway as they all dived for their coats and then stood there thrusting hands into sleeves while thanking Fiona. Flushed with success, she made a point of saying goodbye to everyone but just as she got to Pete she was distracted by someone tugging her arm, and looking down saw Cuthbert presenting her with his drawing, and the next thing Pete knew he was out in the rain, minus her blessing.

Ros stood in the living room window, looking out, with the net curtains draped over her head and back. She was making transparent pink smears on the glass with a cloth soaked with Windowlene and then using a second cloth to buff the window clean. The activity was a distraction while her soul kept a look-out for the return of her son through the rain.

The house took longer to clean these days anyway, and not simply because she just had the two weekdays off work. She and Ted were smoking more so that it was now a house of full ashtrays. She could always smell tobacco smoke on the curtains and when she plumped the pillows there it was again. Whenever she emptied the kitchen bin into the metal bin by the gate she would always hear empty Cinzano and whisky bottles clinking jollily among the slop.

That morning she'd sung along to one of Petula's melancholy ones – Don't Sleep In The Subway – and couldn't remember the last time that she'd dusted the light bulbs. She cursed herself for getting a job at a biscuit factory because now she couldn't stop eating biscuits, and was sure that any day now she'd have to stop wearing knickers and switch to the type of giant pants that her mum wore.

Nowadays when Ted came though the back door in the evening he pecked her on the cheek habitually, replicating old kisses instead of fashioning new ones, and they no longer looked at each other lovingly, let alone into each other's eyes passionately. At least, thought Ros, Ted was a placid drunk, and she often marvelled at his ability to come home after a night in the pub, get into bed and read some more of The Eagle Has Landed, instead of roaring out Welsh hymns in the manner of Richard Burton – possessor, like Ted, of one of the great livers of the 70s – and shouting at her as though she was Elizabeth Taylor.

And the respect was still there, crucially for two people who could look at each other and only see their own troubles. Once, when she was at work at about four thirty in the afternoon, she'd noticed that all the girls around her were riveted by something, and turning round saw Ted standing in the doorway, smiling, with his jacket slung over his shoulder, his shirt undone to the belly button and tiny droplets of sweat silvering the hairs on his chest. Although the girls had never seen Ted before, they guessed who he was from the way he was looking at Ros, and then they'd all looked at Ros with varying shades of envy. Ted barely noticed these other maidens as he went over.

'Hello, Dolly,' he said, holding out his hand, and after

Ros had taken it he lifted it high, raising Ros up and making her pirouette around the desk and into his arms. Then, under the delighted gaze of Ros's girlfriends, the beautiful couple had disappeared through the door, like Taylor and Burton before the drinking began.

By now the sun was yellowing the clouds and the wet street was awash with light. Ros saw Pete coming down the road, squinting through the rain, his shoulders hunched, and – she guessed by the look on his face – frowning at providence. She went into the kitchen, took a freshly washed towel from the laundry basket, and as soon as he came through the door threw it over his head and began to rub his hair vigorously.

'Mum, get off!'

'Your hair's soaked. I told you to wear a hat.'

Reaching up, Ros's arms quickly became tired, and she grieved, sure it was only yesterday that she'd been on her knees, towelling the head of a toddler, but when she released Pete and saw his face – finally liberated from all the effects of acne – and noticed for the first time the blokeish jaw of the man behind the tender chin of the youth, she felt ravished and would have fallen to her knees again, like the mother of God at the Resurrection.

'So how did it go?'

'I suppose it was mildly interesting.'

'Was Fiona nice?'

'Really nice,' croaked Pete from behind a packet of Sugar Puffs.

Ros hooked her finger in the top of the packet and lowered it like a drawbridge, to see better the face of unrequited love.

'You should have chatted her up.'

'I hardly think that would have been appropriate at a meeting of such serious import.'

'Or invited her round for a cup of tea.'

'I didn't get a chance.'

Glumly, Pete finished his cereal and left the bowl and spoon by the sink for his mum to wash up. Then he ascended the stairs of doom and closed the door of his tomb behind him.

Fourteen

Normal life continued in the shape of their annual holiday, this year to Seatown, a small seaside village in Dorset surrounded by a giant caravan park that stretched along the cliffs to the east and the west. After dropping off a set of keys at the yard and leaving a bottle of scotch for the man who was letting them have his caravan for a week, Ted took the traditional holidaymaker's route west, joining the A303 at Basingstoke, crawling past Stonehenge and then turning south towards Bridport, missing out Weymouth. The journey to the coast took over four hours – when it normally took two and a half – because of the holiday traffic, Ted proposing that the best way to solve the problem of congestion around Stonehenge would be to build a tunnel under it, in which everyone could hide if there was a nuclear war with the Soviet Union.

It was a blazing hot day so Ros and Ted kept the front windows down all the way there. The smoke that Ted blew out of the window bounced off the slipstream and into Pete's face, who in between dozes read some more of The

Silmarillion or looked around at all the other refugees from the towns and the cities. He saw a car that had swerved onto the verge and beside it a man holding a little boy's willy, directing the arc of pee into a hedgerow, the little lad looking down at his potbelly and wondering where it was all coming from. He saw other men urinating into bushes and all the lay-bys were choked with cars. A woman with fat, sunburnt arms was trying to pour water into a doggy bowl that a frantic Cocker Spaniel was pushing along with its snout. Now and then they'd pass a car with its bonnet up and steam hissing out of the radiator. They couldn't decide whether the large birds hovering over the central reservations were Kestrels of sparrowhawks and Pete thought, 'Timothy would know.' In his mind he always referred to his new friend as Timothy because the lad had said to him one day – with some passion – 'If you use the contraction 'Tim' it makes me sound even more diminutive.'

Once, when the traffic was stationary in both directions, Pete caught the eye of a little girl whose face was as white as bone, sitting in the back of the car beside them. The next moment, her face disappeared behind the vomit that was spraying all over the window. Ros noticed too and jumped out of the car with a box of tissues, and for a while she and the little girl's mum made a big fuss of the patient, before Ros got back in with a big smile on her face, happy to have helped.

When they were near the end of their journey, bumping down a track between high hedgerows, Ted grumbling that the cow parsley was scratching the sides of his Cortina, it was Pete – with his head out of the window

– who was the first to smell the salt on the westerly breeze and cry, 'I can see the sea!' that ancient cry of landlubbers about to become beach babies once more.

Ted was an old-fashioned husband in that he believed it was his job to do the bad jokes and Ros's to do the cooking, but every morning while they were on holiday he got up and cooked them all a fried breakfast while Ros and Pete were still great lumps under the bedclothes.

The kitchen was in the middle of the caravan, by the door and near the toilet, which they called the compactor because whenever one of them sat in it they felt crushed. The little curtains by the windows and fabric seat covers on the three-sided sofa were of matching orange, while the kitchen cupboards and the breakfast table were made of pine, bleached in patches by the sun. It was shabby but – Ros was pleased to see – clean, and the smell of disinfectant on the linoleum and the lemony scent of air freshener lingered for two days. When they stood in the doorway other smells penetrated, such as grass, salt and seaweed and – if the wind was in the right direction – fish batter and vinegar from the big chip shop in the village.

On the first morning Ted, wearing only navy-blue Y-fronts and with a cigarette hanging out of his mouth, was prodding the eggs and bacon in the frying pan when a dairy cow – with elasticated globules of drool dangling from its mouth – stuck its head through the open door. For a while the two handsome ruminants – the result of millenia of evolution in opposite directions – stood there admiring each other, and then Ted called over his shoulder,

'The welcoming committee's here.'

Ros poked her head out, saw the beast and gasped. Pete padded over and said, 'It's Ermintrude from the Magic Roundabout.'

'Want some breakfast?' said Ted to the cow.

The creature rolled its eyes and expectorated through its nose.

'Get it out,' said Ros. 'It's dribbling everywhere.'

'Git.' said Ted.

The animal didn't budge so he jabbed at it with the frying pan. It was either this motion or the stink of a fellow animal being incinerated that made the cow lurch backwards and disappear.

'Go the udder way!' shouted Ted.

'That was almost funny, Dad,' said Pete, and then went back to bed.

The rest of the day was spent on the beach. Ros, worried about Pete's white skin, rubbed sun cream all over him until he was as slick as a pilchard. None of them could swim but a couple of times all three of them paddled knee-deep in the shallows, feeling like clumsy sea oafs among the shrill children wearing inflatable armbands and the athletes charging out to sea. The third time that Ros suggested they go for a paddle, Ted said 'no', so Ros and Pete went together and for the first time since he was a little boy Pete held his mum's hand when she was almost knocked off her feet by a gentle roller. They grinned at each other and then – feeling bolder – waded further out where they were bounced up and down by the incoming swells.

At lunchtime they wandered up to the village and had fish and chips outside a pub. The people who couldn't find a table sat on a low wall and ate theirs out of styrofoam trays, watched from the thatched rooves of the fishermen's cottages by gulls with greedy yellow eyes. Eventually one of these devils swooped down and grabbed a half-eaten saveloy right out of an old lady's hand – making her scream – but as it flew off it dropped the thing on the road. Pete ran over and brought it back to her while people said to each other, 'Did you see that? Those gulls!' The old lady looked doubtfully at her saveloy – now gingery with sand – but her husband said, 'No need to let it go to waste,' and pouring some of his lager over it to wash it, popped it into his mouth.

Before they went back to the beach they hired an umbrella for shelter and Ted bought some beer, so with his cigarettes, newspaper and Alistair Maclean novel he was set for the afternoon. Ros re-oiled Pete and then asked him to do her back. They'd been lying there for an hour when a man – his bald head as bright as a trumpet from the sun – came over and said to Ted and Pete,

'Do you want to play football? We're two short for a five-a-side game.'

'He'll go,' said Ted, and Pete jumped up and was gone for two hours.

'Where were they from?' said Ted when Pete got back.

'Birmingham.'

Ted imagined the route that they'd taken and said, 'Poor buggers. It must have taken them ages to get here.' He put down his paper, looked out to sea and began his lament of the day. 'The M5. One of the great engineering projects of the post-war era, the combined endeavour of thousands of hard-working men and skilled engineers, at the staggering cost of four hundred trillion pounds, and what happens the day after it opens? It turns into a bloody car park.' Then he went back to his paper and the rest of the bad news.

Hot, sandy and nicely fried by about five o'clock, they went back to the caravan to change out of their swimming costumes and then went into the village and had chicken-in-a-basket for dinner. As a special treat, Ted let Pete have half a pint of beer, which he didn't like. Ros suggested that he try half a pint of cider, which he quaffed.

That night there were plenty of stars and no wind so they all slept soundly.

The next morning they drove along the coast to Lyme Regis and visited a museum where they learned all about fossils and the famous fossil hunter Mary Anning, who lived in the region. Pete and Ros had heard of her but Ted hadn't. Museums made him glum and he was quickly bored by one display cabinet after another full of relics and labels. At one point, believing himself to be alone, he let out a big sigh but Ros was right beside him.

'It's interesting,' she said.

'It's like being back at school. People telling you things you're gonna forget.'

He perked up when he saw an exit sign above a doorway. He stood behind Ros and Pete who were examining the thigh bone of a Diplodocus. Pete was explaining, 'The Diplodocus weighed fifteen tons and was slow-moving,' and Ros was thinking, 'I know how it feels.'

'I expect we'll see Nanny and Grandad soon,' said Ted.

'How come?' said Pete.

'Because they're a couple of old fossils.'

Pete smiled and so did Ros, but only with her mouth.

'You'll be a fossil one day,' she said.

'He's one now,' said Pete.

After lunch they sat outside a pub for a couple of hours. Ted had four pints, smoked and watched the packed beach and the glittering sea. Pete would sit for about fifteen minutes and then wander off again. He'd spot a beautiful girl sunbathing – maybe resembling Raquel Welch in a white bikini – position himself somewhere near to her and then pretend he hadn't noticed her, while hoping that she'd spotted him too and fallen instantly in love, but knowing in his heart of hearts that it could never be and that the whole of life was a tragedy and he'd be better off dead.

Ros sat and wrote postcards, to her mum and dad, the girls in the office, Pauline and Norman, Jenny and Malcolm and Mr and Mrs Morris. Ted didn't have any family but she bought a postcard – of a tramp lying on his back and covered in beer and vomit – that he could send to his mates at the yard. Ted wrote, 'Dear all, have abandoned the wife and son. Free at last! Love Ted.'

The next day Pete played football with the boys from Birmingham again and on Thursday – tired of the beach – the Turners lazed around in picnic chairs by the caravan all afternoon. They had the whole range of English summer weather that day – sun, wind and rain – and at about two o'clock a sudden shower of hailstones crystallised the grass and sent them diving into the caravan, where they crouched in the doorway, their smiles turned to winces by the rattling on the roof.

That evening they went to see a variety show at the hoiliday camp. First on was a magician wearing a blue velvet suit and a white frilled shirt, whose petite female assistant smiled all the time that she was being sawn in half. At the end she was supposed to disappear in a puff of purple smoke but there wasn't enough smoke and everyone in the audience saw her slipping through a trapdoor in the stage.

Next up was the Australian tenor Montague Lambing who – as Ros and Ted informed Pete – had been famous in the fifties but was now notorious for being a heavy drinker. Once, he'd fallen off the stage and landed on his fourth wife, Iris, who – bearing in mind that Montague was almost completely round – miraculously survived. He put real heart into his performance as everyone could tell by the way his head turned cerise when he hit the high notes during Climb Every Mountain, so when he was applauded warmly at the end it wasn't only for nostalgic or sympathetic reasons.

The star act was a comedian, Andy Sausage – 'Admit it girls, you love a big sausage in the evening.' – who was famous for his rapid-fire delivery. He was about sixty years old, short, and wearing a black and white dogstooth suit, a yellow shirt, a purple bow tie and large comical glasses.

'Did you hear about the bloke who went to see a psychiatrist? He said "Doctor, I think I've turned into a dog." The psychiatrist says, "You'd better lie on the couch and tell me all about it." The bloke goes, "I'm not allowed on the couch." … Did you hear about the bloke who walked into a pub with a duck on his head? The barman says, "How long have you been like that." The duck goes, "It started with this nasty little spot on my bottom."'

He went on like that for half an hour and at one

point Ted slid off his chair and onto his knees, while Pete laughed so hard that Ros fell in love with him for the ten thousandth time. Afterwards, Ted got chatting to some men at the bar. When she felt that it was time to go Ros lingered in his eye line but with a jerk of the head Ted informed her that he was having too much fun, so she and Pete went back to the caravan without him. They made cheese on toast and a cup of tea and Ros said, 'Let's listen to Radio 2 for a change.' They heard Laughter In The Rain and Wichita Lineman. Ros said, 'Do you like this kind of music?' Pete was feeling agreeable so he shrugged his shoulders and said, 'It's ok.'

The next day they went to the amusement park. It was a modest affair with fun rides for kids, a lido, a crazy golf course, tennis courts and an artificial pitch where people could play volleyball with a giant, inflatable, multi-coloured ball that floated rather than flew through the air.

They all had a go on the shooting gallery, Ros – to the consternation of Ted and Pete – winning, her prize being a toy poodle that wagged its tail if you wound it up. They had jam doughnuts for elevenses and then played crazy golf, Ros coming first, Pete second, and Ted saying that he needed a drink.

For lunch they all had burgers with chips and beans and decided to visit the beach one more time. On their way out they passed a little audience that had gathered around a large black and white chessboard, about twenty feet square. A man and a girl about ten years old were playing with giant lightweight chess pieces that they picked up with both hands, the king being as tall as Ted and the pawns as short as young children. The man's beery friends were three women and two men, all wearing straw hats and dressed in brightly coloured holiday regalia. They prodded him with remarks such as, 'Don't forget your prawns, Alan,' and 'He's going, call an ambulance!'

The girl, blonde, wearing pink shorts and a T-shirt with a kitten on the front, was clearly some sort of prodigy, so everyone guessed from the way she would stand there frowning in concentration, then suddenly pick up one of her attacking pieces, march stoutly forward and land it behind enemy lines. Her dad watched gravely, with arms folded and head tilted downwards, doubling his chin.

It wasn't long before the girl – knowing she was about to win – was fighting back a smile of triumph. She picked up her queen, put it down besides Alan's king and said, 'Checkmate.' Alan looked unhappy and checked the disposition of the pieces but he knew that he'd lost from the general applause and the way that the girl's dad was nodding tremendously. He shrugged, held out his hand for the girl to shake, but when she looked baffled, patted her on the head and walked off.

The crowd began to disperse but Ros noticed that Pete was lingering. He'd been in the school chess club and had recently told her that he'd played Timothy a few times and – not surprisingly – been trounced.

'Why don't you play?' she said, and before he could answer, walked over to the board and wrote his name under NEXT PLAYER.

'He'll play,' said Ted, pointing out Pete to the girl and her father.

She looked at her dad, who nodded, and then everyone

started picking up the pieces and putting them in their positions.

The girl's father said, 'Winner plays white.'

Pete walked over to the black pieces and the girl moved her pawn to K4.

For the first ten minutes the opponents were evenly matched. The girl brought both of her knights and bishops into play and Pete responded in kind. More and more people stopped to watch and whispered suggested moves to each other.

Ros could tell from Pete's face that he was enjoying himself and that he thought he was in with a chance, but then the girl brought out her queen in a bold move and the audience went quiet. Pete picked up a pawn, hesitated, then put it back. He picked up a knight and hesitated again. As he stood there holding the piece in mid-air, the girl walked off the baord and exchanged a smug look with her dad. Pete was in a pickle and folk in the audience asked each other in whispers how he was going to get out of it.

Ten minutes later, Pete was in serious trouble. He'd made three or four weak moves which had allowed the girl's queen, knight and bishop – working in combination – to menace his king. He castled to relieve the pressure and was grateful for one thing – that his own queen had escaped the melee and was unsurrounded. He caught his mum's eye, shrugged and put on a brave face.

Suddenly the giant inflatable ball from the volleyball court sailed over and landed among the chess pieces, scattering them like ninepins. There was a collective groan and then two young lads in swimming trunks charged onto the board, picked up the ball and ran off, looking sheepish.

'Well these were here,' said a man from the audience as he walked onto the board and righted a rook and two pawns. The girl and her dad started picking up pieces, as did Pete and some other people from the audience. Ted looked around for Ros and saw her in the centre of the melee. She and a burly man had picked up opposite ends of the black queen and were having a tug of war. Back and forth they went until with a savage wrench Ros tore the piece from the man's hands and walked away with it, pink in the face and with her hair in turmoil. She put the piece on a square and stood beside it, guarding it. 'Always wanting to help,' thought Ted, fondly.

When all the pieces were upright again, everyone stood back and a woman said, 'Looks alright to me.'

'Definitely,' said Ros.

The girls father examined the board and looked satisfied as well. Only the girl herself seemed unsure.

'Dad… ' she started to say.

But Pete – whose turn it was – had seen his chance, and instead of wondering why he hadn't noticed it before was already walking across the board with his queen so that he could take a pawn and put the girl in check. She looked wildly around, wondering how it could have happened, but everyone watching knew that Pete had made a killing move. When she moved her king he would take her rook, putting her in check again. If she moved her knight to block this check he would be able to capture her other knight, and while all this was going on she would be unable to develop her own attack at the other end of the board. Her dad was now down in the dumps and unfolded his arms and stuffed his hands into his pockets.

The girl fought on bravely for a few moves but then her shoulders slumped and she gave up. She knocked over her king and looked at Pete with a wan and pretty smile.

'Well played,' she said.

'You too.'

She and her dad joined the people drifting away while Pete stood among the ruins of his victory. Ted walked over and slapped him on the back and Ros put her arm around him.

'Come on, let's get the champion an ice-cream,' she said.

Fifteen

Pete had enjoyed his holiday but he was more glad that he and Timothy were reunited. He went round to his house and told him that he'd got drunk on cider and had beaten a girl at giant chess.

'What opening did you use?' said Timothy.

'I was black.'

Timothy pushed his glasses down his nose so that he could look at Pete over the top of them.

'Alright then, what opening did *she* use. The Ruy Lopez? The Italian?'

Pete had never really believed in the truth of these openings that Timothy was always on about and so he couldn't take them seriously. He tilted his head to one side and rolled his eyes around in their sockets, pretending to search his intellect.

'Now what opening was it? Was it the… Or maybe it was the… I know, it was the nostril.'

'The nostril?'

'That's an opening, isn't it?'

'A nostril is an orifice, not an opening, you giant moron.'

They didn't speak to each other for a whole minute and then Pete said, 'I found another hedgehog in the garden.'

'Did you tell your girlfriend?'

'What girlfriend?'

'Fiona, of course.'

Pete assumed a most serious expression.

'Fiona isn't my girlfriend. She is the president of the hedgehog rescue society.'

Timothy held his head in his hands and sobbed. Once he'd pulled himself together he said, 'Edmunds is going into hospital for an operation.'

'What, on his club foot?'

'No, on the other one. They're going to make it into a club foot as well so that they're both the same.'

'Oh very funny.'

Through this repartee, Pete and Timothy reaffirmed their love for each other. Pete always felt as home at Timothy's anyway because the whole family had made him feel welcome. They were all very academic but couldn't have cared less that Pete was nowhere near the top of the class himself.

Timothy's sister, Jane, was back from university and she came into the room. She was a plump girl with a round, pretty face and black hair that was tied into a ponytail. She wore faded blue jeans, a blue Oxford University T-shirt and big black glasses just like Timothy's. Finding the boys sitting next to each other on the sofa, she looked around for somewhere to sit, couldn't decide where to, so sat on top of Timothy, squashing all the air out of him.

'Did you have a nice holiday?' she said to Pete.

'Great, thank you.'

'What did you do?'

'I was just telling Timothy that I played giant chess.'

'Funny you should mention Timothy because I've been looking for the little fellow. I don't suppose you've seen him?'

By now Timothy had drawn some air into his lungs.

'GET OFF ME, YOU FAT COW!'

'Oh, he was under me,' said Jane, getting up. 'How funny.'

After Jane had gone, Pete and Timothy went back to writing their History Of The Roman Orgy, and after finishing Chapter Four: Lubricants, began Chapter Five: Sheep. Both possessing the pornographic imagination typical of the adolescent boy, they wrote quickly, and even colluded on the obscene diagrams with which they intended to illustrate their pages. Pete became so absorbed that he even forgot Fiona for a while, but even when he was thinking about her she seemed like some heavenly, unattainable creature who he would probably never see again, unless his interest in hedgehogs lasted until the next annual meeting of the rescue society.

In reality, she was not so very far away at all at that moment, about a mile away in fact, sitting on a bench outside the baker's in Earley town centre with her best friend Ruby and about to indulge in an orgy of her own. The two girls had just shuffled along to let a lady sit next to them and were now peeling the greaseproof paper away from their cream and jam buns, preparatory to making pigs of themselves. Soon they were giggling at the dollops of cream on each other's noses and licking the jam off their fingers between munches. Eventually they sat back with great sighs.

'Shall we get another one?' said Ruby, and the girls laughed again.

'I was young and pretty once,' said Barbara Amplethorpe.

The girls turned and looked at the woman sitting next to them. She was middle-aged – they guessed – and was wearing a black trouser suit and sensible black shoes. Her hair was tied in a bun and she had unsightly, protruding teeth, the result of some terrible accident or birth deformity, they assumed. But she had nice eyes and was smiling to the extent that the projecting monstrosities allowed.

'Did you enjoy your cakes?'

Mesmerised, Fiona and Ruby simply nodded.

'We shouldn't eat too many though, should we girls. It's bad for our complexions.'

Both girls were nudging each other and wanted to scream, 'Run!' but were rooted to the spot by an excess of politeness. Fiona, however, was braver than her mournful young friend, so that when the woman took a packet of cigarettes out of her handbag and lit up a Silk Cut, she said, 'You shouldn't smoke either, madam.'

'You're right, my dear!' shrieked Barbara. 'But a few a day keeps the cakes away!'

Their bench was situated at the intersection of four arcades that echoed with the footfall of shoppers and the cries of infants. Concrete tubs full of euonymus were positioned throughout the precinct to give the illusion of gaiety, which was further enhanced by a clown with giant red feet walking up and down selling balloons to children. The walkway beneath his feet was polka-dotted with dark grey roundels of old chewing gum, while the wind – frosty or Mediterranean according to the time of year – had blown drifts of flattened cigarette butts under the benches. Over by the newsagent's a little girl rode a toffee-coloured mechanical horse, watched by her mother, weary already at ten o'clock in the morning.

For a while the attention of Barbara and the two girls was riveted by the costermonger, drawing people towards his open-air stall like a fairground barker. He threw two free apples to some pensioners sitting on a bench, and then held out a cauliflower – in a paper bag that was too small for it – for an old lady, who opened the tartan flap of her two-wheeled shopping trolley so he could drop it in. Soon Fiona and Ruby found themselves in conversation with Barbara, who with gentle questions probed them about their lives: what school they went to, where they lived, did they have boyfriends – 'No.' they giggled – and what their interests were. Fiona replied with more candour than the timid Ruby, happily telling Barbara about her hopes for the future, the concert they were going to buy tickets for, and the place where she worked as a result of her passion for animals.

In the end they didn't have to run away because Barbara herself liberated them – after stubbing out her second cigarette – by rising stiffly to her feet, wishing them all the best for the future and walking away, looking a little lonely the girls thought, and making them feel sorry for her, and proud of themselves for feeling sorry for her after the revulsion they'd experienced earlier.

After this day, the parents of Fiona and Ruby never had to remind their darling daughters to brush their teeth.

A few days later, Pete and Timothy had to endure the trauma common to all new-found friends: the meeting of their mothers. Ros and Julia Herbert stood in the kitchen and wondered how on earth it was that they'd never met before, bearing in mind all the times that Ros had dropped Pete off at Timothy's, and Julia had dropped Timothy off at Pete's. Their fears about each other – Ros's that Julia was a bluestocking, and Julia's that Ros would be just plain dull – were allayed five minutes into their encounter when they both realised that they were going to get on. So instead of being intimidated by Julia's bold, architectural glasses and schoolmistressy manner, Ros thought she was funny, gossipy and – thanks to the wind-blown nest of black and grey hair and too much umber eye shadow – a pantomime from the neck up. Julia couldn't believe how pretty Ros was, or how calm, with a smile like a firework exploding silently, and a robust figure just the right side of chunkiness. And she obviously had a sweet tooth, judging from all the packets of chocolate biscuits that tumbled out when she opened a cupboard and reached in for coffee cups.

For ten minutes Pete and Timothy had to stand there and listen to their mums talking about them as though they weren't there – 'The amount of time they spend in their rooms. I don't know what they do in there' – and then they went up to Pete's bedroom. Despite their embarrassment, the boys were excited about the meeting between their mums because they wanted to be allowed to go and see ELO, whose tour had come to London, and it was this meeting that would decide whether they would be allowed to embark on such an adventure.

Pete kept his bedroom door open so that they could hear the voices drifting up the stairs, their ears pricked for words such as 'London', 'deserve', and 'ELO'. When they were satisfied that the talk was still of earthly matters rather than the possibility of cosmic happiness, they continued with their History Of The Roman Orgy, but it wouldn't be ten minutes before Pete crept out onto the landing again, listening for the magic words. Once, the voices grew suddenly louder as Ros opened the living room door and went into the kitchen, for more milk or something he believed, until he heard a very faint clang and realised that his mum was helping herself to another biscuit on the sly. With the natural wickedness of the boy, he determined to remind her of this moral lapse on her part the next time that she accused him of eating too many Sugar Puffs.

Finally, Pete heard the word 'music' and knew that the arbiters had reached the main item on the agenda. They sneaked down the stairs and Pete – without making a sound – managed to open the living room door slightly, Timothy, the shorter spy, kneeling down and removing his glasses so he could fit his ear into the gap.

'What are they saying?' he hissed.

'I'm not sure. Something about music, though.' Pete listened some more. 'Vaughan Williams. Who's Vaughan Williams?'

'A composer my mum likes. In the English pastoral style.'

By now the discomfort was causing Timothy to pant, as Pete knew by the peanut butter thermals rising up to him. He looked down and saw a most hideous sight: Timothy blinking moleishly, with mouth agape and one half of his face palsied by the pressure against the door frame.

'God you're ugly.'

The conversation in the living room veered back to everyday matters for a while, but then Pete's face brightened.

'ELO,' he said. 'She definitely said ELO.' Then he frowned. 'Sid Pistol. Who's Sid Pistol?'

'I imagine a conflation of Sid Vicious and the Sex Pistols.'

'Conflation?'

'A joining up, accidentally in this case, I'm sure.'

'Does your brain ache when you come out with things like that?'

'If you had a brain you'd know.'

From his towering position, Pete inserted his big toe into Timothy's left nostril. Timothy sneezed and the voices in the living room stopped. Pete heard Mrs Herbert say,

'What's the matter.'

'I thought I heard something.'

Pete expected to hear movement towards the door but when after a few seconds the talking resumed, he sighed with relief.

'What are they talking about now?' said Timothy.

Pete was frowning.

'I can't quite… '

'What?'

'I can't quite believe it but I think my mum is saying that ELO are a punk band.'

'But ELO are a rock band, who achieve a soul-expanding greatness through a combination of harmonious pop, orchestral arrangements and operatic subject matter.'

'I know.'

Shortly, the boys were so uncomfortable that they went back to Pete's room. Timothy said,

'I'm afraid our mums have succumbed to the classic misapprehension of most parents – that all music after nineteen-fifty-five is depraved.'

'Yes, and they think it's a bad influence on the young.'

They sat in silence for a while and then Timothy said,

'Your mum can't really believe that ELO are a punk band, surely?'

'That's what it sounded like.'

'What music does she like?'

Pete had to think for a moment.

'Petula Clark.'

'Perhaps she thinks that everything that isn't Petula Clark is depraved.'

'Well, if she does, then we won't be going to see ELO.'

And with this utterance the bells of hope were silenced.

Down in the living room, Julia Herbert was saying,

'Well, Ros, thanks so much for the coffee but I really must be going.'

Inside, Ros was triumphant, not because Julia was going, but because she'd managed to persuade the woman that ELO were a punk band, a moral danger to their sons, and that therefore to let them go to the concert would be a failure of love. Of course she'd been helped by the fact –

established early on in the conversation – that Julia didn't know anything about contemporary rock, being a classical music buff, but she'd still had to deploy all of her acting skills in order not to arouse her suspicions. Ultimately, Julia had been won over by Ros's suggested – and surprising – alternative. So Ros was triumphant, but at the same time exhausted by her own shamelessness, in the same way that Barbara Amplethorpe had been wearied by trying to lead Mick Burnley away from a life of crime.

In the hallway, Julia cried out, 'Timothy, time to go!'

The boys walked down the stairs like two of the doomed descending into hell.

'Well?' said Pete.

'Well what?' said Ros.

'Can we go and see ELO?'

'I don't know, dear. The tickets are very expensive and we're not quite sure that you're old enough yet, and your dad isn't very keen on the idea either. But Mrs Herbert and me have had a better idea. In fact I've got you the tickets already.'

'To see who?' said Timothy.

Ros and Julia looked at each other and cried, 'The Carpenters!'

Sixteen

A week later, on a balmy evening, Ros drove the boys to the Hexagon theatre in Reading. Even after a day of North African heat, she'd wondered out loud whether Pete should take a padded winter coat and hot water bottle 'just in case it's a bit chilly inside', but after seeing the look on his face, hadn't pressed the point. Sitting beside her in the car, he was wearing a brown shirt with white dots and a big collar, and dark brown brogues, and had slapped on so much of his dad's Brut aftershave that Ros's eyes were watering. In the back, his fun-sized friend looked as smart as a prince in shiny black shoes, yellow trousers, white shirt and red tie, an ensemble that raised Julia Herbert even higher in Ros's estimation.

During the journey, the three of them wondered which of the Carpenters' songs the boys would hear that night – 'Top Of The World, definitely', 'maybe Goodbye To Love', 'Jambalaya?' – and then Ros told them both off for making a suicide pact if any of their friends from school found out where they'd been.

She parked a few streets away and walked with them to the theatre. Outside the foyer was a crowd made up of bubbly teenage girls, smiling young couples, bemused fathers chaperoning daughters and – to Pete's relief – one other teenage boy, looking, like him, bewildered at finding himself outnumbered by so many pretty young women and by the way they still seemed to be able to understand each other even though they were all talking at the same time and making a real din. Pete couldn't smell a thing because of all the Brut he had on, but Timothy was borne along by the warm, heavenly, floral essences that floated off of the girls. Both boys were struck by how beautifully bare their arms and legs were, and how trifling their summery shorts and skirts.

Ros looked at Pete and Timothy's faces and said, 'I bet you're glad you came now.'

They went into the foyer and Ros bought them a programme. It was a foot long and on the glossy cover was a picture of the Carpenters. Richard, wearing a white suit and sitting at a white grand piano, was smiling, his perfectly aligned teeth as white as porcelain. Karen was leaning on him from behind, her arms encircling his neck and her head nestling against his, and looking wistful, frail and beautiful. Ros wondered if all American pop stars looked like benign interstellar travellers.

She watched Pete and Timothy drift across the deep orange carpet and up the stairs with their tickets at the ready, and then went back to the car. She'd planned to drive home and then come back and pick them up later, but now she realised that instead of spending the evening with her morose husband she could sit in the car for the next two hours and watch the world go by instead. She stopped at a newsagents and bought herself a packet of chocolate-coated toffees, and then got in the car, pushed the seat back and opened the window to let the summer evening in. It was so warm that the chocolates melted between her fingers on the way to her mouth.

She sat there for half an hour, roiling toffee after toffee around in her mouth and feeling plumper by the minute. She wondered how the boys were getting on and hoped that Timothy's little legs were pumping up and down to the tune of Jambalaya by now. Pete, she guessed, would be trying to hold himself aloof from music that he'd described as 'wet' and 'girly', but knew that eventually his gentle nature would succumb to the ethereal harmonies of the Carpenters.

While in the foyer, she'd scanned the crowd for Fiona Wren without success but knew that she had to be there somewhere, thanks to the intelligence that Barbara Amplethorpe had acquired during her meeting with Fiona and Ruby at the shopping precinct. But even after this encounter Ros had known that to give Pete the best chance of bumping into Fiona at the concert she'd have to get him seats as near as possible to the girl of his dreams, which was why – when Fiona and Ruby were queuing for tickets – they found themselves in conversation with a lady called Belinda Ogilvy who was buying tickets for her nephews.

Belinda was terrifically old – at least forty, thought the girls – and, thanks to the high blonde beehive with red ribbons, pale blue eyeshadow and yellow floral mini dress, an undying victim of that decade of comical fashions: the

Sixties. Ros had fun creating this new incarnation from a box of old fancy dress costumes, but the dress – being two sizes too small for her – made her bottom look even bigger than Barbara Amplethorpe's, or so she judged from the wolf whistles of scaffolders that had followed her across the plaza in front of the theatre.

Inching along in the queue behind Fiona and Ruby, Ros didn't mean to speak to the girls but in the end she was drawn in by their excitement.

'I hope you don't mind me asking, but these Carpenters aren't one of these terrible punk bands are they?'

Fiona and Ruby looked at each other in disbelief and then giggled.

'They're a pop group.' said Fiona.

'Brother and sister,' said Ruby.

'Ah, that's alright then,' said Belinda.

She'd then introduced herself and explained her mission.

'Well,' said Fiona. 'Seeing as you're next in line, I expect your nephews will be sitting near to us.'

'I'm sure they won't be able to contain their excitement wherever they sit,' said Belinda.

After Fiona and Ruby had bought their tickets and said goodbye, Belinda had gone up to the kiosk and asked for seats near to her friends. After that her only worry had been that Fiona would go home to her mum and tell her that she kept being accosted by strange women.

Ros was parked near the station and could see scores of workers and shoppers hurrying towards the platforms. A group of punk rockers was pouring out of one of the waiting trains and among them Ros spotted that amiable rebel, Lump, and his short, fat, violent girlfriend Sugar. Most of the crew were holding the signature can of industrial-strength cider and those who weren't smoking were dropping their butts onto the concourse. A British Rail cleaner, wearing a black waistcoat over a collarless white shirt, and holding a long-handled dustpan and brush, watched them go by, shaking his head at the future.

As they came out of the station the punks turned towards Ros, and although a part of her envied their carefree attitude she was more frightened by their lawless aspect, and so she sank down in her seat, hoping that Lump wouldn't spot her. He and his friends stopped by a bench and Lump produced a large joint. He poked it into his mouth, applied the flame and – after sucking hard – turned the tightly twisted end into a brief fireball, from which tiny, glowing shreds of incinerated Rizzla floated into the hot dusk.

The joint was passed around solemnly and then the punks set off again, passing in front of Ros's car and heading towards a small street to her right where – she noticed for the first time – other punks had gathered below a sign saying The Pit. Still within earshot, the punks bumped into a fellow traveller with a bright green Mohican haircut, and Ros heard Lump cry, 'Are you coming then, Minton?'

'Where?'

'To see the UK Subs.'

A memory stirred, and Ros realised that The Pit was the old location of a dinner and dance club called The Welcome that she and Ted used to go to in the fifties. She remembered them going down the stairs, leaving their coats with the hat-check girl, walking past the bar glittering with glasses and optics, and being shown to one of the tables-for-two that encircled the small wooden dance floor and faced the stage, just big enough for a five-piece band and crooner or – on men-only nights – a stripper to twirl away her chiffon gloves.

Ted didn't have his moustache back then, she recalled, and his hair was as black as pitch, tightly curled and almost woolly, almost like a black man's Ros had thought, and indeed Charlie had suspected – pacifically, but without letting on to Ted – that his future son-in-law might have Caribbean ancestry. Ros couldn't have cared less because at the end of only her second date with Ted she felt as though she'd climbed a mountain with only a single breath.

Ros's favourite singer around that time was Jo Stafford, while Ted liked Perry Como, and rock-and-roll sort of passed them by. Now and again they would bop around the dance floor but mostly they preferred dancing in each other's arms. And they both liked Frankie Vaughan. Ros had discovered him because of her dad who – after a few pale ales on a Saturday night – would sing Give Me The Moonlight into a dish mop.

One night in The Welcome, just after their marriage, they sat facing each other across the candlelight, both tired and tipsy, Ros with her mouth full of Black Forest Gateau and her eyes full of Ted's big brown eyes and thick, sable sideburns. Something caught his eye and he froze with his fork halfway to his mouth.

'I don't believe it,' he said, gesturing with the fork. 'It's Frankie Vaughan.'

Ros looked across and saw six smartly dressed people sitting in a booth, smiling and looking up at a waiter who was opening a bottle of champagne. Frankie, grinning and tanned – from making a film with Marilyn Monroe in America, Ros knew – was sitting with his arm around the woman next to him, whose fur coat, too expensive to be left with the hat-check girl, was piled in luxurious folds on the shelf behind her.

'I'll get his autograph,' said Ted.

'No.'

'It's your birthday.'

Ted got up, threw his napkin on the table and walked off, and the next thing Ros knew, he was standing boldy but bashfully beside Frankie's table and saying something that made them all look over at Ros and wave, this collective action making everyone else in the restaurant look at Ros too. Feeling a fool, she waved back – not too regally, she hoped – and then Frankie's companions started searching through their handbags and pockets, until one of the men produced a pen so that Frankie could write a message on a napkin. The missive completed and fond farewells exchanged, Hercules – having found his impossible labour to be child's play – returned to his table with a fat smile on his face. Ros read,

'To Ros, the second most beautiful girl in the world, after my wife! Love, Frankie Vaughan.'

By now all the chocolate toffees had gone. She saw the blonde hairs on her arm sticking up, and shivered, realising that the heat of the day had gone and night was falling. The street to her right was empty now, meaning that The Pit had swallowed up the punks. She decided to get a coffee from the station buffet and make it last until the boys came out of the theatre. She got out of the car, looked around to make sure that no one was looking, and plucked the seat of her knickers from between the cheeks of her bum.

A few people were hurrying across the concourse in front of the station and the buffet was nearly empty. While a woman filled her styrofoam cup from the urn, Ros examined the victuals that remained for sale, which at that time of the evening amounted to some chocolate bars, three packets of salt and vinegar crisps, a white roll containing a square of processed cheese, and a currant bun flattened by the heat of the day. She was tempted by the bun, but knew that if she ate it after all of the chocolate toffees she'd start to wobble.

Back at the car she put her cardigan on and lit a cigarette, opening the window just enough to let the smoke out. She imagined that Ted would be cross with her for not phoning home, but at the same time she didn't care a damn about the dunderheaded old crook just then. These thoughts prompted another memory, of him coming home from work about six months after Pete was born, standing in the doorway with his head cocked to one side, listening, and on hearing the baby wailing, saying,

'So he's still crying. Right, that's it. I'm leaving. It was nice knowing you, love.'

Pete had bawled and bawled for the first six months of his life, and even after his christening – where he turned the vicar to jelly – the unholy trumpeting continued, so it took a while for Ted to bond with the little blighter. But once Pete had stopped crying and started laughing, and was heroically plump, Ted did finally fall in love with him, and reverted to infancy himself, so that when he picked Pete up it looked to Ros like a babe in a baby's arms.

It got to ten o'clock and Ros thought that – allowing for encores – the boys should be out sometime soon. She walked over to the theatre and stood with the waiting mothers and fathers, hoping to see Susan Wren so that she could pounce on her, but the woman was nowhere to be seen.

After a while, two of the theatre staff appeared in the foyer and wedged the doors open, and Ros held her breath. The audience came out in ones and twos and then in droves and Ros scanned the throng for the heads of Pete and Timothy. She saw Pete – looking thrilled – and watched him wander to one side while looking around for his friend, who eventually popped out from the forest of legs and stood by him. There they waited – not for her she realised with a leaping heart – but for someone else, and then she saw Fiona and Ruby squeezing through the crowd and walking up to the boys, who they'd obviously already met.

Ros slipped away – while keeping the foursome in view – to give them time to linger. Fiona and Ruby were hugging their programmes to their chests and swinging coyly from side to side, remembering the songs, while the boys faced them, Pete smiling gaumlessly and clearly riveted by Fiona, Timothy doing most of the talking and bringing his awesome analytical powers to bear on the performance, Ros guessed.

After a round of cheery goodbyes, the girls walked off in the direction of the station and Ros realised that their parents had deemed them grown-up enough to travel to and from the concert unaccompanied, which made her feel guilty about chaperoning Pete. Still, when she walked up to the boys he was still looking thrilled.

'Was that Fiona I just saw?' said Ros.

'We were sitting right behind her,' said Timothy.

'And did you like the Carpenters?'

'They were great!' said the boys in unison.

'Better than the Sex Pistols?'

They walked off, Timothy pushing his glasses back up his nose and clasping his hands behind his back.

'That's a very good question, Mrs Turner, and after giving the matter a great deal of thought, my answer must be an emphatic 'Yes'. It was the progessive lyrical phrasing, you see, in combination with the carefully layered harmonies and orchestrated arrangements... '

'Put your seat-belt on, Timothy.'

'Yes, Mrs Turner.'

On the way home, Ros quizzed the boys about the concert and they listed all the songs that they'd heard. It sounded to Ros as though The Carpenters had gone through all of their greatest hits with the addition of Country Roads and California Dreamin' for the sake of variety.

'And did Fiona enjoy herself?'

'Put it this way, Mrs Turner. For a girl who has pictures of The Carpenters sellotaped to the backs of her hair brushes, it could hardly have been otherwise.'

'I saw you talking to her.'

'She was telling us what school she went to,' said Pete. 'And apparently she works at the vet's.'

'I know... I mean, does she?'

'She loves animals,' said Pete with a lump in his throat.

He didn't tell his mum that the last thing Fiona had said to him was, 'You must come round and see my menagerie', because he didn't really know what a menagerie was, but suspected it was a drawer full of lacy underwear.

They dropped Timothy off and then drove home. Pete – tired but elated – went off to bed and then Ros went up herself, and was surprised to find the direct descendent of Ivan The Terrible nicely tucked-up, sober and engrossed in another Jack Higgins.

'So, did they have a good time?'

'Put it this way, Dad, your son is now under the spell of The Carpenters.'

'We'll have to get him into Perry Como next.'

'And Petula Clark.'

After they'd turned the lights out, Ros said into the darkness, 'You'll never guess what.'

'What?'

'They bumped into that Fiona from down the road at the concert.'

'Fancy that.'

'Perhaps she'll be his first love.'

There was a deep silence and then Ros went to sleep with a smile on her face, believing that Pete was on the verge of an apotheosis thanks to Fiona, but Ted went off with a frown, thinking not of love but of all the torments that accompanied that blissful condition.

Seventeen

It was Timothy's turn to go on holiday next and Pete was at a loss, but then he received a phone call from out of the blue. Fiona told him that they needed an extra volunteer at the vet's and asked him if he wanted the job.

'I wouldn't know what to do.'

'Well, I'll be there. In fact I'll be your supervisor.'

Pete could think of nothing better than being bossed about by Fiona and so said, 'Yes,' and at the same moment stopped missing Timothy.

On his first day at work, Fiona collected Pete from his house and they walked the mile to the vet's. The place was called Justice For Pets because it was run by Mr Justice, a huge man with a great red and gold beard, and whose large hands looked as though they'd be better at shovelling boulders than sewing up hamsters.

'So this is the new recruit,' he said to Fiona. 'Another defender of the hedgehog realm.'

'I'm Pete.'

'Well Pete, Fiona will show you the ropes. I'm off to reattach an ear to a Beagle. And don't forget Dr Dolittle.'

Fiona saw the frown on Pete's face and said, 'He means talk to the animals.'

Justice For Pets was a one-man show, quite small. Apart from a nurse who came into assist with operations, Mr Justice's only employee was Margaret the receptionist, a middle-aged lady who always wore a patterned headscarf and large round glasses with tortoiseshell frames, and who had a freckly chest and bosom. The waiting room was a square room with wooden chairs around the walls, from where one door led to the yard and shed where the animals were kept, and another to the surgery itself, another square room with glass cabinets full of medical supplies and equipment, and a central table where the operations and examinations took place. Any member of staff who went into the surgery had to wear a white coat. The one they gave to Pete hung down to his ankles but he felt that it gave him an air of authority and that now he could look a rabbit in the eye.

Their first job that morning was to clean out all the kennels and cages. Fiona saw Pete pulling a face and said,

'Animals have bottoms too, you know.'

'Also diarrhea.'

Fiona looked disappointed, and Pete could tell that she was thinking, 'How can you be mean about poorly animals,' but then, as another shoveful of ordure plopped into the bucket, he got the giggles and saw that the corners of Fiona's mouth were wriggling too.

'It's important to do this,' she said, trying to be serious.

'We're lucky there aren't any elephants,' said Pete, and Fiona collapsed.

The next job was to shampoo a greyhound called Horace who'd come in with a broken paw – now set and bandaged – and then caught fleas. Horace was a placid beast and so didn't give them any trouble while Pete held the hose and Fiona did the soaping.

There were several other dogs, a few cats, tortoises, rabbits, gerbils, two British snakes and a large African Grey parrot with a red tail and a yellow eye, in for beak realignment. For breakfast they gave the cats water, the tortoises lettuce, the rabbits carrots, the gerbils nuts, the parrot porridge and – in an innovation of Mr Justice's – the dogs hard-boiled eggs.

The next morning they had to sit with a dog that had just been operated on. It was a Neapolitan Mastiff whose facial folds had sagged over its eyes to the extent that it couldn't see a thing. It could see well enough now thanks to the operation but Fiona and Pete wondered if Mr Justice was guilty of an over-correction, because now Mulberry wore a permanent look of surprise and it took him a long time to blink.

They would normally finish their work by lunchtime and then walk home. During her days off – Thursday and Friday – Ros got to know roughly what time they would be coming down the road and would be watching from behind the curtains in the living room. When they got to Pete's, he and Fiona would come inside or Fiona would go back to her house on her own. If they both came in – to find a surprised Ros in the kitchen – Fiona would always be chatting away while Pete would be hanging on her every word. Ros would make them a drink and ask them what they'd done that morning and Fiona would reveal all, while Pete stood there looking a little embarassed but proud that such a vivacious girl was actually in his kitchen.

If Pete came in on his own, on the other hand, he would begin to tell Ros about his day without being prompted.

'Hello, Mum,' he'd sing when he came through the door, and then it would be 'Horace' this or 'Horace' that, or 'A tortoise died,' or 'A gerbil escaped and we enticed it with butter,' or 'I shaved the hair off a cat's belly where Mr Justice was going to make his first incision.'

When Timothy came back from his holiday – a maths camp for the large-brained – and observed the new dispensation he was jealous, partly because Pete had an interesting job and partly because he got to spend a lot of time with Fiona, who he was a little in love with himself. On the other hand Pete was jealous of Timothy because he could speak to Fiona on the same intellectual level about science. Timothy was aware of this and would find ways of reminding Pete that he and Fiona lived further up the evolutionary scale than him. He would make a steeple with his hands, bite his lower lip and tilt his head back as though he was the lord of rabbits contemplating one of the great mysteries of the warren.

'Fiona, when you and Mr Justice were operating on that dog the other day – a most interesting case it seems to me – I presume your main concern was not to sever the cranial gluteus nerve.'

Fiona, playing along, said, 'Ah, you mean the troublesome middle glueus of Harris the sausage dog. It wasn't just the cranial glueus nerve that we were worried about, Timothy, it was the whole of the glueus maximus itself.'

Next, Timothy would remind Pete that while Fiona and he were travelling through life at a higher altitude than him, they hadn't forgotten him.

'And while all this was going on, Pete, I presume you were opening a tin of meaty chunks.'

Still, Timothy's jealousy was a puny thing compared to his loyalty, so that he only really wanted the best for his friend when it came to Fiona. He broached the subject one day when they were playing frisbee in Timothy's back garden. Pete was good at catching but Timothy – because of his short-sightedness – kept catching them in the face.

'Well,' said Timothy, as once again the frisbee floated between his outstretched hands and clobbered him on the nose, 'it's back to school soon.'

'Yep,' said Pete.

'You won't be working at the vet's anymore then.'

'No.'

'Who are you going to miss most, Fiona or the animals?'

From the look on Pete's face Timothy could tell that – just like when they were playing chess – he hadn't been thinking ahead.

'I mean you might never see her again after we've gone back to school. This could be it, the end. Perhaps in our world Arwen really does leave for the Undying Lands.'

Pete, thinking unhappy thoughts, threw the frisbee wildly so that Timothy had to chase after it. When he came back he said, 'So you'd better get on with it.'

'With what?'

'Kissing her.'

'Kissing her?' said Pete, grimacing.

'Ah,' thought Timothy. 'So he hasn't kissed her yet but he definitely wants to.'

The same thought crossed Ros's mind whenever she saw Pete and Fiona together. She was also sure that Fiona felt the same way and that her wonderful son was about to replace the godlike Richard Carpenter in the heart of the young girl. At the same time she remembered how – when she was about eleven years old – a tough-looking boy with a big nose and mean eyes used to walk up to her in the playground every morning and hit her over the head with a rolled-up comic, and then stand there with a strange, remote smile on his face before slouching off. Years later, she talked about these incidents with the boy's sister.

'Why did he keep hitting me over the head?'

'It was his way of telling you he loved you.'

Ros prayed that if Pete ever declared his love for Fiona he didn't do so by hitting her over the head with a copy of Lord of the Rings.

She pursued the subject with Ted one night while they were lying in bed. Ted was on his third Jack Higgins in a row and Ros was reading The Thornbirds.

'There's definitely something going on between Pete and Fiona.'

'She's a pretty little thing,' said Ted, his face pink and clean from his wash.

It crossed his mind that Pete might be a chip off the old block after all if he was going to be loved by women.

'I wonder if they've ever... you know... kissed.'

'If there's something going on then he must have done. He's a lad, isn't he? He's probably all over her like a bad suit.'

Ros remained silent and Ted started to worry. They both remembered how cross he'd been when he'd caught her standing outside the toilet and listening to how many sheets of paper Pete was using, this when the lad was about eight years old. Now Ted wondered whether Ros had forgotten the magnitude of his wrath and was planning something really stupid, like taking his binoculars and stalking the young lovers.

Ros had The Thornbirds open in front of her but she wasn't reading. She was trying to imagine the future of her own family.

'Do you think I'll be a grandmother one day?'

For the first time in a long time, the right answer came to Ted straight away.

'The world's best looking one.'

And for the first time in a long time, he was well rewarded for such a remark.

In the next room, Pete was in bed with an Arthur C. Clarke open in front of him but like his mum he wasn't reading and like his dad he was thinking that the love of his life would never grow old.

On the Friday before he was due to go back to school, Pete and Fiona were walking home from the vet's when Fiona said,

'Why don't you come round after lunch and we can take Bruce for a walk.'

Bruce was Fiona's Golden Retriever, an excellent example of the breed with a glossy coat and a regal air, who Pete had seen at the meeting and on one other occasion, the day that Fiona had taken him back to her's in order to give him a hedgehog badge. There, in the kitchen, with the hound looking on and Fiona's mum standing coldly by, Fiona had pinned the badge to his chest herself, standing so close to him that he could see – just below his nose – where the satin of her skin met the silk of her hair.

'Ok,' said Pete with a shrug of the shoulder, as though he was doing the irksome girl a favour, and hadn't really just seen a glimpse of paradise at all.

Fiona had gone back to hers and Pete had gone indoors and up to his room, where he sat on his bed for a while, awed by the turn of events. Now – in his imagination – the wood where Fiona took Bruce for his walks had become the Land Of Lorien, the fairy realm of wonder and romance from The Lord of the Rings.

'What's going to happen?' he whispered. 'Will she let me kiss her? Oh, how do I know? How do I know?'

After a while his thoughts slowed and he fell back to earth, and telling himself that he must make some kind of preparation for the consumation to come, did Fiona the greatest honour that he could think of just then, and changed his socks.

On his way out, he encountered his mum in the kitchen, also preparing to leave.

'Where are you off to?' said Ros.

'I'm going to take Fiona for walkies.'

Ros frowned at the dullard of love.

'I mean, Fiona and me are going to take Bruce for a walk.'

Ros stood in front of him and tugged at the twists in his shirt, while thinking, 'A most interesting development.' Then she took his smooth, spotless cheeks in her fists and

rocked his head from side to side to the tune of, 'You…
great… big… handsome… sausage… you… '

'GET OFF!'

As they walked up the drive Pete said,

'So where are you going?'

'Just to do a bit of shopping.'

They walked in silence until they came to Fiona's
house, where they would seperate.

'So where does Fiona take Bruce for walks?'

Pete gestured towards the wood, where the Broadmoor
tower had sunk beneath an ocean of summer leaves.

'Well, have fun,' said Ros, and walked away.

Before Pete could ring the doorbell, Fiona came
through the side gate with Bruce on his lead. The dog
nosed him in the groin – already tingling strangely – and
lingered over the strange cocktail of odours emanating
from that region, until Fiona jerked him away with an
admonitory, 'Bruce!' and an apologetic look at Pete, who
was now engorged from the neck up.

The glebe was a small, four-sided wood of oak, beech
and holly. Hedgerows of hawthorn and grey willow
seperated it from the estate on three sides and the ruins
of St Michael's church on the fourth. Beneath the canopy
the boles of the trees vanished into a dwarf forest of ferns
into which Bruce plunged as soon as Fiona let him off
his lead, his progress traceable by eddies in the foliage
and the odd glimpse of gold. On emerging, he placed
himself in the middle of the path on quivering haunches,
and staring unshyly back at the watching humans did a
dump, a long-pined for one judging by the dreamy look
in his eyes.

Fiona stood over the dollop, looked down, and then nodded her head.

'What?'

'No worms.'

'Ah,' said Pete, his heart breaking as he realised that this wasn't a romantic walk in the woods at all, but a scientific expedition to test the functionality of Bruce's bottom. 'How cruel girls are,' he thought.

They wandered away and an embarassed silence built up as they realised that all of their small talk had been used up at the vet's that morning. Now and again Fiona would call to Bruce, and there was a moment of suspense when a man appeared with a German Shepherd, Fiona standing in front of Bruce like a human shield.

'That was a close one,' said Pete after they'd gone by.

'Actually, German Shepherds are friendly dogs and very good with children.'

'I can't say anything right today,' thought Pete.

They reached the edge of the wood and saw the ruin of St Michael's church, which God himself had destroyed with a bolt of lightning. Dozens of Victorian headstones were stacked against the graveyard wall. Even Pete – still at the age of innocence – was struck by how quickly things changed, remembering all the lazy hours he'd spent there with Dan and Adrian, and how strange it was that he couldn't give a damn about them now. He hadn't seen them once all summer, not even from a distance.

After standing in silence for a while, Fiona moved off and Pete followed, but a step behind her, so that he could watch her beautiful face without her seeing his sulking one. Soon, he realised, their circumlocution of the wood would be at an end and he would be back in his bedroom again, alone and – as far as Fiona was concerned – just another member of the hedgehog rescue society.

Shortly they could see daylight through the trees, indicating that the place where they would exit the wood was just up ahead. Sensing this, and panting for more minutes of freedom, Bruce stopped coming when Fiona called, or disappeared into impenetrable thickets. Trying to be cavalier, Pete would be the first to plunge in after him, but unable to find him would emerge wearing a crown of twigs and thorns. Even Fiona's temper was tested to its limits, so that her patient calls became passionate and then truculent.

Somehow they found themselves in an unfamiliar spot, an arbor formed by a ring of old oaks. Crispy brown pools of last summer's acorns lay in the hollows, and butterflies flickered through the dappled shade. Bruce, ensared by the scent of some rabbits in a hole, his tail wagging madly, was caught completely unawares and leashed by Fiona.

Straightening up, she came face to face with Pete, but only then said, 'Got him,' so that it was possible for Pete to believe – if only for a moment – that she meant him and not the dog. Slowly, his lips inched towards her face which he realised – blissfully – was not about to be averted. Innocently, the young lovers kept their heads at the perpendicular during these awesome moments – the foreheads touching first, then the noses and then the lips – so that it was more of a gentle headbutt that Pete gave Fiona than a kiss.

They stood there for some moments with their eyes closed, and then embraced, opening their eyes. Far away through the trees Pete could make out a figure – a woman maybe – who'd stopped on the pavement, landed her bags of shopping and let go of the handles to reanimate her numbed fingers.

Eighteen

Ros started to wonder whether Pete knew the facts of life. She guessed that he would have learned about such things at school but wanted to be sure. It crossed her mind to bring the subject up with him herself but she quickly dismissed the idea, imagining the look of terror on his face.

'No,' she thought. 'Ted's the man for the job, but he won't be happy.'

That night they were reading in bed as usual. Ted had the feeling that Ros had something on her mind but because he'd had a bad day at work and been grizzly all evening – even though he'd had two helpings of a steamed jam sponge – the last thing he wanted just then was more reality. Even so, when he'd finished reading, he closed the book, took a deep breath and said, 'What?'

'I'm wondering whether Pete knows about the facts of life.'

'I know where this is going,' thought Ted, and started to panic.

'What do you mean "the facts of life"? He's fourteen years old. He must know all about that stuff by now.'

'Shouldn't we find out?'

Ted started to babble.

'They probably do it at school these days. He probably knows more about the facts of life than I do. No one told me about the facts of life and I still managed to get married and have a kid. And there is such a thing as instinct, you know, a man's instinct.' He turned on his side and settled down for sleep. 'No, he'll be alright. Don't worry about it.'

As usual, Ros opened the curtains to let the night in. Ted, with his back to her, thought that she must have put on a lot of weight recently, judging from the racket she made going to and from the window and the way the bed bounced up and down when she got back in.

'Goodnight,' he said, but there was no reply.

Because the last thing a husband wants to be reminded of is his parental responsibilities, Ted drove to work the next day in a bad mood, which worsened when he found that Wolfie, the Alsation belonging to the nightwatchman, Reg, had left a large turd in the middle of the yard.

He summoned Reg to his office and said, 'Do you know why I've asked you here, Reg?'

Reg, who'd never been hauled in like this before, took his woolly hat off and began to torture it with his hands.

'No.'

'Your animal has left a deposit.'

Reg looked out of the window and saw the mess. He grinned with relief and said, 'I'll go and get the shovel. It won't take long.' He turned to go but Ted called him back.

'Reg, I'm not sure you understand how serious this is.'

Ted could hear himself but couldn't stop himself. 'Your animal has left a large one in the middle of a working area. I have to consider the health and safety implications.'

Reg stood there wondering where the old Ted had gone.

'Put it this way,' continued obergruppenfuhrer Turner. 'If it happens again I'm going to have to give you a warning.'

'Me? Why me? I didn't do it.'

'I can't give the dog a warning, can I.'

'I suppose not.' Reg looked crestfallen. 'Can I go now?'

'Of course.'

Reg had finished his shift but before he left he told everyone in the yard that there was something wrong with Ted and that he'd turned into a tyrant.

Tony, Brian and Chris were able to vouch for this personally after Ted accosted them during their break. They were sitting on some old sofas in a corner of the depot, drinking their coffee and smoking, when they saw Ted approaching and looking down at a clipboard where it said – or so they guessed from the look on his face – that the Germans had won the Second World War after all. He stood before them.

'Can you lot tell me how it is – I mean how it can be possible – that once again, I mean once again, we have run out of axle grease. I mean, are you drinking the stuff, using it on your haemorrhoids?'

The tyrant glared at them for a few moments and then walked off. He'd only taken a few steps when Chris said,

'Everyone gets 'em in the end, Ted.'

Ted heard laughter but instead of turning round, managed to restrain himself. He walked on, trying to assume a noble bearing.

It was Maurice who discovered what was up. He went into the office at lunchtime and observed Ted scrunching up old invoices into balls, taking aim with seething eyes and darting them at the bin.

'What's up, Ted?'

'Nothing.'

'Yes there is. You can tell old Maurice.'

Maurice was indeed old, and like Dickie himself took a fatherly interest in Ted. The tyrant threw a few more balls, heaved a tragic sigh and groaned, 'It's Ros. She wants me to explain the facts of life to Pete.'

Just managing to keep a straight face, Maurice said, 'Christ Ted, is that all?' and left.

Once the laughter around the yard had died down, helpful suggestions started to come in, the first of which was a stack of pornographic magazines left anonymously on Ted's desk. The second suggestion came in the form of an expired membership card for a strip club in Reading's red light district, and the third came from Maurice.

'Show him that film Brief Encounter.'

'Why?'

'Lots of puffing trains entering tunnels.'

At this point, Ted knew that he was on his own.

Once he got home, the evening proceeded normally. He had a satisfactory dinner followed by a cup of tea and a cigarette, laughed along with Pete while they watched It Ain't Half Hot Mum, and after the lad had gone to bed, imbibed three large scotches. At various times he and Ros commented on the clement weather and the industrial action by the unions, agreed that their recent holiday seemed like a distant memory, and arranged to get fish and chips for dinner on Friday. As it got nearer and nearer to bedtime and the subject of Pete's education still hadn't come up, Ted started to think that Ros had simply been venting some anxiety the night before and that maybe she'd forgotten about the matter altogether.

By the time he got into bed, he was pretty relaxed about the whole thing and romped through another chapter of Storm Warning. After some time, however, he became aware of a great silence in the room and realised that, although Ros was holding a Harold Robbins in front of her face, she hadn't turned a page for twenty minutes. Ted yawned, not from tiredness but from fear, a mighty yawn that eclipsed his face.

'Well?' said Ros.

'Well what?'

'Have you thought about it?'

'About what?'

'What we talked about last night.'

'It's at the top of my to-do list.'

'What are you going to say to him?'

'I'll say that if he ever meets a woman as beautiful and virtuous as his mother... '

Ros performed the ritual with the curtains and then got back into bed.

'It's not funny. It's important.'

'Ok, I'll do it tomorrow,' he sighed, and thought, 'And after that my life will be easy.'

As he walked around the yard the next day, his workmates held conversations for his benefit.

'Hey, Chris.'

'Yes Tony?'

'Where do babies come from?'

'I don't know about anyone else, Tony, but my parents got me from a shop at the hospital.'

And,

'Brian?'

'Yes, Matt.'

'What's foreplay?'

'That's an interesting question, Matt. In many countries it is considered to be a highly skilled technique for helping your wife, or girlfriend, or the babysitter achieve the most amazing orgasm, but in this country it is by way of an apology for forgetting your wedding anniversary.'

'Thanks Brian. That was most informative.'

'A pleasure, Matt.'

'Swine,' thought Ted, but then noticing all the posters of busty beauties that the men had put up around the yard, and remembering the number of times that Pete had been there, he said to himself, 'At least the lad knows what a pair of giant knockers looks like.'

Ros and Ted spent the early part of the evening being excessively polite to one another. After dinner, Ros said, 'I'm going to make an apple pie for the weekend,' and left the room, leaving Ted and the unsuspecting Pete alone together.

Star Trek, one of Pete's favourite programmes was on, and Ted decided to let him finish watching it before he said anything. He watched his son and noticed how he was broadening through the shoulders and the waist, and that he had a blokeish jaw and hands that could be made into proper fists. Then he thought he heard some movement behind the door. He tiptoed over, jerked it open but there was no one there. He went down the hallway, poked his head into the kitchen and saw Ros – happy and absorbed – rolling out a circle of pastry. 'Oh,' he thought, but when he went back to the hallway he found two hand prints made of flour on the living room door and said to himself, 'I'll deal with you later.'

When Star Trek was over, Ted said, 'Come with me. I've got a job for you.'

Pete looked bewildered because this was normally the point in the evening when he retired to the sanctuary of his room and gave himself up to morbidness.

'Come on,' said Ted, and Pete followed him out of the back door and across the garden to the shed. Ted went inside and then came out backwards, dragging the lawnmower. Pete had never mown the lawn before and understood that from now on he would have another chore to do – apart from washing the cars – if he wanted pocket money.

It was an old-fashioned motor mower with a rotating cylinder, a rear roller and a front-mounted grass catcher. Where the bright green paint had been chipped off, the metal underneath was orange with rust. It was really too big and unwieldy for the Turners' small garden, but Ted had bought it as a broken-down thing many years ago and for something to do had restored it to its former glory.

He pulled it to the middle of the lawn and showed Pete where to put the petrol and the oil, and then pointed out the significant moving parts. He could tell that Pete was bored but thought that introducing him to the lawnmower was as good a way as any of getting the lad's attention before he broached the great matter.

After the explanations, Ted yanked the start-cord and couldn't help smiling as the motor burst into life and a puff of old dust came out of the air filter. He flicked the brake off, chugged across the lawn in a straight line and then traversed back, making a second neat stripe next to the first. Pete watched closely, attracted by the power and noise of the engine and when his dad had finished his second strip and turned the mower off, looked at him expectantly, hoping that it would be his turn next.

'Fancy a go?'

'Ok.'

'If you get a straight line, I'll tell you a joke.'

Pete swung the mower round, lined it up and after an early wobble got the machine under control and went dead straight until he reached the other side of the lawn. On the way back he got his line just right and was grinning by the time he came to a stop next to Ted.

'How many ears has Captain Kirk got?'

'I don't know.'

'Three. A left ear, a right ear, and a final frontier.'

'That's a good one.'

'Well don't just stand there,' said Ted. 'Off you go again.'

The next time that Pete came back, Ted showed him how to make the mower run faster, and then said, 'This Fiona. Is she your girlfriend then?'

'No,' said Pete, and roared off.

On his next return, Ted said, 'Liar', and Pete blushed before heading off again.

Ted decided to leave him alone for the next few turns. Pete was actually dizzy from the petrol fumes and having to suddenly swing round at the end of each strip, but he was still enjoying himself, so much so that the next time he came up to Ted and his dad said, 'You do know all about that stuff, don't you? Sex, I mean,' Pete looked him straight in the eye and said, 'God, Dad, we did all that stuff at school years ago.'

'Good!' shouted Ted above the roar of the mower, and once Pete had mowed the last edge of the lawn and turned the machine off, he was at peace once more. They stood there and looked at where they'd made a cricket pitch from a meadow. They shook hands and then put the mower back in the shed.

Watching from the kitchen window, Ros couldn't hear what Ted was saying but she was pleased that he seemed to be getting on with it, albeit in a roundabout way. Between the first appearance of the mower and the completion of the mowing, Pete's mood – she observed – had gone from sullen, to interested, to absorbed and then finally, after a couple of outbursts of thunder, to blithe and happy, which was the exact range of emotions she'd imagined him going through as the facts of life were explained to him. And when he shook hands with his dad at the end – the first man-to-man handshake they'd ever shared as far as she was aware – she knew that the principles of human reproduction had been successfully passed from one generation to the next.

In bed that night, she said.

'So how did it go?'

'Put it this way: the lad is fully clued up.'

'What did you say?'

'I said that the lawnmower was a penis, the open door of the shed was a vagina, the oil can was a lubricant and the grass catcher was a condom. I said that if the lawnmower entered the shed with the grass catcher off, it would lead to a life of toil and unhappiness. But if the lawnmower entered the shed with the grass catcher on, it would lead to a life of freedom and joy.'

Ros couldn't believe her ears. Ted could feel her gaze upon him but at that moment he didn't just resemble the greatest actor in the world: he really was the greatest actor in the world.

'You didn't.'

'I bloody did.'

'You didn't.'

'Ask Pete if you don't believe me.'

'I will,' said Ros, but of course she didn't, and so never knew the truth.

Nineteen

When Ted received notification of his court date, there was reassurance from his solicitor: 'A suspended sentence at worst, Mr Turner', and encouragement from Vince: 'They have TVs in every cell these days, Ted', but even so he hit the bottle hard and smoked an extra twenty Regals a day, ten of them during the evenings while he was watching the telly, creating a fug throughout the house that made Ros's eyes water and Pete appeal to his mum for clean air. He even stopped cleaning his teeth – Ros knew by the bone-dry bristles of his brush – so that his teeth began to yellow, as did the patch of ceiling directly above where he used to sit all evening, smoking as though he was trying to grow another lung tumour before bedtime.

Ros didn't give up on Ted, but she didn't want to fight with him either, and arming herself with air freshener and frabric cleaner went to war with proxies in the form of her odoriferous carpets and curtains.

One night Ted left the pub even more inebriated than usual. For a while he stood in the cold, shivering inside his chunky suede car coat and turning up the brown fur collar, and wondering how he'd got there and how he was going to get home, before – miracle of miracles – realising that his car was parked right in front of him. To celebrate, he lit a cigarette, and then got in, but was baffled by the absence of the steering wheel. 'It's been stolen!' he cried, before realising that he'd got in the wrong side. After he'd got into the driver's seat, he tried to throw his cigarette out of the window but because he hadn't rolled it down the butt bounced off and landed under the seat.

He drove off, telling himself to concentrate so as to get home safely, got the car going in a straight line after a few initial swerves and then – realising that the honking motors around him were trying to tell him something – turned his headlights on. After that he gripped the wheel hard and kept checking his mirror to see if he was being followed by detective constable Fenton. It took him twenty minutes to get home and when he stopped on the driveway he cried, 'Made it!', but when he tried to get out a great force kept pulling him back. He struggled and roared but in the end he gave up and fell asleep.

Some time later he heard a tapping on the window. He opened his eyes, saw that the car was full of smoke and thought that he'd crashed and it was the rozzers outside. Then the tapping turned to banging and he recognised his wife's voice.

'Open the door, Ted!'

'It is open.'

'It isn't!'

He unlocked the door and cold air rushed in and smoke poured out.

'You're on fire!' shouted Ros.

'I can't get out!'

'Take your seatbelt off.'

He undid the belt and tumbled out of the car.

'What's going on?' he said, but there was no reply because Ros had dashed into the kitchen. She came back with a washing up bowl full of water and chucked it over the seat. The fire went out but the seat continued to smoulder.

'I thought my bottom was warm.'

'Are you burnt?'

Ted, sitting on the ground, probed his behind.

'No.'

'Are you suffering from smoke inhalation?'

'No,' said the forty-a-day man.

Ros stood over him.

'Don't tell me you drove home in that state?'

'I had the headlights on.'

'I've been waiting for you to come home so you can drive me to the hospital.'

'Why?'

Ros's neck went plump because her heart was in her mouth.

'Dad's had a heart attack.'

'Oh, shit,' said Ted. He got to his feet. 'I'll drive you, of course.'

'In the state you're in? Don't be pathetic.'

Ros got an old towel out of the garage, draped it over the driver's seat of Ted's car and then reversed out and parked on the road. While she got her own car out of the garage Ted went indoors and drank a pint of water. He found Pete in the living room and could tell the boy was frightened. Pete saw his dad swaying in the doorway and said, 'Grandad's had a heart attack.'

'I know. We're going to the hospital. Will you be alright here on your own?'

'Of course.'

'Don't set fire to the house or anything.'

Pete looked at his dad's smouldering bottom and was about to say, 'You can talk,' but thought better of it.

'All hell has broken loose,' said Ted, and went upstairs to change.

Pete was peering through the living room curtains as his mum and dad got in the Mini. Mr and Mrs Morris had come out into the cold to see what all the fuss was about. Mrs Morris called out,

'Is everything alright, Ros?'

'Dad's had a heart attack. We're going to the hospital.'

The two old dears clung to each other in horror. Mr Morris had a large head on a small body tapering to tiny feet. In his padded beige dressing gown and scruffy grey slippers he looked to Pete like an old owl. Mute from Parkinsons, he saluted instead of calling out as Ros and Ted drove off.

By now Ted was no longer inebriated, just drunk. Realising that the night had only just begun, he lit a cigarette to fortify himself.

'Can't I have one?' said Ros.

'Of course.'

He held one out for her but she was leaning so far forward – wincing at the oncoming headlights – that she didn't notice. He lit one and poked it into the corner of her mouth, where it stayed, making her look like a floozy, he thought. Gradually the car began to fill up with smoke, but thinking only of their destination they failed to spot the irony.

Ros, frightened for her dad, drove down the Reading road at sixty miles an hour, which was twice the official speed limit and three times the rate that she normally trundled along at. It sobered Ted up fast and he sat there with clenched buttocks, glad that there were hardly any other cars about, quizzing Ros gently for details of Charlie's illness.

When they got to the Royal Berkshire hospital they ran up the steps and into the reception area. It was quiet and two cleaners with long mops and wheeled metal buckets had just swiped the linoleum floor. The smell of antiseptic stung Ted's nostrils as Ros inquired passionately for her dad's whereabouts. They were directed down a long, brightly lit corridor with windows onto the wards, Ted having to almost run to keep up with Ros. They squeezed into a lift beside a gurney piled high with white linen and light blue blankets, and ascended.

Ted – who had always been fond of Charlie – was worried what they might find when they got to the ward, and knew that Ros – watching the floor numbers above the door illuminate in sequence – was also fearing the worst. He tried to give her hope by saying, 'He'll be alright,' but between the metal walls of the lift his voice sounded hollow and doom-laden.

Charlie was in a room of his own. Before they went in they stopped to look through the porthole in the door. He was lying on his back with his eyes closed and an oxygen mask over his mouth. He looked ashen but his perfectly round tummy was rising and falling slowly beneath the bedclothes. Betty was sitting beside him, holding his hand, her head tilted back against the wall.

As they opened the door Ros let out a sob. She took her mum's hand and stood by the bed, looking down at Charlie. There was a deep frown on his face as though he wasn't going happily into the abyss. She looked at the monitor where a flowing white line leapt in time with his heart. Without thinking, all three of them synchronised their breathing with the rise and fall of Charlie's tummy, to keep him out of the grave.

'It was a heart attack then?' said Ted.

'A big one,' said Betty. 'Two arteries are blocked. If he lives, they'll operate.'

'Did you find him?' said Ros.

'No, we were sitting on the sofa watching the telly when he rested his head on my shoulder. I said, "You soppy git, do you want a cuddle?' He didn't say anything and then he sort of tipped over until he was face down on my lap. I felt his face and it was cold and clammy. That's when I called the ambulance.'

Ted found chairs and he and Ros sat down. She took Charlie's hand and leaned over him, whispering encouragement. Ted said, 'You'll be up and about soon, Charlie,' and then went to get teas from the cafeteria. It was closed so he got three cups from the nurses' station. A nurse came back to the room with him, checked on Charlie and said, 'He's fighting,' and left.

When they ran out of things to say it was quiet in the room apart from the sound of Charlie's breathing and the electric hum of the heart monitor. Ros imagined Pete sitting up in bed with a bowl of Sugar Puffs in his lap, worrying about his grandad but having a midnight feast all the same.

After two hours it was decided that Ted would go home to be with Pete while Ros would stay the night and be collected by Ted in the morning. They visited Charlie the following night, which was Friday, and then Ros spent practically the whole of Saturday and Sunday at his bedside. She got used to the coming and going of the nurses in their silent white shoes, and the grave smiles of the doctors as they took Charlie's pulse or held a thermometer up to the light, so that by Sunday night she felt as though she'd been sitting beside the still-comatose Charlie for years, watching him slowly deflate for lack of solid food.

The pattern continued throughout the following week – evening visits by both Ros and Ted – but on the Friday Ros said to Pete, 'We'll take you in to see Grandad tomorrow.'

Pete didn't look very enthusiastic so she said, 'What's the matter?

'Me and Timothy were going into Reading tomorrow.'

'Why?'

'To buy Peter Gabriel's new album. It's got Solsbury Hill on it.'

Instead of pointing out that he'd got his priorities mixed up, Ros came up with a solution.

'Well go and buy your record and then get the bus down to the hospital. It's not far. Timothy won't mind waiting if he doesn't want to go in with you.'

'Ok,' said Pete.

That night Ted – instead of going to the hospital – gave himself a night off without consulting Ros and went to the pub. When he got home – moderately drunk – and went up to bed and asked after Charlie he recieved no reply from the recumbent Ros and so presumed she was asleep, not realising that she was lying there wondering if a wife had ever murdered her husband with a crochet hook.

On Saturday Pete and Timothy went into Reading and bought copies of Peter Gabriel's new album. They had burger and chips for lunch in a Wimpy restaurant and then wandered around the shops, eventually coming to the walkway – high above the street – that linked the shopping centre and the multi-storey car park. Here they came across a crowd that had gathered in the bright sunshine to watch an atrocity in progress. Some punk rockers – among them Sugar and Lump from Pete's neighbourhood – had fallen upon a Teddy Boy and were dangling him head first over the abyss, at the bottom of which, in deep shadow, another crowd had gathered. A group of men had burst into a department store and appropriated a mattress from the home furnishings section, and chased by a young assistant manager frantically trying to put a Reserved label on the item, were now trying to place the mattress directly beneath the Teddy Boy, who was watching their progress more eagerly than most. Leaning over the parapet, Pete and Timothy could clearly hear the men with the mattress saying to each other, 'Left a bit!' 'No, right a bit!' and then one of them said, 'Let's get another one!' and they dashed off again.

Miraculously, despite his inverted position, the Teddy Boy remained immaculate, with his pink tie – clipped to his shirt – still in place between the black velvet collars of his blue zoot suit, and the wave in his quiff, thick with grease, also firmly in place. Lump had him by one ankle, another punk rocker by the other ankle, and Sugar was screaming, 'Drop Him! Kill him!' but fortunately for the Teddy Boy Lump was only acting in a spirit of fun, and giving the drainpiped legs a shake, sent a comb and some coppers raining into the gulf.

The next thing that everyone saw, was a squad of coppers bursting onto the scene, the Teddy Boy being hauled to safety, Lump being truncheoned to the ground and Sugar biting the ankles of one of the coppers.

By now Pete and Timothy had lost track of time, so that they were halfway home on the train when Timothy said, 'Weren't you supposed to go and see your grandad?'

Pete's heart sank and he walked home from the station like a condemned man going to his execution. When he went through the door, Ros said, 'Hello, is Grandad better then?' but then she saw the look on his face.

'I forgot.'

Ros realised that after all the progress Pete had made over the last few months, he was still just a selfish little boy at heart, just like his father. She walked out silently, leaving Pete alone.

For the next three days it was winter in the Turner household. It was so cold that when someone opened the fridge door the kitchen got warmer. Ted found himself sleeping on the sofa and had to make Pete's dinner, while Ros made her own. She also drove to the hospital on her own, without reference to Ted.

On the fourth day Ted said to Pete,

'You know what you need to do, don't you?'

'Go and see Grandad. But when?'

'Go tomorrow after school.'

'But Mum will be expecting me home after school.'

'I'll tell her that you're at Timothy's and that you told me about it but forgot to tell her.'

'Why don't I just tell her that I'm going to see Grandad?'

Ted, the old tactician, said, 'Because it's better if it's a surprise.'

When Ros got home from work the next day and found that Pete wasn't there she began to worry, and by the time that Ted got home she was frantic. She had the wild idea that because she'd been cross with Pete he'd run away from home, to London, and was being held captive by tramps.

'Sorry,' said Ted. 'I forgot to tell you. He's round at Timothy's.'

'Why didn't he tell me?'

'He must have forgotten. You know what lads are like.'

Pete came through the back door at half past seven. Ros was so relieved to see him that she could only pretend to be angry.

'Why didn't you tell me that you were going to Timothy's?'

'I didn't go to Timothy's.'

'Where have you been then?'

'I've been to see Grandad.' The tears came into his eyes. 'He doesn't look very well, Mum.'

And in that moment she forgave him for everything.

The next evening they all went to see Charlie and when Ros saw him sitting up in bed she cried harder than if he'd been dead already. To the visitors he looked older, smaller and terribly weary, but they knew that the old Grandad was still here from the brightness of his eyes, eyes that had seen freighters and frigates exploding during Atlantic snow storms, the face of his two-year-old son Jonathan dying in his arms, but also little Ros running up and down the garden in her yellow wellington boots and a hundred summer sunsets over Weymouth bay.

Betty explained that when Pete had come the previous evening he'd sat and talked to the unconscious Charlie for half an hour without stopping.

'And this morning he woke up.' she said.

'The doctors say I've got to lose weight.'

'You've got portly,' said Betty.

'You can talk,' said Charlie.

'You've both turned into roly-polys,' said Ros.

They could tell by the look on her face that if they didn't cut down on the biscuits there'd be serious trouble.

Ted put his hand on Pete's shoulder.

'So it was Pete who brought his grandad back to life.'

Pete blushed, and to hide his face sat on the bed with his back to them all.

Twenty

When Pete was two years old they had gone on holiday to Bournemouth for a week. They had all the usual types of English weather for late spring – hail, drizzle, sunshine and showers – but because they had such an adorable little boy with them they hardly noticed.

And Pete was adorable, the most adorable little boy who had ever lived according to the landlady of the hotel they were staying in. When they entered the breakfast room in the morning, Pete dressed in navy blue shorts and a white woollen cardigan with wooden buttons, and wearing shiny black shoes with silver buckles, and his hair combed to perfection, Mrs Gibson would cry, 'Here's the happy prince!' and everyone would go, 'Ahh,' including the guests who had children of their own. On these occasions Ted couldn't have been happier but at other times he would get cross with Ros for pampering the boy, and decided that if she made him look any more like Liberace he would put his foot down.

Away from work Ted was bored but the happiness

of Ros and the child was the main thing so he bore his burdens willingly. Her mum and dad had bought them a new camera so Ros took lots of photos to memorialise the young Plantagenet's first holiday, the start of a tour of the kingdom that would last a lifetime. When they took him to the shoreline the water was too cold for his toes but he seemed pleased by the sight of the sea.

They had photos of him sitting astride a blue elephant on a roundabout, and next to his mum on a large model steam train, his hood up and his mittens on because it was raining. He looked happiest on the back of a donkey, this time wearing a bobble hat and with a blue sky behind him, his mum and dad supporting him from either side and pulling comic faces.

After dinner on the first two evenings they left Pete in his room for half an hour and sat in the bar downstairs. This bright little parlour was staffed by the landlady's husband, Sergeant Gibson, formerly of the Life Guards, a tall, ginger-haired old warrior with a long blonde moustache. After a few gin-and-angostura bitters, he entertained the guests by playing the Radetzky March on a row of brandy glasses. Ros would smoke two or three cigarettes and then go back to the room, leaving Ted with his beer and – as the evening wore on – his port and brandy. When he came back upstairs he'd kiss the sleeping Pete while smelling of booze and a cheap cigar that some rep had given him.

On the Wednesday morning, down by the fun fair, they found the Ben Hur ride. It was made up of six tracks that flowed around a small arena which was supposed to resemble the stadium in the film Ben Hur. On each track was a little chariot with four wooden horses in front, each chariot being connected by a rope to a turning handle positioned on one side of the arena. Six little children were strapped into six little chariots and pulled along the tracks by their fathers madly rotating the handles, and cheered on by a bloodthirsty crowd who made bets among themselves.

Ted had trouble with his handle to begin with and Pete was last until about three quarters of the way round, at which point he put on a sudden burst of speed and finished a glorious second behind a little boy whose father – Ros guessed when she saw his biceps – was a coal heaver.

The kids didn't know what was going on – they were all crying as they crossed the finishing line – but the grown-ups had enjoyed themselves, as was obvious from the hoarseness of the mums by the end of the race. Ted and the coal heaver shook hands and walked side by side to where the mums were gathering up the charioteers.

In the afternoon they bought a pink balloon and tied it to Pete's wrist. They found the public gardens where there was a great lawn with circular beds of summer flowers – pansies and petunias – and wet roses silvered by the returning sun. Eventually they found a bench and sat for an hour, Ted at one point going off and coming back with an ice cream cone, Pete's first. They took a photo of him holding the vanilla nectary in both hands, looking awed, not by the gift itself but by his own mightiness in being able to hold it up.

They wandered away and came to the Pitch And Putt. Ted went over to a little wooden hut and bought tickets from a man wearing a blue and white boating blazer and a straw hat. He handed them a putter and a lofted club each and they began to hack their way round, leaving Pete in his pushchair by the side of the fairways and greens.

Ted played some good shots but Ros kept swinging and missing, and by doing so reminded Ted that she'd never been a sporty lass. In the end she picked up her ball and threw it towards the green, saying, 'Am I allowed to do that?' a philosophical question that Ted felt it was beneath his dignity to answer.

Each green was surrounded by Box hedging topiarised into fantastic representations of castles and mountain ranges. Ted reached the last green – the Chinese Pagoda – in one, while Ros, after chucking her ball halfway down the fairway, had decided to putt it the rest of the way and was assuming the position. She made a good connection for once and the ball bounced along the fairway and skipped over the green towards where Pete was idling in his pushchair. There was a nasty little thock – the sound of ball hitting bone – and at the same moment a man's head appeared over the top of the hedge like a rabbit sitting up.

In the ensuing silence Ros dropped her putter and ran towards Pete who – judging from the way he was screwing his face up – was ready to wail, but after a few short croaks the fit spluttered out. Ros picked him up, looked into his eyes – which focused on hers – and sighed with relief.

'Is he alright?' said Ted.

'I think so,' said Ros.

'Is he alright?' said the man.

'I think so,' said Ted.

They took their clubs back to the wooden shed and then left, Ros carrying Pete in her arms so that she could watch his face. There was a pink mark on his forehead where the ball had struck him but no lump yet. He was quiet and seemed absorbed by a knitted piglet that he held in his hands.

They hadn't gone far when he turned white and threw up. He went limp and his eyes kept closing and slowly opening. They asked a man and a woman where the nearest doctor was and the man pointed the way.

'It's not far.'

'He looks poorly,' said the woman.

'He was hit by a golf ball,' said Ted.

'Some people,' said the man, presuming the perpetrator was elsewhere.

They burst into the doctor's and the receptionist showed them in straight away. The doctor stubbed out his cigarette and examined Pete while Ted went over what had happened. Ros was speechless with dread and even Ted, the steadfast English yeoman, talked in a trembling voice.

'He's had a concussion,' the doctor said. 'He needs to go to hospital for an X-ray. I can call an ambulance if you want but if your car's nearby it might be quicker.'

'We'll take the car,' said Ted. 'Where's the hospital?'

By the time they got Pete to the hospital he was unconscious. He was taken for an X-ray and was gone for about an hour. Ros and Ted were sitting in the waiting area outside one of the wards when they saw him being wheeled along the corridor on a bed. He was taken into the ward and through the glass they could see his bed being pushed against the wall by the porters and then two nurses leaning over him and smoothing down his bedding. Only Pete's head was visible above the bedclothes. He was still and grey. Then they closed the curtains around his bed and Ros was reminded of a day with her parents by the coast, when they couldn't see the sea because a mist had rolled in.

They stood up when a nurse came out, expecting to be shown in, but she shut the door behind her and stood in front of it. She was wearing a starched, white nurse's uniform over a grey short-sleeved blouse and balanced on the back of her head was a white hat of indeterminate shape, like an iced cake collapsing in on itself. She explained that Pete's skull wasn't fractured but he did have a concussion and so would be kept in for a few days. Ros stood there wringing her hands and Ted kept nodding his head, trying to convince Ros that everything the nurse was saying pointed to a good outcome. When the nurse stopped speaking there was a silence while they waited for her to step aside but she remained there, blocking their way.

'Can we see him then?' said Ros.

'We don't think that's a good idea, Mrs Turner. If he wakes up and sees you he might get agitated and that could affect his brain.'

'But what happens if he wakes up and his mummy isn't there?'

'We'll be there. We'll make sure he stays calm.'

Ros begged to be allowed to see Pete for just one moment but the nurse repeated what she'd said before. The next thing Ros knew she was standing outside the hospital in bright sunshine.

'He'll be alright,' said Ted, taking her by the arm and leading her away.

They walked for a while and then sat at a table by a kiosk. They were served tea and buns and sat there without speaking to each other, tormented by the shrill holiday crowds flowing past them, and batting the wasps away from the buns. They went back to the hotel at eight o'clock, when it was still light. Ros lay on the bed, flicking through a magazine, while Ted sat by the window smoking.

The first time that anyone in the hotel knew that something had happened was when Ros and Ted appeared in the breakfast room the next morning without Pete. They told a grief-stricken Mrs Gibson and everyone else that Pete had hit his head and was concussed and was unconscious in hospital. People commiserated and then went back to their breakfasts, the unspoken words 'permanent brain damage' and 'what kind of parents are they?' hanging in the air along with the fried bacon.

Ros and Ted went to the hospital and were told by a different nurse that Pete was still unconscious but stable. Once again they were limited to looking through the window at his bed, still with the curtains closed around it. Ros had brought Pete's knitted piglet and she asked the nurse to give it to him. The nurse obliged by going into the ward, disappearing behind the curtains around Pete's bed and then re-emerging with a nod to say that Operation Piglet had been successful.

When they left the hospital the sun was shining again, meaning that once again all the other holidaymakers were happier than they were. There was nothing for them to do but walk, and sit, and drink tea until the next visiting hour in the evening. This time a young doctor told them that Pete's condition was the same and they wouldn't be allowed to see him.

They went to the hospital the following morning,

walked for a bit and then went to a pub as soon as it opened. After four pints Ted said for the hundredth time, 'He'll be alright. Don't worry.' Ros had three port-and-lemons and smoked as doggedly as a tart.

The next day they went to the matinee of Dr Zhivago. Ros could tell from the stillness of the audience that everyone was entranced, and Ted – mesmerised by Julie Christie – forgot Pete for a while, but as soon as they left the cinema they forgot all about the film and started walking quickly to the hospital.

When they were told, yet again, that they wouldn't be allowed to see their son, Ted – who up until then had been mighty and silent – began to seethe.

'Surely we can see him for one moment.'

The young doctor had blonde eyelashes, pinkish ears and a hairline that had receded early, adding to his paleness. He shook his head gravely while holding on to both ends of the stethoscope that was hanging around his neck.

'We still think it's too early.'

'At least let his mum see him.'

'As I said… '

'I want to speak to the captain.'

'The who?'

'The captain. The person in charge. I mean, you're just a corporal right? Get me the captain. See what he says.'

'Mr Turner, I am in charge of this case… '

'Or the general.'

'I am quite capable.'

'NOW!' roared Ted.

On the other side of the window the nurses and the

conscious patients looked up, and all along the corridor people poked their heads out of doorways. The young doctor lifted his chin defiantly and tried to say something but couldn't find the words. A matron started to walk down the corridor towards them and the doctor went to meet her. They whispered to each other for a few seconds and then disappeared into a room.

Ros made Ted sit on the bench and held his hand. She'd never heard him shout like that before and it had scared her, but at the same time it thrilled her to know how much Pete was loved. After a while the matron came to see them. She was about forty years old, sturdy, with hips for perching babies on and arms for lifting invalids, but with a large open face and eyes that were benevolent and brown, and the moment that Ros saw her she knew that their fortunes had changed.

The matron leaned down and squeezed Ted's arm.

'You wait here, Mr Turner. Is that ok?'

Ted nodded obediently, looking a little embarrassed, but still with a stubborn look in his eye, reminding everyone that further explosions were likely if Ros didn't get what she wanted.

The matron led Ros into the ward and over to Pete's bed. She opened the curtains and beckoned Ros to follow her. Pete was lying on his back with his eyes closed and his arms outside the coverlet. Ros, conditioned by her recent interactions with the hospital staff, resisted the urge to run over to him and instead looked at the matron hopefully. The matrton nodded and pointed at the chair next to Pete's bed.

Pete had good colour and was breathing slowly

but deeply. To Ros he looked as though he was sleeping normally. They'd positioned the knitted piglet in the angle made by his neck and shoulder and she adjusted it so that it was facing Pete. She took his hand and then, after a quick look at the matron to make sure that she wasn't breaking any taboos, used her other hand to make a parting in his hair.

'When do you think he'll come to?'

'We don't know,' said the matron. Realising that she might just as well have said, 'Maybe never,' she went on, 'Soon, Mrs Turner, I'm sure.'

Ros looked at her and knew that – unlike the young doctor – she was talking from experience.

She sat there for a few more minutes, holding the boy's hand, until a sign from the matron told her that it was time to go. She didn't kiss him but leaned close in the hope that he'd open his eyes, but the touch of her breath didn't wake him.

When Ros came out of the ward Ted could tell from the look on her face that Pete was ok. She explained that he had a little bump on his forehead but was sleeping like a baby. They went back to the hotel for dinner and then Ted went into the bar for a drink and Ros went into the lounge and chatted with some of the other guests. Twenty minutes later Ted came in, having only had one drink. For once he was looking for quietness and so sat there and drank coffee and listened to Ros talking to two ladies.

When they went to the hospital in the morning they were both taken in to see Pete because the boy was awake. His face lit up when he saw them but when Ros embraced him he blubbed.

'You've been in the wars, old son,' said Ted gruffly, fighting back sobs of his own.

The matron touched his arm and led him outside. She told him that Pete would make a full recovery but that he should stay in hospital for two more days. Ted phoned the hotel to ask if they could stay for longer and his work to tell them that he'd be back two days later than scheduled.

The next day the sun shone all morning and all the holidaymakers looked happy but Ros said,

'I'm never coming here again.'

'Me neither.'

They went to the matinee of The Sound Of Music and this time it was Ros who forgot Pete for a while, and for ever afterwards it was her favourite film.

Two days later, after Mrs Gibson had given Pete a bag of sweets, they all went home.

Twenty-One

R os didn't cry very often. She'd cried the third time she made love to Ted, and on her wedding day, and the time when – three years after Pete was born, when they were trying again, Ros hoping for a little girl – they were told that she couldn't have any more children. Even now, many years later, when she saw a mother with a little girl she moaned to herself in a way that no one could hear. And she'd cried when, hoping to meet some other mummies – in the days when the estate was still only half-built and she hadn't known any of the neighbours – she'd pushed Pete all the way up to the play area to find the empty swings bobbing on the breeze and not a child or a woman in sight. But if she wanted to make herself cry she had only to remember the holiday in Bournemouth, when she'd almost killed Pete with a golf ball.

And so it was that when Dickie's wife Brenda came into Reading for her weekly afternoon tea at Hudson's department store, she found the new Elizabeth Taylor – blinded by tears – staggering around outside the entrance.

'Ros, what on earth's the matter?'

Ros tried to say something but only squeaks and beeps emerged from her stricken throat. The doorman in his dark grey crombie and top hat had been watching Ros suspiciously for a while, but now that the regal – and familiar – Brenda had hoved into view he offered his assistance.

'There are seats in the vestibule, madam.'

'Thank you Steven,' said Brenda, taking Ros by the arm and leading her inside.

In the dark hallway Brenda embraced Ros, who was holding a soaking wet ball of tissues over her face with both hands, and whose sobs were muffled by the thick red carpet. Looking over Brenda's shoulder, Ros could see a large oil painting of the rich Edwardian haberdasher who had founded the department store, and below that a hollow elephant's foot stuffed with umbrellas and walking sticks. Eventually Brenda stood back and peeled Ros's hands away from her face so that they could look at each other – Brenda with kindness, Ros with gratefulness – and both women realising at the same moment how ugly Ros looked, they laughed.

'Oh Ros, you've got freckles!'

'Has my make-up run?'

They took the lift to the top floor and Brenda led Ros to the ladies' room. While Ros dried her eyes and re-powdered her cheeks she admired Brenda in the mirror. She was sixty-five years old, she knew, but looked forty, naturally for someone who was primped, manicured and massaged on a daily basis. She was wearing a matching dark blue skirt and jacket, a white, ruffed satin blouse and a single loop of pearls around her – relatively unwrinkled – neck. Ros was most impressed by the tall, aristocratic coiffure tinted the faintest mauve, and tickled by the brightness of the red lipstick, applied with the boldness of a courtesan, but most of all Ros liked the large brown eyes which – she remembered – looked fondly on pretty much everyone.

'Well, my dear, I didn't expect to find you here today. What a surprise.'

'And I didn't know you came here for afternoon tea,' said Elizabeth Taylor.

Ros put her make-up back in her handbag, lifted her shoulders and then dropped them with a big sigh.

'Now,' said Brenda, taking Ros by the arm again. 'Let's go and have tea and you can tell Brenda all about it.'

In the tea room a waiter led then to a table by the window and took Brenda's order of afternoon tea for two. From this high up they could see the forest of Windsor in the smoky distance, and down below people in miniature idling along the sunlit high street. All the other tables in the room where occupied by ladies and gentlemen with their guests or friends, talking in a relaxed, gossipy way, muted by the atmosphere of decorum. Brenda nodded to aquantancies as she peeled off her white, elbow-length gloves, the type that she'd been wearing since the 1950s when her beauty was at its height.

'I've been coming here for years,' said Brenda. She pointed to the west. 'You used to be able to see the yard before they built the new shopping centre. Now that's a monstrosity if ever there was one.'

A waiter arrived with a teapot and cups and placed a silver, three-tiered cake stand on their table.

'Shall I be mother?' said Brenda, lifting the lid of the pot to see how black the tea was. She nodded at the cakes. 'Don't wait for me, Ros.'

Ros tonged a piece of Battenberg onto her plate and then sat back as daintily as possible for a girl with giant thighs that were about to get even larger, and when Brenda – having poured out the tea – added a slice of chocolate cake and a Florentine to her Battenberg while saying, 'We're not going to worry about our weight today, darling,' Ros found herself grinning like a little girl.

Prompted by Brenda, Ros explained that she'd been wandering about all morning, in tears, because Ted was in trouble with the police and she didn't know what to do. She knew that he was worried as well, but like all great oafs he didn't want to unburden himself in front of his wife, meaning – thought Ros – that their marriage had been nothing but a fantasy all along. She added that Ted was practically an alcoholic, was surly all the time, and spent many hours in the company of Vince, a dubious character from the bad old days. Finally she said, 'And then I sort of ended up here.'

During her speech Ros had still managed to consume the dainties on her plate, and now – feeling empty – she helped herself to a miniature meringue and a Portugese custard tart. Brenda hadn't stinted on the victuals either, so that between them they'd emptied the top two tiers of the cake stand, leaving just the bottom tier laden with scones, cream and jam. She'd been quiet and attentive while Ros was talking but as her young friend returned the tongs to the stand she smiled at this revelation of an ancient truth: while men live to eat, women eat to forget.

Then she laughed – a great, sudden, 'How do we put up with them?' laugh – reached across the table, took her companion's hand and said, 'Dear Ros.'

When Brenda let go she noticed some crumbs on the sleeve of her jacket. She brushed these onto the tablecloth, swept them up and then dusted her palms, so that the sugary particles – glinting in the sunlight – rained onto her plate, and all so that she could stand her elbows on the table and rest her chin on the sill of her hands. With the wryness of the woman who'd seen it all, she began to tell Ros about the past.

'Well as you probably know, Dickie started the business during the war, after he was invalided out, shot through the hip at the first battle of El Alamein. He was depressed for a long time because he missed his mates but I was glad to have him back. He was just a mechanic back then, with his own little garage, and we did alright – me doing the books, him doing the dirty work – and everything legit apart from the odd barrel of black market engine oil that came our way, and which I, as the conscience of the business, turned a blind eye to. Then near the end of the war Dickie pals up with this American army sergeant who looked like Tyrone Power. It was the first time I'd seen someone drink Bourbon and chew gum at the same time. The next thing I know, Dickie comes home one night with a big smile on his face, driving an American army truck still with a white star on its side. "Where did you get that from?" I said. "I bought it!" he goes. "How much?" I ask. "Ah!" he says, tapping the side of his nose like a comedian. A few months later he buys another one, after five years we've got ten lorries and the yard, and after twelve years we've got fifty lorries and eighty staff. By this time we've bought the manor house in Hertfordshire, put the stone lions on top of the pillars at the end of the gravel driveway, had three kids, bought a Roller and two Beagles, and every time Dickie comes home there I am, floating down the curved staircase in a cocktail dress so I can make him a Martini.'

At this point a waiter came along to clear away the tea things and the two trencherwomen – their blood fizzing from all the sugar – watched the empty cake stand sail away, satisfied that they'd let nothing go to waste.

'Can we have an ashtray please, Robert,' said Brenda.

After Robert had placed a cut glass ashtray on the table, Brenda took out a packet of cigarettes, offered one to Ros and then poked a gold-banded St Moritz Menthol into her silver cigarette holder. She lit them both up with what looked like a small, oblong diamond and then blew smoke out of her mouth with an upwards-and-sideways jerk of the head, in the manner – thought Ros – of Bette Davis chewing the scenery.

'To put it another way, I was glad I'd married the dear fellow, even though I'd never been particularly ambitious and had believed Dickie to be more a safe pair of hands than an entrepeneur. Then we started to diversify, so that Dickie's not just a haulier but an agent as well, a middleman, selling construction equipment to the Arabs who are building all this infrastructure in the desert where they'd discovered oil. That's where the trouble started. The Arabs had so much money that they quickly got tired of buying second-hand trucks from us and bought them straight from the manufacturers instead. So there we were with a load of equipment we couldn't sell and a half a million pound loan that we couldn't pay back. It burst our bubble alright but we didn't go under, and now we've built it back up to where it is now.'

With the afternoon sun shining through the window and replete from all the cakes, Ros felt drowsy and hot, but was intrigued by Brenda's tale, if doubtful of its meaning.

Seeing the look on her face, Brenda said, 'My point, dear Ros, is that I'll never know where the money to buy that first truck came from, or what happened to the American sergeant, though my guess is that he's the sort of multi-millionaire who ends up in jail. Nor do I understand how Dickie finances the works these days, and neither do I want to know because it would probably turn my hair white. After the war, Ros, British industry was rebuilt thanks to a financial underworld and immoral alliances between businessmen and crooks. Or to put it simply, there's always something funny going on in some yard somewhere.'

They stubbed out their cigarettes and Brenda called for the bill.

'Thanks for the tea,' said Ros, taking her purse out of her handbag.

'Put that away, Ros. The best thing about having a successful business is being able to treat my friends.' Brenda leaned across and took Ros's hand one more time. 'I'll have a word with Dickie about Ted's little problem.'

'There's no… '

'Oh I insist,' said Brenda, and the gold-plated clasp of her handbag closed with a click.

She'd left a five pound note on top of the bill and when Robert came over she said, 'Keep the change, dear.'

The grateful Robert summoned a fellow waiter and the chairs were whisked from beneath the rising women with a ballroom flourish.

Halfway to the lift Brenda stopped, looked Ros up and down and said, 'Perhaps you can pay me back after all, dear'

'How?'

'By looking over some things I've come to buy.

They took the lift down to the ladies' floor and walked silently across the thick viridian carpet, past women just browsing or examining their tilted reflections in free-standing mirrors. On islands built of giant formica cubes cashmere cardigans were heaped neatly and display dummies wore satin underwear or floor-length chiffon evening gowns. When they came to a rack of fur coats they stopped and thrust their hands into its midst, their fingers making their warm, frictionless way to the cold silk linings inside.

'Don't tell anyone,' whispered Brenda. 'But I've got one of these.'

She led Ros to a corner where they slipped behind a curtain and entered a large dressing room walled with floor-to-ceiling mirrors. A tall, elegant young man with black, Sicilian hair came out from behind his desk and greeted them deferentially. He had a tape measure hanging around his neck and a row of pins stuck into the left cuff of his jacket.

'Well Guiseppe, is our creation ready?'

'We sewed on the last button only yesterday, Mrs Ford.'

Brenda went behind another curtain and Giuseppe waved Ros into an armchair. After a few minutes an old lady holding a pin cushion pulled the curtain aside and out came Brenda wearing a floor-length grey silk evening gown with an empire waist and a sequinned bust. Giuseppe pursed his lips, dimpled his chin with a finger and circled Brenda while the old lady got down on all fours and fussed with the hem. At last Giuseppe clapped his hands and cried 'Perfect!'

'What do you think, Ros?' said Brenda.

It wasn't Ros's style at all and made her think of old and forgotten German princesses but even so she was impressed.

'It's magnificent Brenda.'

'What about the jacket, Giuseppe?'

He stood behind Brenda and helped her into a black lace bolero, so that now – to Ros – she looked like an old Spanish princess.

For a few minutes Ros and Giuseppe oohed and aahed while Brenda rotated slowly before the mirrors, looking over one shoulder and then the other to gauge the flow of the silk. At last she said, 'Yes, that'll do nicely,' and disappeared behind the curtain.

Giuseppe returned to his desk while Ros waited in the chair. She loved how forthright and young at heart Brenda was, and then reflected how only certain people seemed to possess the energy required to keep hold of wealth once it had been acquired. Part of her envied her older friend, but the rest of her was exhausted just by thought of how many plates Dickie and Brenda had to keep spinning in the air to keep their empire intact.

When Brenda came out again she was holding a baby-blue evening dress with long full sleeves and a high neck, and a pair of toeless white shoes.

'I found this hanging up in there, Ros. I reckon it would suit you.'

Giuseppe, sensing another sale, got up and looked from Ros to the dress and back again.

'I definitely think madam should try it on.'

'I can't afford it,' said Ros, mesmerised by the lovely dress.

'Who said anything about buying it?' cried Brenda. 'Just try it on, for fun.'

Behind the curtain Ros got undressed, made the blue gown into a pool and stepped into it, pulling it high and fitting in onto her shoulders. Looking bashful and a little off-balance in the unfamiliar shoes, she re-entered the mirrored room to the gasps of her little audience. The old woman looked at the hem and said, 'Up two inches,' while Giuseppe stood behind her, zipped her up and then slid his hands under her armpits, indicating that the bust needed to be loosened.

Ros examined herself in the mirror and even did a little twirl. She could only agree with Brenda that the dress was perfect for her, not least because it made her look a lot slimmer. Lost in thoughts of her own, she didn't notice that the old woman was on her hands and knees again, pinning the hem up, or that Giuseppe was writing code on a little notepad, or the great winks that Brenda was giving them both.

Behind the curtain again, she took the dress off, and after telling herself not to be so silly because she was never going to see it again, held it against her face and stood there in silence and darkness while the silk flowed over her skin.

When she re-emerged she was in too much of a daze to notice Brenda, Giuseppe and the old woman breaking apart as though from a huddle, or the look of complete innocence on their faces. Brenda took her arm and led her through the ladies' department and out into the sunny street.

'Now are you feeling better, dear Ros?'

'Yes. Thankyou. And I'll try not to worry.'

Brenda leaned in and kissed her.

'Perhaps there's no *need* to worry.'

Ros watched her walk away and then turned for home.

Twenty-Two

After he'd been back at school for a while, Pete noticed a new recluse in the library. A boy called Noblet, a year younger than him, had developed bad acne during the summer holiday and was sitting in a corner on his own, suppurating quietly and reading Asterix the Gladiator. Pete kept looking at him and in the end couldn't resist going over.

'Oi, Noblet,' he said, cheerfully. 'What are you reading?'

Noblet looked up and Pete could see a pustule on one of his eyelids. In his expression there was surprise that Pete – one of the clear-skinned – was talking to him.

'This,' said Noblet, holding the book up.

'Aren't you a bit old for that sort of thing? Why don't you try… ?'

Pete wandered off and came back with Volume One of Lord Of The Rings. Noblet looked at the book and recoiled, as though he'd been offered a mirror.

'I don't like fantasy.'

Pete thought, 'When you look like you do that's all there is,' but said, 'Try it,' and walked off.

A few days later Pete hailed Noblet again. The afflicted one was sitting in his usual place in the darkest and most unvisited corner of the library, with its sections on knitting, childcare and personal hygiene. The book he was reading was Lord Of The Rings and Pete was pleased to see that his riveted face had cleaved the book in two.

'So how far have you got?'

'Almost at the end of the first volume,' said Noblet with a big smile on his face.

'Ah, so the Fellowship is seeking sanctuary in the land of Lorien.'

Whenever he visited the library from then on, Pete was aware of the proximity of Noblet, who – like a cur – crept closer to his beloved intercessor day-by-day. Pete didn't want to be friends with the boy, and so in between making polite enquiries about his progress with the book, was distant with him. On the other hand, he was proud that he'd introduced an innocent to the greatest book in the world, some mitigation for the torment of having a face that looked like one of his mum's burnt moussakas.

At the end of one hot, drowsy afternoon, during which Noblet had sat next to Pete the whole time, the bell for the end of school sounded and Pete got to his feet. Noblet dragged his eyes away from the book, looked up at Pete and said, 'See you Monday.'

Pete looked down at Noblet and pronounced loftily,

'When you've finished that, you should read The Silmarillion. I've read it twice.'

As he was walking out of the school gates, Pete looked around for Timothy but couldn't see him. He loitered for a while, facing the stream of boys leaving school, now and again asking someone, 'Have you seen Herbert?' and then set off after him, reckoning that he must be up ahead somewhere after all.

Soon he saw that the stream of blue blazers had slowed and thickened near the earthen path that led back towards the railway line. A boy was standing on tiptoe to see what was going on. Other boys – noticing this – stopped to see what he was looking at and then joined the tributary that was heading down there.

Pete had an uneasy feeling and hoped that the reason for the commotion was a boy with a pornographic magazine – the usual reason for a clot in the stream – or a fight between two enemies rather than a case of bullying, but then he distinctly heard the name 'Herbert' and new that Timothy was involved.

He began to push through the crowd, elbowing smaller boys into the man-high weeds and brambles that bordered the path on either side. He noticed scholastic debris on the ground – a pen, a book of chess problems, an exercise book, a glasses case – and then saw a circle of about thirty boys facing inwards. Adrian was there and when he saw Pete he said, delightedly, 'Your new friend's about to get squashed!'

Pete barged through the crowd and found Dan, his tall, good-looking friend of old, and Timothy – his new little friend – facing each other in the middle of the circle, Timothy looking crossly up at Dan who was emptying his briefcase item by item.

'And another one,' said Dan, dropping a heavy tome on the ground. 'And another one. And… what's this?' On the cover of the book was a picture of the bug-eyed Einstein with his famous nimbus of wild hair. 'Is this your fucking dad, Herbert?'

The watching boys snorted and sniggered, and Timothy cried.

'No, but he was the father of modern physics!'

For the first time Dan noticed Pete. 'Oh hello,' he said, and frowned, clearly unable to understand how anyone could be friends with a nitwit like Herbert.

Every time that a book was dropped, Timothy would pick it up and stuff it into the bundle under his arm, until the bundle became too heavy and flew in all directions. When he reached down once more, Pete – more concerned for his his friend's dignity than anything – said crossly, 'Don't!' and went to pick the book up himself.

'Don't what?' said Dan.

'Just leave him,' said Pete, straightening up.

Dan paused with Timothy's bag in his hands and looked squarely at Pete for a moment, as though considering the request for old time's sake, and Pete thought, 'Good old Dan,' but then Dan's eyes turned cold. He looked at Timothy, spat, 'Fuck off, Herbert!' and threw a book straight at him, hitting him on the forehead. Timothy reeled back and clutched his head. When he took his hands away everyone could see a livid welt between his eyebrows.

Pete stood in front of Dan and shouted,

'What did you do that for?'

Dan grabbed Pete by the collar and hissed,

'Because I felt like it.'

The next thing Pete knew, they had each other by the throat and were staggering around in circles, grunting into each other's faces and kicking up dust. Pete was surprised to find that he was equal in strength to Dan and was holding his own, but he knew it wasn't much of a fight from the derisive comments coming from the watching boys and the way some of them were walking off.

With a final, giant effort Dan pushed Pete and said, 'Fuck off, Turner!' Pete rocked back on his heels and stood there, looking Dan in the eye and panting hard and wanting to touch his neck where Dan had pinched his flesh, but resisting the urge. Inside he was thinking, calmly, 'We could go back and forth like this forever but I'm just not scared.' He knew that their friendship was definitively over now, not because of the wrestling, but because for the first time ever Dan had called him by his surname.

A shout was heard and Mr Bolger, the deputy headmaster, came charging up. Finding nothing much going on, he sent everyone packing and five minutes later Pete and Timothy found themselves walking down a quiet road on their own. After a while Timothy said,

'Are you alright?'

'Yes. Are you?'

'Oh, I'm alright.'

They didn't say anything more, taking comfort from each other. Timothy knew that from now on he could take courage from his friend, in the same way that Pete had taken courage from him when Pete had been just another lonely boy in the library. When they parted they said goodbye without making eye contact, each boy feeling a sob rising into his throat.

That evening Ros and Pete ate their dinner alone, Ros

informing Pete that his dad had gone out for the evening with his old friend Vince. Pete had met Vince on many occasions and liked him because he was jovial and generous with his money – he'd tipped Pete fifty pence every time – but he also understood that his mum thought the fellow crooked somehow, and so didn't press for details about their whereabouts.

The two petty criminals were, of course, in the wood-panelled snug, sitting on their usual stools but this time with their backs to the bar, facing the small audience that had gathered around to hear Vince's latest joke.

'So there's three blokes sitting in the pub and one goes, "What's the fastest thing in the world? I reckon it's electricity because as soon as you press the light switch, the bulb comes on." The second bloke goes, "No, I reckon it's speech, because when you say something, another person can hear you straight away." The third bloke goes, "No, the fastest thing in the world is diarrhea." They say to him, "Why's that?" He goes, "Because the other night I had diarrhea, and before I'd had time to tell anyone or turn the light on, I'd shat myself."'

There was a roar of drunken laughter and cries of, 'Nice one, Vince!' and 'Vince the slayer!' but Ted – in a world of his own – only pretended to laugh. Vince stayed for another half an hour and then left along with most of the other fellows. Ted, left alone at the bar, picked up his pint and gave the stew of his life another stir.

After a while he realised that a man had sat down next to him. He'd noticed the fellow earlier, sitting on his own and apparently happy in his own company, and then had forgotten about him. He was about sixty, Ted reckoned, with healthy, light brown skin, pinkish cheeks and silverish hair. He was wearing an expensive-looking, dark blue, pinstripe suit and no tie, and was handsome, if fat around the middle: Ted could clearly see a diamond of hairy white belly bulging from between the buttons of his shirt. But what attracted Ted to the man was the fact that he was smoking a long, thick and obviously Cuban cigar, which at that very moment he was ducking thoughtfully into the ashtray, brushing it against the Zs and Vs of dead butts to dislodge ash. The man was drinking port from a glass bowl balanced in the palm of his hand, the stem slotted between his fingers. Ted thought,

'If he's rich, what's he doing in here?'

The man put down his glass, rummaged around in his trouser pocket for change and said, 'Fancy another?'

'Don't mind if I do,' said the forlorn one.

'Two more, please,' said the man to the barmaid. Then he looked at Ted. 'And I'm guessing you're a whisky man.'

'How did you know?' burped Ted.

'Because you live in the Wild West.'

Ted frowned so the man continued.

'Your gunfighter's moustache.'

'Ah.'

'With that thing you could hold up a bank without using any guns.'

Ted laughed until he got the hiccups.

'That's the best thing that anyone's said to me for years.'

So the man bought Ted a whisky chaser and they had an exchange about their favourite westerns – Shane, High Noon, Red River – Ted listening more than talking and still fascinated by the man's cigar, from the burning tip to the end damp from slobber. Belatedly they gave their names – the man was Roger – and then questioned each other about their lines of work.

'What's a troubleshooter?' said Ted.

'Oh, you know, when a business is in trouble I come in and help sort things out, from a legal point of view.'

'Big business?'

'That's where the money is.'

Over Roger's protests, Ted bought the next round.

'My boss is a successful businessman.'

'What's his name?'

'Dickie Ford.'

'Oh, I know Dickie,' said Roger.

'You don't.'

'I've known him for a long time.'

'Great man, Dickie. We get on well. My wife reckons he treats me like the son he never had.'

'Yes, I knew Dickie had three girls.'

The barmaid rang the bell for last orders and Ted went to to the toilet. When he came back he saw that Roger had got the final round in.

'So how are things at Dickie's?'

Lulled by all the booze, Roger's cigar smoke and patrician air, Ted entered the confessional.

'Not good to be honest. Some hot fuel pumps came my way and I was overcome with greed.'

'It's a shame you didn't steal the toilets from the police station.'

'Why?'

'The police would have had nothing to go on.'

Ted rested his head on the bar and cried. By now he

wanted to leave Ros and live the rest of his life as Roger's catamite.

'I presume you've come to the attention of the boys in blue?'

'I don't know how.'

'Local police or county police?'

'Local. Detective sergeant Naylor is the man in charge of my case.'

'I know detective sergeant Naylor.'

Ted looked at Roger with even more respect. He was nodding his head as though thinking to himself, while looking at the optics and plucking a shred of tobacco from his lower lip.

'Another overworked, middle-aged police sergeant who's never going to make superintendent.'

'How do you know him?'

For the first time Roger looked at Ted shrewdly, almost coldly.

'There's no need for you to concern yourself with the details of our relationship with the constabulary, Ted Turner.' Then he smiled again and patted Ted's knee. 'Perhaps you're the little piggie whose house is built of straw.'

'What do you mean?'

'I mean that it could all blow over.'

Ted wasn't sure what this meant either, and neither was he sure that he'd told Roger his surname, but he was too addled to figure it all out. The barmaid coughed politely and Ted looked round to find that he and Roger were the only punters left.

'Last man standing again,' said Ted, flattening his palms on the bar and trying to lever himself up.

'Steady old chap,' cried Roger, catching him.

They weaved their way to the door, tried to squeeze through side by side and then popped out in each other's arms. Ted took out his car keys but Roger came over all serious again.

'I don't think you want to drive home tonight, do you lad?'

He led Ted to a maroon Jaguar XJ12, luxurious and gleaming under the street lights. Ted wondered why they were both getting in the back seat until he saw a man sitting behind the steering wheel. He was about Ted's age, had a completely bald head and was wearing a white shirt, a blue tie and a grey V-neck jumper like a grown-up schoolboy.

'We're going to drop my new friend off first, Les.'

'Right you are, sir.'

There was a faint vibration and the car moved off in silence. Roger opened the window – he still hadn't finished his monumental cigar – while Ted leaned back against the leather head rest and closed his eyes.

'Thanks for this, Roger.'

'Just as long as you get home safely.' After a while he said, 'It's the next on the right, Les.'

Ted thought, 'I don't remember telling them the way.'

When they arrived home he had trouble getting out of the car so Les helped. Ted forgot all about Roger until the morning, when he realised that he'd have to catch the bus into Earley to pick up his car. Four days later he received a letter from the police informing him that all proceedings against him had been dropped, and that the matter of the stolen fuel pumps was closed.

Twenty-Three

Dickie and Brenda came over in their old Daimler and drove Ros and Ted up to see Barbra Streisand at the Talk Of The Town. Ted sat up front alongside Dickie as they thundered up the M4, both dressed in black suits and bow ties, and smoking panatellas, Dickie wearing a black silk cummerbund around his fat waist for a touch of class. His platinum hair flowed in silky waves around his ears and was thickest at the neck, but his eyebrows were black. With his healthy brown skin – testimony to fifty Caribbean holidays – and big aquiline nose he looked like the Roman general who conquered Spain.

That morning, Ros had answered the doorbell and found a delivery man standing there with a large, square cardboard box tied up with pink ribbon. When she opened it she saw the baby blue evening dress that she'd tried on in Hudson's, and with it a note from Brenda that said,

'Darling Ros, wear this tonight or we'll go without you.'

Ros took the dress into the living room and held it up to the light pouring through the front window. The feel of the silk made her feel dreamy and drowsy, like a little girl having her hair brushed before bedtime. She said out loud, trying not to fall under its spell, 'I can't possibly accept this,' but this prick of her conscience was quickly overpowered by desire, meaning that for a second time Brenda was accosted by the new Elizabeth Taylor, on this occasion by phone.

'Brenda, I... '

'Now don't be silly, Ros... ' There was the sound of a hand trying to muffle the mouthpiece, and Brenda saying – to company, Ros guessed – 'It's her!' Brenda continued, 'That dress was made for one girl and one girl only. And that's you, Ros.' From the background a woman called out, 'Do as she says, Ros. We have to.' There was laughter and Brenda went on, 'You see.'

'Brenda... ' said Ros, but before she could continue she heard love and rudeness combined exquisitely in the sound of the line going dead.

Brenda was wearing the dress created by Giuseppe, with the addition of three strings of pearls, rings on every finger and diamond earrings the size of crystals in a chandelier, making her equal in rank and dignity to the Roman general. She and Ros had drunk one sherry and one Cinzano each already, so that Brenda – who could talk to crowds anyway – was talking to Ros even more than usual, while Ros was happier than ever just to sit and listen. Ted had bought her a packet of Regals so she knew that she could smoke as much as she wanted that evening, and had lit up one of her own instead of taking one of Brenda's menthols when offered.

Brenda was telling Ros about some renovations they

were having done to the mansion. Apparently a roofer had fallen thirty feet and broken an ankle. Brenda had jumped in the Daimler, which she'd never driven before – her Alfa Romeo being in the garage – and had got the man to hospital before he bled to death.

'I can't believe he survived,' said Brenda.

'I can't believe there weren't any scratches on the Daimler,' said Dickie.

At this point he was steering with his knees while he poured capfuls of brandy for him and Ted from his hip flask.

'Do you two want one?' said Dickie, passing the flask over his shoulder.

'Not 'alf,' said Brenda.

'I couldn't,' said Ros.

'You bloody could,' said Brenda.

After she'd thrown the brandy down her throat Ros sat very still for a moment, and then gasped, before laughing so hard that she had to wipe her lips with the back of her hand.

By now they were coming into Kensington, past long terraces of grand and shabby mansions with porticoed entrances. The Daimler slowed among the growling buses and jostling cabs bearing theatregoers and dinner dates up west. Dickie and Brenda started telling Ros and Ted about all the great entertainers they'd been to see.

'We saw Judy Garland at Carnegie Hall,' said Dickie. 'Who else, love?'

'Frank Sinatra in Vegas. Matt Monroe in Philadelphia.'

'Tom Jones here in London.'

'What about you, Ros?' said Brenda.

'We saw Freddie And The Dreamers,' hiccuped Ros. 'Does that count?'

Dickie parked in Soho and they walked to the venue, sidestepping piles of rubbish and the odd prostitute silhouetted by a naked bulb in a hallway, Ros and Brenda lifting up their dresses to step up onto the pavements, the click of their heels echoing in the alleyways. Ted and Dickie – walking faster – stopped now and then to let the girls catch up, Ted wondering what it would be like to be Dickie, armoured by wealth and success and being able to afford everything.

Ros gasped when she saw Barbra Streisand written in orange light bulbs across the front of The Talk Of The Town. Above was a giant head-only picture of Streisand, her blue eyes defined and elongated by black liner, giving them an Egyptian air. The empress of the musical world looked down at the well-dressed crowd with a smile like an opening note.

Ros and Ted caught each other's eye and raised their eyebrows in a 'How did Dickie manage this?' kind of way when the waiter led them to a table in front of the stage.

Dickie ordered champagne but when he produced more cigars for him and Ted, Brenda said, 'Not now, Dickie. Let's at least have a prawn cocktail first.'

Ros looked around at all the beautifully dressed men and women and whispered to Ted,

'Do you think any of them work in a biscuit factory like me?'

He shook his head and held out his hands so she could see the oil under his fingertips.

'I think I'd better keep these in my pockets.'

They grinned at each other like a couple of kids who'd sneaked into a party for grown-ups.

Ros had her hair up – just the way Ted liked it – but there was nothing demure about the way she chomped through her steak and wolfed down her Black Forest gateau.

Dickie noticed and said to Ted, 'She eats well, doesn't she.'

'She's worse at home.'

Ros burped and held out her glass for more champagne. Brenda filled it and said fiercely,

'It's all on us, Ros. It's all on us.'

The lights went down and the orchestra began to play a medley of some of Streisand's hits, including People, Evergreen and Happy Days Are Here Again. Then the place went dark and the spotlight hit Barbra standing at the front of the stage, only a few feet from Ros's table. She was wearing a long black cocktail dress with an off-the-shoulder neckline trimmed with black ostrich feathers. She was smiling sweetly, almost shyly but in her eyes – thought Ros – there was fearlessness and pride. Ros held her breath, riveted by the sudden, spellbound silence in the theatre and her thrilling proximity to this world-famous entertainer.

Streisand turned to the conductor, shrugged and said,

'Well, what are we waiting for?'

Before the band could play a note some men – zealots from the Barbra Streisand fan club – rushed past Ros's table and up to the stage, reaching out to try and touch the goddess who was tantalisingly out of reach. One man almost got up onto the stage and Barbara looked down at him and said in her Brooklyn accent, 'Take it easy, buster.'

As soon as the men had been herded back to their tables the lights came up and Streisand went straight into 'Don't Rain On My Parade'. For the next forty-five minutes she sang classic after classic and for many weeks afterwards Ros could hear the words of 'My Melancholy Baby' in her mind, and still feel herself swaying from side-to-side to the tune of 'It Had To Be You'. During 'Who Will Buy?' Ros noticed Ted frowning, trying to place the song, and putting her lips to his ear – his hair tickling the end of her nose – she whispered, 'From Oliver.' He draped his arm over the back of her chair and stroked her arm, and at one point – when in the same moment they noticed Dickie and Brenda holding hands – they looked at each other as though to say, 'Let's hope we're like that at their age.'

As the orchestra played the opening notes of 'Just In Time', Streisand turned to the conductor and said, 'Make this one swing, Joe.' She introduced another song by saying, 'Funny how love lasts forever but falling in love takes no time at all.' The final song of the first half of the show was the Judy Garland classic, 'Get Happy', and this time Dickie joined the group of men who went up to the stage and reached out to Barbra, hoping for a touch of magic.

He came back to the table and said, 'She looked right at me, right into my eyes.'

A waiter went by and Brenda said, 'Get me a bucket of water I can throw over my husband.'

Dickie produced more cigars for him and Ted and said, 'So what do you reckon? Is Barbra Streisand the greatest singer of the twentieth century?'

'Don't forget our Judy,' said Brenda.

'What do you think, Ted?'

'What about Ella Fitzgerald? Or Billie Holiday?'

'Who's the best out of those two?' said Brenda. 'It's impossible to say.'

'Ok,' said Dickie. 'We'll do a top five but agree that they're all as good as each other. So we've got Billie, Ella, Judy and Barbra. Who's the fifth?'

They all put their thinking caps on and then Ros said, 'What about Karen Carpenter?'

A man at the next table snorted and they all turned to look at him, but because he didn't look back they presumed the snort wasn't directed at them.

'She's certainly got a great voice,' said Brenda.

'Our Pete went to see The Carpenters,' said Ros. 'He and his friend had a great time.'

'But has she got one of the great voices of the twentieth century?' said Dickie. At that moment he caught Ted's eye and saw that the big man wanted Ros indulged. 'Well, now I come to think of it, I reckon she has! So our fifth greatest singer of the twentieth century is Karen Carpenter!'

The man at the next table snorted again and they all looked round to see him staring at Ros and shaking his head. He was a big man, completely bald and with thin lips, and was so drunk that his eyeballs were floating in liquor. His wife sitting next to him had a rotund figure and a pleasant face but looked scared by her husband's mood.

'Karen Carpenter one of the greatest singers,' sneered the man in a Texan accent. 'I've never heard anything so dumb in all my life.'

Ros was so drunk and happy that instead of being appalled she laughed out loud, at the man's comical rudeness, but at the same time took pity on him for what

Ted was bound to do next. There was a strange glint in her husband's eye, a hungry smile on his face. To Dickie he looked like a lion licking its lips at the sight of a buffalo trapped knee-deep in a mud hole.

Ted had his back to the man and now turned round in his chair to face him.

'You need to apologise,' he said, blandly.

'Why?'

'For being a berk!' said Brenda.

The man looked at Ted, thought for a moment and then nodded. 'Ok, I'll apologise.'

Then he smashed his cigarette into the ashtray. 'Like never.'

'Harry,' said the man's wife. 'Take it easy.'

Now Ted got out of his chair and stood over the man. He held out the palm of his hand with the fingers curled upwards.

'Do you know what this is? said Ted, softly.

'Your brain?'

'It is my hand. The hand that in a moment is going to grab you by the testicles… '

'Balls, I think they say in America,' said Brenda.

'… that is going to grab you by the balls, lift you up by the balls, and carry you out of here by the balls with your feet off the ground.'

From the way the man was staring at the hand it was obvious to everyone that Ted's words were having the desired effect.

'Ok, bud, take it easy.'

Ted put both hands on Harry's table and leaned close.

'No, apologise properly.'

'Ok, I'm sorry!' shouted Harry with a writhe.

'There's a good boy,' said Ted, and sat down again.

Brenda looked triumphantly at Harry and then patted Ted's knee.

'I hope no one breaks into the yard while you're there, big boy.'

'Big boy,' said Ros, and got the giggles.

Streisand started the second half of the show with On A Clear Day You Can See Forever, and then sang People. Ros kept thinking how beautiful she looked and how unself-conscious she seemed to be, but she also wondered whether more humdrum thoughts crossed her mind while she was singing, such as whether her mum was feeling better after her cold, or whether her assistant had remembered to cut the crusts off of the tuna mayonnaise sandwich that would be waiting for her in the dressing room after the show.

For the rest of the performance she alternated between songs from her new album and classics from the great American songbook. Finally she said, 'This is for my friend, Bob Redford,' and sang The Way we Were. By the end of it a lot of people in the audience had gone weak at the knees and so couldn't get up to applaud straight away, but when everyone was on their feet the ovation lasted for fifteen minutes. There was one encore – a Foggy Day In London Town – and then she was gone.

The lights came up and people rose to go, leaving tables covered with empty glasses, full ashtrays and thrown-down napkins. Ted retrieved Ros's handbag from under the table but just as he was giving it to her, Dickie said,

'The evening's not over yet.'

'What do you mean?' said Ted.

'I've got passes to see her backstage.'

Dickie and Brenda looked at Ros and Ted standing there gormlessly, and laughed. A man about Dickie's age waved them over and led them round the back of the stage, and along a series of corridors where they squeezed past mops and buckets, rails hung with costumes and musicians with their instruments hurrying home. There was a hubbub up ahead and when they turned a corner they saw a crowd of people standing outside an open door and peering in. Above all the heads Ros could just make out Barbra Streisand standing in front of a mirror while an assistant unpinned her turban and lifted it off her head. Barbra was talking fast, greeting people, thanking others and signing programmes that were thrust towards her.

Slowly, Dickie's friend eased his way through the crowd, dragging Dickie and Ted with him, while Brenda – just behind and holding Ros's hand – kept up until it became too much of a tight squeeze and she and Ros had to let go of each other.

With Dickie, Ted and Brenda in the room, Dickie's friend said, 'Barbra, this is my friend Dickie.'

Barbra looked at Dickie and sang, 'Well, hello Dickie!' to the tune of Hello Dolly! Then she saw Ted and said, 'Hey, Mike, you didn't tell me Burt Reynolds was here tonight. My, aren't you handsome!'

Ted, who was already pink from all the booze, blushed like a baby and looked back at Ros with a helpless smile. Brenda looked back at her too and mouthed, 'Poor Ros, you got left behind.'

Gradually, more men and women squeezed past Ros,

forcing her to walk backwards step by little step, until – finding herself standing in the corridor on her own – she thought to herself.

'Oh I hope I get to see Petula Clark one day.'

Twenty-Four

In early October Ted's birthday came around. Standing on the tips of her fluffy yellow mules in the bathroom, Ros could see that a vast marmalde inflorescence had replaced the bright green canopy of the wood. In a few weeks millions of the leaves would have changed to the colour of her hair, and by Christmas the Broadmoor warning siren would be looming over it all.

It was Saturday morning and she was alone in the house. Pete was round at Timothy's and Ted had just left with an, 'I'm Off', on his way to the garage to treat himself to some sporty alloy hub caps. In the sink some droplets of water were trickling towards the plughole from when they'd all had their morning washes and brushed their teeth. Two tubes of toothpaste stood upright in a plastic pot. She knew Ted had been strict with the boy recently concerning his untidiness, warning him that if he didn't stop treating his mother like a beast of burden he'd tell Fiona that he was still a big baby. Ros had already checked the toilet and found the vitreous china unstained.

In Pete's room she made his bed, picked up a pair of Y-fronts and dropped them into a tall, snake-charmer's wicker basket. She moved about freely, the old heaps of things that used to cover the floor having long ago been reconfigured into tidier stacks, whether of clothes or books. On his desk she found evidence of study: an open exercise book and a neatly written paragraph under the heading, 'Othello: jealousy vs hubris'. On the wall the hedgehog picture had long gone, to be replaced by a glossy poster of astronauts exploring a cave on Mars, testimony to Pete's new-found obsession – thanks to Timothy – with the literature of Arthur C. Clarke and Robert Heinlein.

Ros had overheard a conversation between the two boys concerning the chance of Man landing on Mars in their lifetimes, Timothy saying, 'You do realise that by Mars I mean the fourth planet from Helios, not a chocolate bar.'

'At least if I got to Mars I'd be able to see it, Mole boy… '

She made herself a coffee, took it into the garden and smoked a cigarette while looking for the final colours of the year. She saw white anenomes, Flamingo-pink Nerines and a cluster of carmine water-lily dahlias among the ghosts of shrubs. She remembered walking around the garden with Fiona, naming the plants for her, Pete following glumly behind. The following day he'd crept up to Ros and said, 'What were the names of those plants again, Mum?'

Mrs Morris's head appeared over the hedge.

'I've got a present for Ted.'

'You shouldn't have.'

Mrs Morris pushed through the shrubbery on her side and a bottle of whisky appeared in the air. Ros reached over and took it.

'He'll be pleased with that. Thankyou.'

'Well, we know he likes a drink.'

'Actually, Mrs Morris, he hardly drinks at all these days.'

'Well he can drink it at Christmas then, can't he.'

'I'm sure he will.'

'And are you still having a party today?'

'Yes. Mum and Dad are coming, and Pete's friends, and Pauline and Norman said they'd pop their heads round the door.'

Ros went back inside and got ready to go out. For lunch she was making jacket potatoes with cheese, coleslaw or coronation chicken, had already bought a cheese and onion quiche and made a salad, but needed to pick up Ted's birthday cake from the baker's in Earley. The exhaust had fallen off of her car, so to catch the bus she walked down all the alleyways of the estate to the Reading Road and waited by the stop, searching the distance for the green, double-deckered Number 41.

The grey sheet metal of the shelter and the signpost itself were covered in spray-painted names, The Slits, The Clash, The New York Dolls, the headliners of the zeitgeist, Ros presumed. Inevitably she thought of Lump, and admitted to herself that she quite fancied the boy – his good looks and lazy smile – and believed that underneath it all he had a gentle nature, like Pete, and that his desire to go out in a blaze of glory was probably down to outside influences: a suffocating upbringing maybe, or the demonic Sugar.

When the bus came the bottom deck was full so she climbed the stairs and found another October cloud, this one created by about twenty smokers. She found an empty seat across the aisle from an old lady and thought about lighting up as well, but then told herself that she'd be getting off in five minutes. The narrow window above her was open and she felt cool air on her face as she watched the world go by. She remembered that she'd have to improvise a piping bag to decorate Ted's cake, and thought how funny it would be to pipe Happy Birthday, Burt Reynolds instead of Happy Birthday, Ted.

She was in such a daydream that at first she didn't notice the man who'd sat down next to her. It was only when the smoke around her became more dense and acrid that she became aware of the old gentleman smoking a pipe. He certainly seemed a gentlemen, thought Ros, with his richly textured overcoat and white shirt and tie, and was smoking his pipe in the innocent, self-absorbed way typified by all the pipe smokers she'd encountered previously. The pacific Ros thought, 'A man with an expensive coat on a bus? Ah, he's lonely and out of a job.' A second later the prim Ros thought, 'Lucky for me the bloody window's open.' In the next instant she realised that the bus hadn't stopped since she'd got on and that there could only be one explanation for the man's appearance next to her. 'Another pervert.'

She felt the pressure of his thigh against hers and prayed that the bus would go faster. The man kept taking the pipe out of his mouth and examining the bowl, and eventually some ash fell onto her dark blue raincoat, over her knees, and lay there quivering with the motion of the bus. For a whole, tense minute they watched it until he said, 'Sorry, my dear,' and with a brush of his fingers turned the grey maggot of ash into a streak of the faintest pink.

'Excuse me!' shouted Ros, rising to her feet, and the next moment the old lady across the aisle shouted, 'I saw that!'

The man took the pipe out of his mouth and looked from one woman to the other.

'I don't know what you mean.'

The old woman stood up.

'You touched her! You planned it! You were sitting back there and then you sat down next to her.'

Now the man stood up.

'How dare you.'

'Get out of my way!' shouted Ros, and barged into the man, forcing him into the aisle.

She and the old lady stood together, facing the man. 'Fiend!' cried the old woman, waving her fist at him. All the other passengers were watching by now. The bus lurched beneath them as it slowed down for the stop outside the baker's. Ros never knew where she got the idea from but she snatched the pipe out of the man's hand and popped it out of the window. She just had time to register the look of horror on his face before she found herself running down the stairs with the old lady behind her. The doors opened, they skipped down, but instead of witnessing the man rampaging down the stairs after them, they saw the doors close and the bus drive off, meaning – they both realised – that the now pipeless pervert was a coward as well.

Ros stood there, breathing heavily, waving her hand in front of her face and saying, 'My God!'

'Well, we saw him off,' cried the old lady. She squinted at Ros. 'Are you okay, dear?'

'I think so,' she said, suddenly recognising this defender of the innocent – by her stoutness and grey cardigan – as Mick Burnley's granny.

The woman looked at Ros for a bit longer, making sure she was ok, and then turned to the queue of women outside the baker's and cried, 'One down, ten million to go.'

Then she turned and walked off, crunching her teeth and delving in the lump-filled pockets of her cardigan for cigarettes, leaving Ros to reflect that true eccentrics were the most human of us all.

Ros didn't remember going into the baker's, chatting to the women behind the counter or the walk home with the cake. The next time she was aware of anything was when she came to in her kitchen, just as she was putting a tray of large potatoes into the oven.

The birthday boy came home, looking pleased with his new hub caps. 'Need any help?' he said to Ros, who was stretching some clingfilm over a bowl of salad. The plan was that all the food would be laid out on the dining table, people would go up and help themselves and then eat off their laps in the living room.

'You can take these through if you like. I've put the tablecloth on.'

Obeying these orders without question, Ted made several trips between the kitchen and the living room. Eventually he stood in the doorway, watching Ros wiping the counter top down and picking up a cherry tomato from the floor.

'Is that everything?'

'Just the potatoes to come out of the oven.'

Ted picked up the kettle, squeezed past Ros and filled it up at the sink.

'Let's have a coffee before the hordes arrive.'

They stood next to each other while they drank their coffees, looking out of the kitchen window. Ted held his mug in both hands, quite close to his face, so that when Ros looked at him she saw droplets of steam on his moustache.

'So how are your hub caps?' she said.

Ted took this enquiry in the spirit in which it was asked – lovingly – but at the same time, as a husband and veteran of a thousand grim silences and fruity exchanges, he knew that what Ros had really said was, 'While I'm of course happy that you've bought yourself something for your car instead of a new exhaust pipe for mine, didn't it cross your mind, just for a moment, that the money you've squandered might have been better spent on a dress for me or a new racing bike for Pete?'

'After I've given them a shine,' said Ted, 'you'll be able to look in them and see your beautiful face reflected back at you in all its glory.'

'So you really bought them for me?'

'Of course. Who else?'

For the next twenty minutes they stood there without saying a word while they finished their coffee. Ros remembered the day she'd spent squeezing acne ointment out of Pete's old tube and refilling it with Wort Of India, the day on holiday when she'd moved his queen to a killing square, and the evening when she'd taken the hedgehog that she'd stolen and released it under the noses of her husband and son. She recalled how her and Ted had walked up to the post box together the night before – with a card for Jenny who was in hospital – and then walked all the way back again without saying anything to each other. She remembered similar but much longer walks around the time they were first going out together, when a whole hour would go by without a word being exchanged. She began to suspect that those times were the happiest of her life, and that all she'd ever really wanted from a marriage was the quality of side-by-sideness.

Ted's next chore was to go and pick up Charlie and Betty, who were catching the bus from Reading but wanted to be picked up from the main road so they didn't have to walk all the way through the estate to get to Ros's. When they got back Ted came in first and then disappeared, giving Charlie the opportunity to pin Ros against the fridge and get a few tickles in before Ted came back. Thanks to a strict new regimen, Charlie was pinker and slimmer than he'd been for forty years, as was Betty who'd supported her husband by adopting the same regimen. Their eyes shone brightly in their fat-free faces but their necks were wrinklier.

'We're allowed one piece of birthday cake, aren't we Betts?' said Charlie.

'You can have one between you,' said Ros. 'Half now and the other half in some tin foil to take home and have next week.'

Charlie put his head on Betty's shoulder and sobbed, 'How could we have brought up such a cruel, heartless girl?'

With the unerring instinct of starving adolescents, Pete, Timothy and Fiona arrived just as Ros was taking the jacket potatoes out of the oven. They went into the living room to greet Charlie and Betty, and then going to where all the food was laid out pounced on the crisps, the Wotsits and the Twiglets. Ted came in and they all started to help themselves. Pete and Timothy took charge of Ted's plate and made sure that he got a sample of everything, piling it high until it was a perfectly conical hillock. They crowned it by poking a miniature pork pie between the two halves of the baked potato on top.

'Like a pearl in an oyster,' said Charlie.

Ros handed out napkins and made sure everyone was fully laden before serving herself. They were all happily in the trough when Pauline, Norman and Jane burst in.

'Happy birthday, old chap,' cried Norman, holding out a crate of brown ale to Ted. He nodded at Ted's glass. 'I see you've started already.'

'Actually, this is ginger beer,' said Ted.

Norman laughed in disbelief but then saw from the grave faces of the company that it was true: Ted was dry. Ros looked on like Cleopatra, happy that Mark Anthony had returned safe and sound from the wars.

Fiona put her arm around Jane and led her to the food table, where Jane selected miniature sausage rolls and lots of crisps. The girls and the boys ate in silence mostly while listening to the adults, feeling dutiful but wishing they were up in Pete's room listening to records. Once everyone had finished eating, Ros and Pauline went through to the kitchen to put the kettle on, followed by Betty with a stack of empty plates.

Not long after Ros had handed out the teas, she went out and came back carrying Ted's birthday cake. Everyone started to sing 'Happy Birthday,' as she processed towards

Ted and held the cake out to him. The pink candles stuck in the white icing formed the words, 'Forty-One Today, Hooray!' and with a mighty whoosh he blew them out, provoking cheers and a round of applause.

After Ted had made the ritual incision, Ros divided the cake and handed it round. While everyone was eating there was a silence punctuated by Mmms of delight. Ros went out to the kitchen, to put some dishes in the sink she believed, but found herself crying. She heard someone coming and grabbed an onion from the vegetable rack to explain her tears.

'What are you smiling at?' said her mum.

'Oh, nothing,' said Ros, but she meant, 'Everything.'